The Spirit of the Age

DECOPUNK

THE SPIRIT OF THE AGE

EDITED BY
THOMAS A. EASTON
AND
JUDITH K. DIAL

PINK
NARCISSUS
PRESS

DECO PUNK: The Spirit of the Age
© 2015 Pink Narcissus Press

Cover illustration & design by Duncan Eagleson

Published by Pink Narcissus Press
P.O. Box 303
Auburn, MA 01501
pinknarc.com

Library of Congress Control Number: 2015930208
ISBN: 978-1-939056-09-2
First trade paperback edition: June 2015

CONTENTS

INTRODUCTION

Steampunk is da bunk. It's passé. It's past its prime.

The times demand something newer and better and more in tune with the 21st century! We therefore raise our fists in the air and cry "Manifesto!"

Sure, some good stories fit under the steampunk label, and a lot of elegant imagery has made its way onto book covers and into costumes. But, really—a top hat with motoring goggles or a steam-powered dirigible? Or a steam-powered computer, when almost as soon as steam engines were in wide use, they were being used to generate electricity?

Oh, well. What makes steampunk steampunk is that it is stuck in the Victorian era, from about the birth of the telegraph to the end of the 19th century. That era was admittedly marked—at least in Europe—by ornamentation and elegance. Some people consider it a time of innocence, which ended with the carnage of the Great War.

It thus provides a nice setting for modern fantasies of zombies and vampires. Sometimes it's a game whose players ask, "If the Victorians had thought of doing this, how would they have done it using the technology they had at their disposal? Certainly they'd have done it more prettily!" But no matter how good the story or ingenious the inventions or elegant the setting, steampunk can't help but strike a modern sensibility as quaint. It's also a bit of a prettified cheat, for all that steampunk imagery is polished brass and wood and rope and sexy leather when anything to do with real steampower was marked by black grease and soot. And social relations were marked by racism, sexism, and the oppression of labor. Life was not pretty if you were not a member of the gilded class.

If you're a fan of technology, we can lay a further charge against steampunk: It is static. Further advances are not permitted, except as variations on Victorian themes.

This has been very nicely illustrated by two non-steampunk books. In 1986, Isaac Asimov published *Futuredays: A Nineteenth-Century Vision of the Year 2000*. It was a compendium of cigarette cards published in 1899, and its vision of the future was marked by commuters in personal airplanes with fabric wings. Albert Robida's *The Twentieth Century*, first published in 1882, has personal travel based on balloons. In both cases, it is as if the futurists were saying "Whatever we do, the future will do it better." In the case of steampunk, many writers throw their minds backward in time and say the same thing.

If there is more advanced technology, as in Karl Schroeder's Virga series, it serves as a frame or context supplied by outsiders, inside which people rely on primitive, Victorian-level technology. At the heart of the steampunk ethos is denial of the nature of technology as endless improvement and change. The Victorian era lasted quite a while, but by the end it was rapidly giving way to oil, gasoline, and electric power. The first few decades of the 20th century saw an explosion of new technologies, of which the most dramatic were the automobile, airplanes, and radio. By the 1920s, the explosion of interest in such things gave rise to modern science fiction.

Not that Hugo Gernsback called it "science fiction." He proposed "scientifiction" and presented it initially in the pages of *The Electrical Experimenter* (founded 1913), which became *Science and Invention* in 1920, and only later in *Amazing Stories* (founded 1926). He conceived it as a way of teaching the youth of the day the basics of science and technology. Not surprisingly, the early stories —including his own, of which *Ralph 124 C41+* is the most famous—were exceedingly didactic, given to great wodges of explanation, some of which was even reasonably accurate (for the time). But there were also a great many ideas—blasters and rocket belts and shrink rays, among others—that could not possibly be explained accurately. They were fun, they aroused enthusiasm for science and technology in many of the youth of an age when scientific and technological wonders filled the air. But they were pure fantasy, and they have remained that ever since.

But let's be fair. For all that many of the ideas in the science fiction of the 1920s and 1930s (and later) were nonsense, they did not present science and technology as static. *Progress* was the watchword! The world was full of wonders now, but even more wonders, more wondrous than ever, were just around the corner.

Through the dreary Depression years, science fiction kept the dream alive for many. Then came World War II and an explosion of technological achievement, capped by the very literal explosions that ended the war. By the 1950s, progress was once more the watchword. The economy was humming, computers were shrinking in size thanks to the replacement of vacuum tubes by transistors. The Consumer Society was off to a roaring start, and although people were generally delighted with the fruits of the technology boom, they almost immediately began to notice problems. Pollution was one. So was the Cold War, and as people (like myself) grew up under the shadow of the atomic mushroom cloud, there developed a pervasive malaise. Technology, it seemed, could be dangerous. It could even threaten the survival of us as individuals and of us as a species. There had to be a better way!

Many people have sought that better way by looking toward the future. To them the answer must be more science, more technology, ways of understanding and counteracting problems such as pollution and cancer and a great deal more. Some people, however, have looked backward. They have sought a simpler time, with safer lifeways. In the sixties, they were hippies and back-to-the-landers. Later, they were (and are) off-the-gridders. In literature their yearning for saner, simpler times fed the burgeoning of fantasy over science fiction. And in the 1980s, some fantasy took the form now called steampunk.

But steampunk is old. It's static and antiprogressive.

If the wish for a safer, saner world has any part in its appeal, it's a lie at heart, for the Victorian era was less than sane or safe. Racism, sexism, and oppression were pervasive. No one knew about such things as treating sewage and chlorinating water supplies often drawn from the very rivers into which raw sewage was dumped. It didn't have antibiotics, either, so it's no wonder that life expectancies were a lot less than we are used to today.

It is therefore time to replace steampunk with something a little more contemporary. That replacement should not be static, nor antiprogressive, nor backward-looking. Let's move up the timeline a bit to the 1920s, when modern science fiction was born.

This was a time when kids played with crystal radios. Crystalline vacuum tubes powered larger radios that occupied pride of place in the living rooms of the day, much as wide-screen televisions do today. Blown-glass tubes filled with violet glows and giving off sparks (violet ray devices) were medical marvels. Science fiction celebrated diamond lenses that could look into the heart of the atom. Crystals powered spaceships (dilithium crystals were not the first) and superheroes ("Doc" Smith's Lensmen wore crystalline lenses). All very sparkly and shiny, not at all like brass and wood and rope. We can keep the sexy leather.

The post-steampunk revolution needs a name. Perhaps, since the 1920s were the time of the Art Deco movement, "Decopunk" would do. It would certainly provide a host of images for cover designers and writers to play with, all of it distinctively different from the images of steampunk.

***

If you find yourself nodding at the idea that steampunk has had its day and needs replacing, then this anthology is for you. We asked our contributors—all modern writers of note—to think in terms of Art Deco, the 1920s, the period between the two world wars, to play with the world as it was then with a modern sense of what happened to it.

Did we wind up with a glimpse of what post-steampunk science fiction and fantasy might actually look like? Maybe. Maybe not. But everyone involved seemed to think the basic idea amounted to a nice sandbox to play in. And once they started playing, they built some astonishing sand castles—er, stories, that is. We hope that some of those stories will strike a chord with you, our readers, and with other writers. Perhaps they will be the seeds of a new genre, and perhaps we will all call that new genre "Decopunk."

But set aside our editorial delusions. Any anthology lives or dies by the stories within its covers, and *Deco Punk* has some great stories! Start with Debra Doyle and Jim Macdonald's "Silver Passing in Sunlight," which evocatively passes the baton. Sarah Smith's "And Every Pebble a Soldier" brings mechanical nightmares to strange life. Paul Di Filippo's "Airboy and Vooda Visit the Jungles of the Moon" considers the question of the relationship between superheroes and their wonderful machines. Nikola Tesla inevitably shows up, notably in Jeff Hecht's "Mr. Tesla's Radio Rainmaker." And more!

They are also fine examples of what really may turn out to be a new post-steampunk genre.

Thomas A. Easton & Judith K. Dial

SILVER PASSING IN SUNLIGHT

DEBRA DOYLE AND JAMES D. MACDONALD

Midnight in Denver, Colorado. The year is inching toward midsummer, but it isn't there yet. Almost a month to go until the longest day of the year. And in the Union Station marshaling yard, that vast steel network of cold iron riveted, welded, bolted or spiked, four men approach a train.

It isn't much of a train, not in these days of sixty-car freights pulled by four-eight-oh steam combinations. Just three cars, three articulated cars, but they gleam, stainless steel reflecting like silver in the moonlight. The first man speaks.

"Do you have it?"

This is Ralph Budd, president of the Chicago, Burlington and Quincy Railroad. He had not been at the party in New York in 1895, thirty-nine years and six days before, but he knew people who had.

"If we didn't have it, we wouldn't be here."

That's H. L. Hamilton, of General Electric. He hadn't been at the party either.

"The question," Hamilton continues, "is whether we can get it from here to Chicago before night falls again. Once we're out of Denver, nothing will protect us but the sun."

"For the love of all that's holy," says the third man. This is the Most Reverend Urban John Vehr, Bishop of the Diocese of Denver. He would not order anyone to carry what he's carrying now, so he has it himself: a square wooden box, stained with earth and water. It's wrapped in a white sheet, but still the smell of mold rises from it.

"Take the thing. Be done with it. It is beyond what I—what any man—can do, to finish this business." Needless to say, he had not been at the party.

"You're sure the power is there?" Budd asks, directing his question to Hamilton, while waving his hand vaguely eastward.

"If it's anywhere, yes," Hamilton replies.

"Then let's get aboard and see this thing done," says the fourth man. He is an old man, late sixties, but still spry. He speaks with a Boston accent. This is Charles Dana Gibson, the artist, once publisher of *Life* magazine. He *had* been at the party.

"I still don't see why we couldn't have hired an airplane; the money's not an issue," Hamilton says.

"Because Satan is the Prince of the Powers of the Air," says Bishop Vehr. He is wearing gloves with crosses embroidered, white on white, across their backs. "Staying in contact with the ground seems prudent."

They clamber up the steps aboard the train, entering at the third car, the observation car. The five picture windows on its boat-tailed stern glow with the lights of the rail yard—arc lights at the sidings, where cargo is being shifted; signal lights red and green, above semaphore arms marking open and closed switches.

Budd looks at his watch, a large pocket watch, a prosperous watch, that he wears on a chain across his vest. "Sunrise is in two hours, morning twilight a bit sooner."

"First light," Hamilton says. "When the sky goes gray in the east, the wheels must not stop rolling until the thing is done."

The bishop places the box onto a small trestle table, equidistant from the windows at the rear of the train. Three cars, in honor of the Trinity, he thinks. A hopeful thing. But the five windows mark a pentagram, with the little table in its center. The bishop can only hope that Budd knows what he's doing.

Ahead, at the next car, Negroes are heaving baggage aboard. Heavy trunks, lighter suitcases. They do not know what is in the last car. The Negroes standing in stiff white jackets at the buffet just back from the baggage compartment don't know either. The white men don't know. The reporters don't know. No one knows but these four men. The engineer arrives, climbs to his cab all the way forward, behind the great steel engine's aerodynamic face, and checks his knobs and levers. All correct. He turns the knob that activates the air-start system and the huge diesel just behind him, eight cylinders in line. They turn and pump, catch and fire, with a heavy roar. The diesels spin a generator and the electric lights in the three cars spring to life, glittering, crystalline. It is a marine engine, designed for diesel-electric submarines. Ten years hence, similar engines will nearly starve Britain into submission. Today, this one has a different purpose.

The cars lurch. Forward to the platform, last stop before Chicago. More passengers embark. Dignitaries. Reporters. Citizens. All passengers, are encased in welded steel.

Gibson leans on his stick, then takes a seat on one of the rearward facing benches. He is one of the last alive who had been at the party. Stanford White, who hosted the party, is long dead, shot in the face by Harry Thaw on the roof of Madison Square Garden. Thaw has been in and out of madhouses and prisons ever since. Now Gibson gazes at the box, pulls from his pocket a sketch pad and pencil, and commences a portrait, drawing from memory a girl's face.

The bishop sits heavily beside him. "That's her?" he asks.

"It is."

"A fair face, to carry so much darkness."

"She was no Eve, and no Salome, either."

Only a dancer in black chiffon, Gibson thinks, and later in nothing at all, but dancers were commonplace, if seldom so young. Just as Stanford White had been a libertine and a satyr and the architect who created the face of New York at the century's turn; but nothing more than that, not an adept who could summon up spirits from the dark beyond. But *something* had been summoned on that night, nevertheless, and it has never lain entirely quiet since.

***

A commotion at the baggage car. The *Rocky Mountain News* has presented Mr. Budd with a mascot, a donkey named Zeph. Now a representative from the newspaper is insisting that the donkey ride on the train's maiden voyage. Mr. Budd himself is called forward by the head man from the baggage car, holding a list of tariffs for "birds" and a manifest that lists Zeph as a "Rocky Mountain Canary."

Budd takes in the scene. "Why not?" he says. Nothing must delay departure and he still has much to do. "One more jackass on this train won't make a difference."

Now Budd makes his way forward through the baggage area, through the post office, past the engine compartment, all the way to the engineer's cabin.

"All's well?" he asks.

"So far," the engineer replies.

"Once we start, do not stop," Budd commands. "Not for flags, not for whistles, not for torpedoes."

"The stations? The grade crossings?"

"Leave those to me." When a man owns a railroad he is king of the entire right-of-way. "Your job is to see how fast you can go. Nothing else."

Budd does not say why, nor does the engineer ask. He would not understand the answer, even if given a truthful one.

The engines throb with power.

Budd's next stop is at the telegraph operator's desk in the post office section. "Send to Denver Operations," he says. "Sidetrack all traffic from here to Chicago. Station masters to personally check the line in their blocks. Place flagmen at all level crossings. Open all switches and lock them open."

The telegraph operator nods, and taps his key.

***

As he stands at the buffet, contemplating a champagne breakfast, H. L. Hamilton thinks back to the telephone call that had set this trip in motion.

The implications and ramifications of that call Hamilton understood only in part. He doubts that any man now on the train with him understands them all. He himself knows only enough to wonder what fool had thought to name the General Electric pavilion at Chicago's "Century of Progress" World's Fair the "House of Magic," and call the show within, "Wonders of the Invisible World."

***

Gibson walks back to the shrouded box, and pins his pencil sketch to the sheet that covers it. "Let that do for a memorial," he says to the bishop. "What do you know of her?"

"Only that she died in Denver's Union Station," the bishop says. "Waiting for an eastbound train."

Gibson knows this much: the year of her death had been 1906 and the day had been the twenty-sixth of June, the same day and year that Stanford White had died on the island of Manhattan. And whatever dark spirit had been riding her homeward, chose for a while to rest.

"Her heart had stopped," the bishop says. "Though she wasn't yet thirty."

She'd only been fifteen at the party in New York, but Stanford liked them young. Gibson, for himself, had no interest that night in anything below her shoulders, except, perhaps, as a figure study. The photographers and artists and poets and architects who attended the party, though, many of them had looked, and touched, and more. Not Frank Wright. He hadn't been invited. Something else Frank Wright hadn't been invited to: designing buildings for the Century of Progress. But the others, the ones who had been at the party, or who belonged to the schools of those who had—they built the tall, angled, multi-hued buildings on the artificial island in Lake Michigan, and illumined the Century of Progress with light from the star Arcturus.

Was it their triumph, Gibson wonders, that roused the dark thing from its restless sleep in a Denver potter's field, and sent it once again looking eastward? He is an artist, not a scholar in such esoteric disciplines; he knows enough only to be sure he cannot know.

Gibson whistles a bar from "Sing a Song of Sixpence"—he had heard it at the party, and now the tune plays again in his memories. Budd looks at him sharply, the sound of the artist's whistling sounds like steam escaping from a faulty boiler.

No boiler on this train. Six hundred electric-and-diesel horses run before them, pulling on the cars. The stainless steel shells of the cars, the light-weight construction that allows the engine to drive on so fast, are fabricated with a new kind of patented electric weld that holds the gleaming rolled sheets together. Architects designed the fluting on the sides of the Zephyr, not just to beautify it but to strengthen its thin steel flanks. Budd is convinced that the age of steam is done, however strong it now appears.

"Ten years ago," Hamilton says, "We couldn't have made this run."

"Two years ago," Budd says, "we couldn't have built this train."

***

The sun is up, the sky is blue, and children stand in the fields to watch and wave as the Zephyr rolls down the line in a streak of silver, faster than any train they've ever seen. The crossing gates are down, each one guarded by a flagman. The station platforms are empty, all guarded. By police, by the National Guard, by Boy Scouts.

Viewed from ahead, the Zephyr's nose looks like a cathedral. Within the cathedral, engineer Jack Ford lights a cigarette, says, "Let's see what this baby can do," and twists the throttle lever all the way to the right. The speedometer spins. Ninety, one hundred, one hundred and twelve; the land speed record is one hundred and fifteen miles per hour. The sun is moving faster than he is; and he is running against the sun.

In the observation car the four men gather, facing away from the box. Two to each side, Budd and Hamilton; one behind, the bishop. And Gibson facing forward, his back to the box.

***

Across Iowa in three hours and a half. Across the Missouri river. The sun is behind them now, falling toward sunset in the west. Gibson is tired; he can no longer stand, regardless of how smooth the ride. He sits on one of the benches, like pews facing the sunset behind them. The colored rays touch the white sheet draping the box, giving it the warm, pink hue of living flesh. He remembers the cigar smoke, and the wine.

***

The city of Chicago builds around them. They must slow. Budd looks at his watch, at the sky, and back to his watch. Hamilton is sweating despite the air-conditioning of the car. The bishop is telling his beads. Gibson's hands are in his pockets to conceal their trembling.

The Zephyr glides into Chicago's Union Station with sunset minutes away, then travels onward, barely pausing, to the center of the great exposition on its island in the lake. The tracks extend into the fairground, passing through the precise and boldly delineated geometric shapes, the strong colors, the banners and the electric lights of the fair, bringing the Zephyr onto the stage of the Wings of a Century transportation pageant, masking the trip's deeper purpose in a celebration of scientific and industrial progress.

While the watching crowd applauds, while the engineer Jack Ford lights another cigarette, the four men debark on the Zephyr's other side. The box is again carried by the bishop. Hamilton leads the way; he knows where the General Electric pavilion is located.

They advance in a tight diamond, like an honor

guard: Hamilton in front, Budd just behind him to the left, Gibson to the right with his stick in his hand, and the bishop behind, holding the white-draped box.

They go to the General Electric pavilion; the doors are closed to all but them. Inside, where the Theater of Electricity stands open, the stage is bare, and all but two of the thousand seats of the amphitheater are empty. A man and a woman sit together in front row at center stage. The four men approach the pair with their burden.

"Mr. President," says Hamilton.

"I hope you'll forgive me that I don't stand," replies Franklin Roosevelt —patrician New York accent, cigarette-holder clenched in his teeth. "I called you here for a reason. You responded, as true Americans."

Roosevelt had not been at the party.

"We are honored," says Budd.

The bishop has always been a New Deal Democrat. He nods, but does not let go of the box.

The woman seated to Roosevelt's right does stand. Gibson takes her hand and bows over it—an old-fashioned courtesy, from another era, but more than anyone here, he is an old-fashioned man.

"One of the fan dancers," Roosevelt says, "from the Parisian Café on the Midway. She does not mind disrobing, but is neither an artist's model" (here Gibson's mouth quirks downward, remembering that night) "nor a lady of...ill repute, but as true an American as anyone here."

She had not yet been born when the party took place.

"Mr. Hamilton?" the bishop says.

"Give her the box," Hamilton says.

"Thank you," says the young woman. She speaks with a southern accent, marred with a lisp. She throws off her robe, then accepts the bishop's burden. He steps back, averting his eyes.

"No," Gibson admonishes him. "You're a part of this, too. All of us must bear witness."

The bishop turns his gaze back to the woman, looking only at her face.

"Come with me," says Hamilton to the woman. The two of them—the man in his dapper traveling suit (rumpled with thirteen hours on a train car; he thinks thirteen hours strangely appropriate), she naked, yet pacing with stately grace—go up the stairs stage left and across the bare platform to the center of the stage, directly before the four who wait below.

"Here," Hamilton says, pointing to a spot. The woman stands there alone.

Hamilton leaves her and walks to the wings. He throws a switch, and with an electric hum a ball descends above her, a ball with a sharp spike depending from its lower surface.

A hum. A crackle. Blue light dances on the sphere. An aurora surrounds it. Bolts of electricity snap and fly. The woman raises the box above her head and lightning descends. She and the box are alike surrounded by a nimbus of cold fire. The bishop thinks of St. Elmo, even as he prays to St. Mary, as the woman on the stage and her burden are surrounded by the electric display.

Within that display, concentric circles form, parallel to the stage, running upward, faster and faster. The woman stands like a figure of marble. The box glows bright, then brighter still, and appears, to those watching from the front, to dissolve into a shower of sparks, green fireflies that swirl and form a column of light ranging from far above, in the blackness above the proscenium, to somewhere below the stage.

A snap, a break, a boom, and all is still. The light vanishes. The box is gone. The woman lowers her arms. The sphere above her rises again out of sight.

Hamilton approaches her from the wings, takes her arm, and escorts her to the stairs. Gibson is waiting below, her wrap over his arm, and drapes it about her as she descends. Her eyes are wide, vacant, as if seeing a long distance.

"I shall meet the men who circle the earth in half the time than you took to cross Iowa," she whispers. Budd hears her, and wonders. He takes her other arm and guides her back to her seat in the front row.

"It's over," says Roosevelt. "Thank you."

***

Budd walks alone from the pavilion, back across the Midway, up to the Wings of a Century platform. He leans back against the side of the Zephyr, reassured by its steel, its reality.

Reporters crowd around him as he lights a cigar.

"How was it?" one asks. "How was the trip?"

"It was a sweet ride," Budd replies.

***

Back in the General Electric pavilion, Roosevelt's aides enter. The president's son pushes a wheelchair.

"What was it?" Hamilton asks. "I've done everything you asked, never questioned why, but I must know. What was it?"

It isn't Roosevelt who answers, however, but Gibson: "The spirit of the age."

AUTHOR'S NOTE

Debra Doyle is a science fiction and fantasy writer living in far northern New England. She has a Ph.D. in English literature from the University of Pennsylvania, and does freelance editorial and critique work when she isn't writing. Her forthcoming works (co-written with James D. Macdonald) include the novels *The Gates of Time* and *Emergency Magical Services: First Response*, both forthcoming from Tor Books.

James D. Macdonald is an sf/fantasy author, stage

magician, and EMT living in Colebrook, New Hampshire. He is the co-author, with Debra Doyle, of the Mageworlds space opera series, recently re-issued in electronic form by Tor Books. Their most recent publications include the short stories "The Clockwork Trollop" in *Beneath Ceaseless Skies* and "The Devil in the Details" from Tor.com.

SYMMETRY
SHARIANN LEWITT

That summer we ate the sparrows. Poor little birds, singing fearlessly and too easy to hit with a homemade slingshot, but when one starves one is not too particular. We would have preferred the rats—more meat on them, even the stringy ones—but they were too smart and therefore hard to catch. I got three, I am not proud to say, when Herr Grunler died in 4B and they came to feast on his corpse. Frau Bencker, the landlady, found him by the smell and the two of us trapped the rats that were too slow to turn away from their repast. We made quite a fine soup for a week on those rats, but usually they were impossible to catch and we had to make do with the dwindling songbirds.

This night there were no rats or sparrows. Richard brought a can of beans from the American at the Adlon and we added a bone that I stole at the kitchen door at Café des Westerns. I found some dandelion greens in the Tiergarten and we added some of the garlic we found in Herr Grunler's pantry. That night we dined as well as anyone in Berlin, as well as anyone not rich or foreign.

"And how is your clock, Herr Doktor?" Frau Bencker asked Richard. That always made him smile, though he has maybe a year to go before he finally earns that degree. For myself, newly come as a graduate student only this year, Richard has become more than a friend and support. I am more of a mathematician than a physicist, truth be told, and Richard always refers to himself as a "tinkerer." We have truly become collaborators, with our complementary abilities and the easy way we follow each other's thoughts.

Sometimes my ideas look crazy, even to me. I see the theorems and they feel right, pure, correct. They make sense. And yet what they suggest about the physical universe makes no sense at all. I dare not even tell most of my colleagues some of the ideas the theorems and proofs indicate, but I have told Richard and he listened to me. He never called me crazy; he tilted his head to one side and looked off at the wall and when I was quite convinced that he was paying no attention to me at all he turned back and looked directly in my eyes. "You do know what you are saying," he said. "If you are right about this, then somewhere there has to be order in the very large nucleus."

I knew what I was saying. I just didn't think anyone would believe me. It was too wild, too crazy, even in a universe where time was a function of gravity. But Richard listened and took my ideas, my equations, seriously.

And so there was the project of the clock. Richard closed his eyes and leaned his head back on the delicate lace edged antimacassar. "The clock. Well, I think we are starting to make progress. Sometimes I see that peculiar glow that is consistent with the strange rays you predicted."

"Broken symmetry," I said.

Frau Bencker shook her head. "Is it broken?"

I don't know why we ever try to explain physics to my landlady, whose competence with mathematics begins with making change and ends with household accounts. "Symmetry. Think of it as balance. Say you balance an egg on the tip of your finger. We call that unstable. The egg can fall in any direction, and all directions are equally possible. When the egg does finally fall, it defines the new state and gives off energy as it moves from a higher state, on your finger, to a lower state, on the floor."

Frau Bencker shook her head. "My eggs never did that. They only broke, and we cannot afford that now. If we had a nice egg I would beat it into the soup." Then she turned to Richard. "But be careful with that clock. You stole it. You shouldn't go bragging about it."

Richard had the grace to look ashamed. It was true that the clock was stolen from the city. There had been many, maybe even a hundred of them over Berlin, but they had become too expensive to run and had been taken down. Richard had helped himself to a few for the uranium, as he explained. He had some ideas for experiments and he couldn't get uranium at the university, and the city was only going to store the clocks somewhere or dispose of them.

Frau Bencker raised her ladle and announced dinner. We ate in silence, savoring the only decent meal any of the three of us had had in days. The soup was delicious and I lingered over every spoonful to relish the richness of the broth and the beans. My stomach became full, so rare an event that I wondered if perhaps I was unwell. But no, it was only the lovely feeling of having eaten as much as I could hold.

I had wanted to talk more about our work after dinner, but Richard put on his hat and headed out for the Adlon. Again. He said he had a date but I know precisely what kind of date it was, for all he calls me *maedchen* and treats me as if I am twelve. I am neither.

I should have stayed in Gottingen. If nothing else, there is more food there, closer to the farms. Professor Noether had said, "Renate, you are truly talented. You belong here, in Mathematics, but if you insist on going to Physics I will speak to Professor Born on your behalf. Einstein may be in Berlin but he does not take students and you will be isolated there."

She was more right than I could have known, and she did not speak of the constant hunger and cold. Last winter we broke up the old chairs for kindling to keep warm, and now only one chair and the bedstead and the larger table remain in my room. The smaller table and the two spindly, uncomfortable chairs went in January and then February when we could not buy coal.

Frau Bencker brought them down to her rooms on

the ground floor, one at a time, and permitted me to stay with her while she burned them in her stove. The chairs lasted for nearly a week each, the table for two. So I sat in Frau Bencker's over furnished front room with her great Biedermeier sofa and chairs and heavy carved sideboard and thick oak table that we could not have broken up in any case, warm, bent over my books.

At least I could study, and when I went to the deep place where I saw protons and neutrons alternately fighting furiously and then dancing coherently in the nucleus of the uranium atom. There I could forget the hunger and the cold. Most of all I could forget the reason I could not remain in Gottingen—Franz Meyer, the most talented graduate student in the department, destined for great things. No one would ever believe me.

I never admitted what had happened to anyone. I almost told Professor Noether, once, when she mentioned that she might be interested in taking me as her student. But then, at the last minute I hesitated and thought that she, too, would never believe me. Franz Meyer was such a favorite of everyone, and so I kept silent and so here I am. Hungry. With only one chair.

But there are reasons I am thankful even so. Since Spring arrived we are no longer frozen. That night Frau Bencker served a good soup in her elegant Dresden bowls, a soup rich with a marrow bone and full of a can of American beans. I still had two cigarettes left from the extra tobacco Richard scavenged from his last visit, and I thought I could trade them for eggs or bread the next day if Richard hadn't smoked them.

So well fortified, I got my coat off the peg in the front hall. "I'm off to the lab," I called to Frau Bencker.

She came out of the kitchen, wiping her hands on a dish towel. "It's too dangerous out there, there is a big rally and the politicals will be fighting all night in the streets. You can go tomorrow."

I shrugged. "I am hoping that some of the new data I need has arrived. Some of the street lights still work. And

I've got the paring knife in my bag. Really, I'll be fine. I'll avoid the main streets."

I avoided Oderberger Strasse because the Socialists blocked one of the buildings and I expected there would be a clash with some other group. The various marching political groups were more dangerous than random men on the street and any group chanting slogans was looking for a fight and would find one. I have no politics. Politics seems to be about which color shirts the thugs wear, but they all beat each other and anyone who happens to be in the way. All they stand for is danger and hurt, all of them.

On the next block over, Communists had taken over the nearest U-bahn station and threw rocks at the former Freikorps who threatened them with old weapons from the war. I quickly darted down a side street to avoid stragglers. The next U-bahn station seemed clear enough. Some nights were worse than others, but this had been the worst in months. With the warming of the Spring the pent up anger of the political thugs found targets in anyone on the street.

Frau Bencker had been right, I shouldn't have gone out. I would have to spend the rest of the night in my dingy basement cell of an office. The streets were too dangerous, too wild.

I let myself into the building and went down the dark stairs to the basement where I had my closet. I did not work in a proper lab. In the University of Berlin, unlike Gottingen, women are consigned to the basement and are not recognized as peers and colleagues. Professor Noether must have known that when she warned me away from this, but she was not aware of my lack of choice. How I miss her, and Gottingen, and my friends, and the bright airy rooms that I shared with Ilse Kreuger who studied philosophy. Every time I came down to this dark hole I wanted to cry. How I wished Franz had left Gottingen and I could leave Berlin.

Instead, I turned on the light and prepared to work like the other two women in the Faculty of Physics banished to the dungeon. Here on my desk was a new stack of paper, data from the most recent experiments, bombarding uranium with neutrons. The French researchers Frederic and Irene Joliot-Curie reported such a procedure had created a new element, and here Otto Hahn and Lise Mietner (one of these women down in the basement) were recreating the work. I was interested in the mathematics of what this means. Professor Noether has worked extensively in Symmetry, which revealed the connection between symmetries and conservation laws in physics.

And it must apply to the nuclei of atoms as well, even those large, strange atoms like uranium that behave so strangely. In all their chaotic unpredictability. I knew there must be some highly ordered low energy states, some kind of sense or order. The mathematics told me so, and the math never lies. I knew this even though every other senior physicist has told me that I was just wrong, that we could not predict, let alone control, the emissions from that nucleus as it degrades. Just as space and time curve around the gravitation of stars, so must space and time and energy and matter interact in ways we do not expect inside the nuclei of atoms. The mathematics I had done pointed in this direction even though everyone except Richard thought that I was wasting my time.

The work was slow with so little experimental data. I could look, I could work out the mathematics when I was not too cold or hungry, but I needed observations. We had so very few. I needed more data on the energy levels of uranium atoms, and there were only preliminary results.

Neutrons and protons are so similar that they are exactly alike except for the slightest difference in mass and, of course, their charge. I thought their similarity is more important than this difference, as if they are the same thing seen in a funhouse mirror in a symmetrical relation.

Radioactive elements are particularly interesting in this regard. Their nuclei are so large that the strong force cannot hold them together and constituent particles may escape. In the unstable nuclei when too many protons escape and there are too many neutrons left, the neutrons themselves decay into electrons and protons, and something else that we cannot yet identify but that I know must exist in the maths. But what I find most fascinating, and most beautiful, are the multiple ordered low energy states in the nucleus. Intriguing because, with broken symmetry, all of the low energy states are equally probable.

This would be my dissertation, though I dare not tell anyone. Some days I quiver with the greatness of it, thinking that it could change our thinking about everything. I have written a letter to Professor Noether, but it lies in the middle drawer of my desk under a blank pad. The letter will be more convincing when I can include the full substantiation. Then, perhaps, she will ask me home. Then, perhaps, they will dismiss Franz and I will be able to return, to leave this city of stone and shadows where women must work in the dark.

I should be more alert. The doors should be locked but sometimes people get in—I should pay more attention. But there are always shadows and movement, most from rodents. I looked at the data and then my equations, and then I was no longer in a dingy basement working under the light of a single remaining bulb (as we cannot afford to replace those that burn out). I can see into the working of the unstable uranium atom, the neutrons and protons squashed together and pushing apart in their oversized nucleus, pushing and pulling, repulsed and attracted and fighting like Communists and Freikorps on Friedrickstrasse. And, like the political fights on Friedrickstrasse, sometimes, when just cold enough, a regular pattern emerges for a moment before chaos swallows it again.

And then I heard a crash just behind me and I jumped and was surrounded by shadows in the basement again. Only I knew I was not alone and something was very wrong.

"*Maedchen?*"

A whisper, not really a voice. A hiss. I wanted to run, to cower under the desk deep in the dark. But there is glass in the door and the light was on. Whoever was out there had seen me.

All I could think was that it was Franz, come all the way from Gottingen to find me.

"*Maedchen?*"

I forced myself to think, think beyond the fear that froze my brain. Only Richard ever called me *maedchen*. Franz knows that I am not one.

Still, I stayed in my seat, motionless, waiting for the worst. For death, for a desperate thug in an old Freikorps uniform to burst in with a gun and shoot, though I have never thought of the Friekorps here. They belong in the streets fighting Communists, not physicists.

I heard my own breathing, harsh, ragged, go on for what seemed like minutes. I forced myself to approach the door carefully, in the shadows, so anyone looking at the glass might not see me. I looked out into the gloom, but of course there were no lights on out in the corridor. All I saw were reflections.

I grabbed the knob and opened the door, half expecting to fall under truncheons. What I found was Richard lying on the floor leaning up against the wall. I rushed to him, to bring him inside, but he flinched from my touch.

"Let me help. What happened to you? How did you get here?" I asked.

Richard rejected my support and crawled painfully across the threshold and into the wan light of my closet. Only when he got fully inside did I notice that what I had taken for shadows on his face were actually blood. From the way he moved and the ash gray of his skin, I believed it was his own.

I helped him lay gently on the floor and poured a glass of water from the tepid pitcher that someone left from earlier in the day. He drank thirstily and I got him a second glass and then a third before he slowed down.

I gave him one more glass of water that he drank slowly while I took yet more water and a wad of the paper Reich marks that we use to wipe our hands or to catch crumbs and washed his face. He winced but I went gently, and finally his face was mostly clean. Most of the blood had come from a scalp wound, I think, though there was a gash under his eye and the left side of his face was badly bruised. Poor Richard. He sets such store in his good looks, and his "dates" often pay in food and hard currency, not to mention the cigarette stubs he scrounges.

"What happened? Who did this?"

"Too many questions." He wheezed. I took off his jacket and saw his best white shirt also stained with blood. I touched gently and he winced and turned even whiter. I shimmied out of my slip and tore it into a long strip to bind his head wound. At least the blood seemed to be clotting, dark and not so fresh. He tried to refuse to permit me to touch his chest at all, but I managed to get the buttons of his shirt undone. Underneath he was horribly battered and I was sure some ribs were broken, but he wasn't bleeding that I could see. At least not externally.

"You should go to the hospital."

"Can't."

"You're not a Communist. Did your date beat you?"

"No. Freikorps."

"At least let me fetch a doctor."

"This place is full of doctors. I'm almost a doctor." He tried to laugh at his poor joke, but it came out as a cough and obviously pained him horribly.

"Let me take you home. We can go in a taxi."

"Reni, no. Dieter knows where I live. "

"You need medicine. You need a hospital. I'm afraid you have internal injuries."

"It's too dangerous out there," he said. "For you, and definitely for me. Too many former Freikorps. It's too dangerous for the taxis too."

"Who is Dieter? Why does that matter? You need to

rest." He needed a hospital, but I didn't know how to get him to one, not if there were no taxis in the streets. He was right. Even through the tiny basement window I could hear the political chants coming closer.

"I found the solution to the clock," Richard said.

"Tell me more," I prompted him. Of course I was interested in his work, but I could hardly concentrate on that now. I wanted to keep him talking because I knew that people with head injuries should be kept conscious. The only thing I know that kept him interested and made him truly, purely happy was thinking about physics.

"I think I've found a way to tune the temperature variations so the uranium nucleus oscillates between the normal ground state and the anomalous low energy ordered states. The strangest thing is that the oscillation is amazingly stable. Or it appeared amazingly stable when I got the temperature right."

He remained silent for so long that I was worried that he had slipped into unconsciousness. Then he spoke very softly. "Time is affected by gravity. We know mass and energy are related. Twenty years ago these were separate categories that could not be crossed and now we know they are all, in fact, all parts of some great whole."

"Yes, that is what my theory implies"

"More than the maths. Nothing is separate. Nothing is unconnected."

He looked at me in such a way that I thought he meant more, but it could have been only the lighting, or the hour, or the circumstances.

"Yes," I agreed with him, and touched his hand. His flesh was cold in a way that frightened me. "Symmetry."

He smiled, and then he fell asleep and I had to rouse him. I wondered if the violence in the street had died, if I could get him to the hospital. I ran up the stairs but stopped before the door. I could still hear rocks being thrown and the screaming mob. Impossible.

So I cushioned him as best I could with the sparse supplies that lay around the office, the bricks of Reich marks that were worth less than scrap paper for minor calculations and notes, a wadded up lab coat that someone had left in a corner, two left gloves that had been on the top of a filing cabinet since the end of winter. A paltry collection, but by the Spring of '23 we were accustomed to so little that this seemed like a reasonable supply.

"Richard, wake up." I was terrified. I went upstairs for another pitcher of water, icy cold, and washed his face in it. That brought him to consciousness. "You can't go to sleep on me. I need you to tell me about how you tuned the temperature variations and how we can understand the theory in light of this data."

"It is just as you predicted, *maedchen*. Neutrons and protons, they are not precisely the same thing, but when they are cooled to the right state they become the same, some third particle that is only very slightly different. When they come into that harmony the whole glows a very pretty lavender."

"You are a genius to be able to make it work!" I told him.

"You are the genius, *maedchen*. You figured out that it should exist. I only built the device."

"No, Richard, no, I can't do any of this without you. Pay attention. I need you to help me keep you alive. You have to try to stay awake." In truth I was desperate. I could think of nothing else that could hold Richard awake, alive. "Explain to me how you cool the uranium. This is important. If we cannot reproduce it we cannot prove it."

He had lost consciousness again. Stamping boots still sounded on the avenue but I no longer cared. I had to get him to a hospital. I no longer cared how dangerous the streets were. They were no more dangerous than staying here.

I slapped him. He opened his eyes as if raising the lids were the hardest thing he could possibly do. "No, *maedchen*. Please, no." I tried to hook my shoulder under his armpit but he whimpered in such agony that I could not bear it.

"The trenches. The influenza," he said as I let him down gently. "Just promise me you will get the clock. As soon as it is safe you go to my room and get it. Key in my pocket. Promise."

"Don't die on me, Richard. You can't die on me."

I sat on the basement floor holding his hand until it turned to ice and I knew he was gone. I sat there, tears running down my face, rocking, as the gray dawn light penetrated the tiny basement window. If only I had forced him to the hospital, if only I had been strong enough to carry him up the stairs. But in the light of day I saw the blood soaked through his jacket and down his trousers, and touched the place where his skull seemed soft. And I cried again until I was sick and there was no comfort.

But I had made him a promise, one last promise, and I knew I had best keep it before lost my nerve.

***

Richard rented a room in one of the horrible tenements in Prenzlaurberg, in one of the old courtyard buildings where the light never comes down the narrow shaft and the courtyard itself is rented for some commercial work. In Richard's building the commerce in the courtyard was a laundry, and his room was so cheap that you had to cross the laundry to get to the back stairs to go up in the dark. There were worse establishments than a laundry; at least the smell of the soap was clean if caustic and the vats of steam were warm.

Richard's room was a barren, dingy hole, much as I remembered it. I had only been there once or twice to pick up a book or a clean shirt with him. He preferred to study with me, and add his few supplies to suppers with Frau Bencker's magic touch. I took his pillowcase and stuffed in what I found: his two other shirts, those books and notebooks that did not live in his office, and a cigar box that was full only of personal papers. Those I thought I would save and see if he had any family I should send them to.

Where was that clock? I didn't see it with his tools,

neatly stored in a tin kit, or among the homemade apparatus that had taken over the table. Where had I missed? I did one last sweep of the room and checked under the mess of pornography under the bed and there I saw it. A uranium clock, sitting on top of a metal box.

Before the inflation Berlin had public clocks glowing across the city. A modern city for the new century, the uranium clocks meant that everyone always knew at a glance what time it was. The clocks, along with the street lights and the public toilets (now closed) made up an urban landscape that had been comfortable and convenient, or so I heard from those who had lived here. I had come only in the past year so I had only lived in the harsh, poor Berlin of the hyperinflation.

And with the hyperinflation the toilets had been closed and the clocks had been taken down. They were too expensive to run.

It didn't fit in the pillowcase. The sheet from the bed covered it sloppily and I tied a loose knot to make a handle. The box, which must have been the cooling device, was even heavier than the clock. This would be hard to maneuver, but I couldn't possibly leave it. For good measure, I draped the blanket over it as well.

I had a lot to carry down four flights and across the laundry and through the port gate out to the street. I didn't notice the large men across the street in their gray Freikorps uniforms until they came back over, stopping the one mule cart, and surrounded me.

"I see you are coming from the building where a friend of ours lives. We have not seen him in some time and wonder if you know him? His name is Hans Richard Schullman."

"No, I don't know any Hans Schullman."

"Oh, you must. All the girls like him. Though he doesn't like girls." The man who spoke before snorted as if he had been funny.

"I told you, I don't know any Hans Schullman. Let me pass."

The big one who had been so threatening turned red and angry. He pulled the bundle out of my hands and started to grab my breast the way Franz Meyer had. Only with Franz I had been younger, frozen, afraid. I had known him. He had worked with me, encouraging me to try harder problems than we were assigned in class and going over the work with me. Only later, only after his repeated assaults, did I learn that he used more than my body. He had used me to solve the equations he needed for his dissertation, that he himself could not accomplish.

This time anger flooded my brain, more than fear. I kicked, hard, at his knees, at his soft bits. I kicked his cock as if he were Franz who used it on me when I screamed after he used my mind. I clawed at his face and scratched at his eyes and bit down hard on his fat fingers.

"Dieter, let her go. She's a good German girl and she doesn't know Hans. It's a big building. See, she just has clean clothes, probably from the laundry." The speaker was also Freikorps, but smaller, not quite so stuffed with sausages. Still, he managed to pull Dieter off of me. Or maybe my own defense had had an effect. Dieter did not look pleased.

"Fraulein, please accept our apologies. We have been searching for a deserter who had been in Dieter's unit at the end of the war. We do not assault decent German women." He snapped me a salute and Dieter, still surly, stood aside.

"Thank you for your good manners," I replied. "What is your name, so I can thank you properly?"

"I am Otto Koenig and this is Dieter Grieg, who usually is the soul of decency. Though tracing a traitor and deserter has naturally made him far more edgy than usual. We are with the Organisation Consul."

"I thought you had been disbanded?" I tried to make it sound as if I would have been sad.

"It only appears as such. For the sake of the political. You understand, as a good German girl."

"Yes, of course. I thank you again. But now I really

must go." I retied the bundles and tried to walk with some dignity though I wanted only to run to the S-bahn station, hide my face in the soft pillow case and weep. Instead I kept my steps slow and deliberate until I had turned the corner and gone a full block before I ran.

Richard had said Dieter's name, had said they knew where he lived. This overfed evil worm had killed Richard.

Had Richard really been a deserter? I wondered. That would make sense. It fit his strangeness at times, his reluctance to speak of anything other than our work and his time in Berlin. But any young man had likely been in the war and all of us had learned not to ask. Those that had come back were all haunted and had shadows.

I took Richard's small bundle, and the clock, down to my office. I did not want to explain anything to Frau Bencker. Only when I returned to my basement hole and saw that Richard lay as I left him and looked as if he were asleep I took out his clock and leaned it on the wall above my desk. Only then did I begin to cry.

I cried as I had not cried before, for Richard and for myself, for my fury at Dieter and Franz Meyer and the war and all the evils around us. I cried for being exiled to the basement when men with half my ability had respectable places above.

The basement grew softly lighter and I lifted my eyes to the clock, amazed. Around it the air glowed softly lavender with the strange rays Richard had described.

I smiled with grim pleasure. I had an idea, and I knew where the old Organisation Consul had their headquarters.

People think that because I look young and wear my hair up in braids, because I wear no lipstick and do not pluck thin arches in my brows and wear sturdy flat shoes I am sweet and innocent. No one in this city can afford innocence. I took the clock and wrapped it back in the threadbare blankets. I took out a blank note card and wrote Dieter's name on the envelope and inside wrote a thank you card that I left unsigned. And then I brought it down to his headquarters and asked the boy on desk duty to see it delivered as a "token of appreciation" from a "grateful citizen."

Four weeks later I "ran into" Otto Koenig. By then Spring was well advanced and dandelions blooming all over the Tiergarten. I only needed my sweater on the coolest evenings and down in my basement, which held a chill. I had made a habit of wandering by the area of the headquarters and had run into Otto a few times. Had he not been Freikorps he would have been a pleasant person.

So Otto and I took a walk along the Spree and he told me what he considered very unsettling news. "I don't know if you recall Dieter Grieg," he began. "He was a decent comrade most of the time, though not the most brilliant man I ever served with. Still. I do not understand what happened to him. He started to see things, to insist that he was being haunted. That Hans Schullman came to him in his room sometimes and told him things, crazy things. That he actually saw Hans when he was wide awake, before he went to bed, and once in the middle of his dinner. Naturally we did not know what to make of it all and thought perhaps he had given in to shell shock. He had not shown any signs before, but some of our old comrades have fallen prey to it lately.

"Anyway, Dieter hanged himself last week. One of the boys went to his place to find him when he hadn't reported for three days. Dieter was reliable, he would never just not show up unless something was very wrong. We sent the boy to see if he was ill, and there he was, dead."

I said nothing and we walked on. "I am sorry," Otto said finally. "Perhaps I should not have burdened you. It was hardly your place, or mine to tell you. Please forgive me if I have distressed you."

"Not at all." I replied. "One becomes used to distressing news in Berlin these days. Thank you for telling me. I would rather know."

And with that we walked around the block one more

time and then I left.

I felt no responsibility. I had not killed Dieter. His own guilt had done that. Nor had I intended him to die.

There is symmetry in the universe, and it goes deeper than anyone knows, anyone except Richard and me. I have the maths to prove it and mathematics is never wrong. Mathematics alone has shown me the clear, safe place where knowledge is true and eternal. Mathematics never dies. Matter and energy are one. Neutrons and protons are the same particle with only a different charge in a fun-house mirror, and Richard found that at just the right temperature oscillation, for a few moments at a time, they became some third particle, yet to be named. And it was beautiful.

***

Two days later I received a letter from Gottingen in a familiar hand. I read it in the evening after eating Frau Bencker's delicious stew. I knew better than to inquire what was in it.

The letter was from Ilse, my former roommate. She had remained to marry a young junior professor, silly girl. Her letter was rather long, full of her tutoring girls in town, her new husband and how much she enjoyed her marriage, and learning to keep a kitchen garden. At the very end, though, she had added a bit of news from my old department.

I know you will find this news very strange and perhaps upsetting. I know you disliked Franz Meyer and would not hear his name spoken in your last months at school, so perhaps you would be amply rewarded. But even in your anger you could not hope for what transpired. After all the fine work Franz had done, he became incompetent. It was quite sudden, and there were rumors that he had some disease or had become psychotic and should go to Vienna perhaps, but he could no longer do mathematics at near the level he had achieved before. It was as if part of his brain had gone missing. He failed his defense twice over and could not explain the major theorems he had supposedly proven. I heard rumors that suggested plagiarism.

In any case, he was dismissed without his degree. I heard that he committed suicide shortly thereafter, though dear Gregor will not confirm these stories. He says it is not our business and is a sad thing if a man loses his mind in such a manner, and we should only pray for him.

Still, I thought you would want to know.

Ilse

Symmetry.

AUTHOR'S NOTE

Writing this story gave me the opportunity to indulge two of my passions—Weimar Germany and promoting knowledge of great women in math and science. Weimar lasted barely twenty years, but in that time saw an explosion of both the arts and sciences along with extreme political unrest. And then there was Emmy Noether, who was one of the great mathematical minds of the early 20th century. Anyone who has studied algebra knows that her later work laid the groundwork for modern abstract algebra, but sometimes we forget that her earlier revolutionary work in symmetry is absolutely foundational to particle physics. When most people list the people who changed thinking about the physical world in the early 20th century, many skip Noether and that is a great injustice.

QUICKSILVER

LINDA TIERNAN KEPNER

They were near Carthage when Carfelli snatched the chicken.

Victor Carfelli stepped warily, clinging to the shadows as he approached the rotten wooden lean-to where they had spent the night. Only New York State would have had the nerve to call that dung pile a cabin.

Carfelli heard the clink of metal. In his softest voice, he murmured, "Black."

"Yeah." The hood of the truck closed with a quiet *clunk.*

"Breakfast."

Henderson Black sighed. "I'll get the campfire up. The pots are clean."

"Keep it low," Carfelli warned. "This camp's closed for the winter."

"Yeah, yeah." The tall, hefty silhouette stood and stretched in the cold grey light of dawn. *He must've tinkered with that truck half the night*, Carfelli thought. "Let me fill a canteen."

"Mine, too."

Black prowled off, searching for clean water. Carfelli retrieved his knife from under the truck seat. He slid into the bushes with his sack, gouged a trench, and decapitated the freshly-killed chicken.

"Trench still open? I've got hot water." From the radiator, no doubt.

"Yeah." They doused the chicken, cleaned, and pin-feathered it. Feet, guts, everything went in the hole. Last thing they needed was some neighbor's dog coming home with a knife-cut chicken head in its teeth. They wiped everything down with one of Black's greasiest rags; it went in the hole, too. "One thing I'm good at, diggin' and fillin' trenches," Carfelli commented, and heard Black chuckle.

Black poured fresh water in the radiator. That hot water gave them the edge applying for jobs where other men looked filthy, but they were clean. Since they were out of butter, too, Carfelli boiled the chicken, with their last vegetables and dried herbs he scrounged. The air filled with the aroma of chicken stew.

"You've got the gift," said Black.

Carfelli told him, "Last of our supplies. Happy New Year 1925."

"Where do we go from here?"

"North, I guess. Alex Bay. Rumrunnin'."

"As good as anything." Black nodded.

A tree limb cracked. Alarmed, Carfelli reached for a rock, and palmed it.

"Easy, boys."

A uniformed man, badge clearly visible, stepped into the firelight. No doubt there were more, out of sight. "Howdy, Deputy," said Carfelli.

"Theft, trespassin', an' assaultin' an officer," stated the Deputy.

No explanation was needed. They were going to be shot. The posse would look like heroes for killing dangerous tramps.

"What gave us away?" Henderson Black asked quietly.

"Tracks in the snow." The Deputy aimed his rifle...

HONK! HONK! HONK!

The truck's lights flashed as well, startling him. A witness!

Carfelli threw the rock with precision, hitting the Deputy in the face. Black dived out of the circle of light and wrought havoc as only he could. A shotgun blasted. Men yelled. Carfelli hurled himself out of the firelight, aimed in another direction with yet another sizable rock, and struck paydirt.

Something hit him in the middle of his back. He wrestled with his attacker. Then, Carfelli felt the body jerk away, and heard solid blows. "Awright, Hend, quit it!" Black never gave quarter, probably why he still survived.

Black dropped the body. "Unconscious."

"Check and see if any of 'emare shamming. Let's get outta here."

"Right."

Swiftly, Carfelli packed while Black piled the unconscious bodies together. Their gear went under the bench-seat of the truck, and battened down in cargo cases in back.

Carfelli shoved the tin pot between them, their only towel beneath it. He sliced chunks of stew as the truck bounded down the gravel-covered, single-lane dirt roads. Black took food from the blade as presented to him, but otherwise kept both hands on the wheel and his speed up as high as he dared.

"God *damn*," Carfelli swore. "County deputies. What county were we in, anyway?"

"Jefferson."

"Well, let's get into the next one."

"Saint Lawrence."

"…and give two County Sheriffs turf to fight over, fine." Carfelli regarded Black, and saw an unfairly handsome face, a fierce glare at the road, a set jaw. "Black, how could we *not* have seen 'em? You may have had your head under the hood, but goddamn it, I was sneaking around, stealing chickens."

"You didn't see them because they weren't there." Black slammed the truck into third gear. "That's why I asked how they found us. I brushed our tire tracks away when we first arrived."

"That's right, you did. There wasn't no tracks. And why did the truck honk?"

"I was playing with the electrical system, trying to find a method to start it from a distance."

Carfelli snorted. "The method's called 'getting up off your ass, walking over to the truck, and putting your key in the ignition.'"

"Maybe," Black allowed. "Still, it would've been nice if we could've called a transport over to spots where we've been pinned down, and got in under cover."

"It's a pipe dream, but a good one," Carfelli admitted. "Find us a general store, with a Work board. We need jobs."

"We've got a few bucks," said Black, reaching in his pocket. "I rolled 'em."

Carfelli counted the bills, and snorted. "Twenty-seven dollars. No wonder they wanted a bounty. But it's twenty-seven more than we had. What did you keep back?"

"Ten for me," Black admitted. "If there's a garage—I need oil and hardware." They held out on each other honestly.

Their reasons for tramping in this desolate Adirondack land were different, but never discussed. Black drove on.

***

Carfelli had the dream again: *Coming home from the trenches, duffle bag over his shoulder, walking through New York happily, reaching his house, still in uniform—finding strangers there, his family all dead and gone, home gone, money gone*—Carfelli woke, gasping.

"Nightmare." Black understood.

"Worse. Where we goin'?"

"Watertown Post Office."

"Should change license plates."

"Later." Black got out his Service match-case.

Carfelli pulled out tobacco and papers, and dexterously rolled a cigarette one-handed. Only two matches left. "We gotta get supplies."

"We will, somehow." They stopped at a general store with a nearly bare Work board. Black bought matches, then read, too. "Just mining jobs. Doubt we could do that, with our lungs."

"You boys veterans?" The storekeeper had overheard.

"Yeah."

"Where'd you work last?"

"Railroad, south of Utica," Carfelli replied.

"Mines pay well."

"And kill you doin' it."

"Well, that's true. Dollar to unload the truck for me."

They regarded each other. "It's a dollar," Carfelli told Black.

"…one dollar for the two of you."

"It's still a dollar," Black told Carfelli.

As they piled sacks in the storeroom, Carfelli saw Black's gaze travel to a big industrial thermometer on one wall. *And we'll make up the difference tonight*, he thought.

Black's truck sounded different now. He trained it to do more tricks than a puppy, like the horn-and-lights thing. At the Watertown Post Office, they climbed out stiffly.

"Have you a letter for Black?"

The clerk turned to a rack. "First name?"

"Henderson."

"Yep, two from Canada, saying, 'To be Left Till Called For.' What took you so long?" Postal officials were chatty; it was prudent to reply.

"I told my friends I was job-hunting in Watertown and ended up in Syracuse."

"Whereabouts?"

"Solvay."

"The foundry." He nodded sagely. "What brings you here?"

"Friends got a fishing shack, invited us up," Carfelli cut in.

"Well, enjoy your vacation, boys."

"Thanks!" Carfelli spoke with false cheeriness.

Back in the truck, Black slit open one envelope.
"*Ducem Nigri, Reversus in domum suam. Duo anni.
Homo est in malo, Cartaginem. Mira res accidit in lacum
Saranac. Pacata ne Lake. Caveat auctor.*" There was no
signature.

Black's lips twitched in a smile. "Done reading?"

"I thought at first it was Italian. Is that Latin?"

"That's how we communicated when I was a POW. I
couldn't speak German, they couldn't speak English, but I
attended Latin school so they called in a priest to
interpret."

Carfelli's heart sank. "Aw, Black, tell me you ain't a
spy. I wouldn't believe it." They had first met in an English
military hospital, then again on a Westchester County
roadside as Carfelli hitched from the city.

"I'm not a spy." Black started the engine. Carfelli gave
him the first puff of the new cigarette, a sign of
camaraderie. Black relented. "I was an experiment."

Now Carfelli understood. "The hand. And the feet."

"Yep, I lost mine when my plane was shot down. So
the Huns tested these on me." Black rolled back the flesh-
like covering on his left wrist, exposing metal rods
beneath. "Dogs and Yanks. Experimental animals." He
rarely sounded this bitter. Black opened the other
envelope with his thumb while he drove. He glanced at it,
then groaned, "Aw, shit."

"*Soror autem tua quaerunt te.*"

"Am I reading that right?" Carfelli stared at the
paper. "That doesn't say 'Your sister is looking for you,'
does it?"

"You know it does."

"You've got family!" Carfelli felt the ache of his own
loss.

"She *must not* find me."

***

If a passerby saw Carfelli asleep on the truck bed at
the roadside, he might think the driver was just taking a
nap. Meanwhile, however, Black had their sacks and his

little glass jar, doing some shopping of his own. The sacks bagged junkyard dogs until Black finished his scavenging; Black was as good at that as Carfelli was at chicken coop raiding.

"Get outta here, ya goddam tramp!"

A large rock landed on the truck bed, near his head. Instinct made Carfelli roll and grab the Remington. He was aiming at the other truck's tires before he actually woke up.

"Sunnuva bitch, he's got a rifle!"

Crack.

First shot in a front tire. Second shot in the windshield. The panic-stricken driver did a two-wheel turnaround. Third shot in the rear tire.

Their truck rolled on the muddy slope. Four boys staggered out and ran away. "Goddamn kids," muttered Carfelli. Papa would be here soon, looking for his vehicle. Carfelli had never tried driving this rig. He shoved his bedroll away and hopped in, praying...

Black looked in the driver's window, grinning. "Want to drive?"

Carfelli slid to the passenger seat gratefully. "Let's get outta here!"

"First things first." Black had scavenged SL license plates from the dump. Carfelli buried the old JF plates while Black screwed on new ones. "Now we're from Saint Lawrence County."

Carfelli sighed. "The mines?"

"No choice. Toolbox."

Carfelli opened the toolbox. From his pocket, Black pulled the glass jar with its stopper, now more than half-full of liquid silver. Mercury. He had gone back on foot and bled that thermometer, to add to the jar.

"Ain't that stuff poisonous?"

"Then don't drink it," said Black.

***

Now, they avoided the main roads.

Carfelli reloaded the Remington using one of Black's inventions—a strip of birch bark with pine-tar holding cartridges in line, one yank of the strip and the chamber was loaded. It prevented cartridges from flying everywhere when they hit a bump. "These roads would be great for a horse and cart," Carfelli grumbled. Calmly, Black kept control of the vehicle as it bounced over a wretched cow-track off the main highway.

Suddenly, a bullet smacked into the windshield and struck between them. A car appeared over the rise, heading straight for them.

Black, as surprised as Carfelli, wrenched the steering wheel. "Hang on! I'm running off the road."

"Yeah." Carfelli gripped the dash as they galloped over a hillock. Their war instincts were still good; *never stop and stare*. Black slumped over the wheel and played possum. Carfelli slid out his door, now invisible to the road, ready to return fire. The car passed by, and continued out of sight.

Black sat up. "What the hell was *that* about?"

"Search me! I expect if we was civilians, we'd be dead now. We gonna see what we weren't supposed to witness?"

"May as well." Black smoothly returned to the roadway. The truck began a slow uphill climb on mud-filled, weed-choked ruts that led to a slovenly farm.

Carfelli stared. "How can they tell the shitty house from the barn?"

"Nobody cares out here." Black stopped the truck. They got out. "That's where the car was. They spun their wheels, getting out of here."

"I'll say." Carfelli raised his voice and hallooed. Silence. They walked over to a dirty, broken door with a leather latch. "Anyone home?"

Black opened the door. "Carfelli!"

Carfelli caught the familiar scents immediately. Blood, guts, and gunpowder.

They entered the shack and stopped, flabbergasted.

A man sat at a table, in a puddle of blood. His wife lay on the floor, her guts blown away.

"Over here." Black had stepped behind a hanging wool blanket.

Five dead children, blood spattered everywhere.

"Got the parents first," said Black. "Kids were trying to hide under blankets and beds."

"I gotta get out," said Carfelli hurriedly. Outside, he gulped air. "No wonder they didn't want witnesses."

Black, just as pale, examined the ground. "Are we accounting for all the footprints?"

Some prints headed toward a pasture, some toward a chicken coop. They heard sounds. Wordlessly, Black inclined his head toward the coop. *Feel like I'm securing a French farm again*, Carfelli thought, gripping the rifle tightly.

Black called, "Anyone here? Come out. Please. We won't harm you. Those men are gone." They opened the coop door, and squatted down to see the figure underneath the roost.

It was a girl, hidden in straw, whimpering with terror.

"My God, you're alive," breathed Carfelli.

Black remained still. "I'm Hend Black, and this is Vic Carfelli. We're railroad workers. We heard you were selling chickens, and we wanted one for supper." Black kept his words simple and his lies plausible.

"What happened?" Carfelli asked gently.

At last, the girl spoke. "I got two roosters. Pa would let me sell one for two dollars if I give him the money."

"Honey," said Carfelli, "where your Pa is gone, he don't need two dollars."

The girl began to sob.

Carfelli reached out. Perhaps because he was smaller and scruffier than Black, she responded. She could barely stand after so long in hiding, and she stunk. Her clothes were ripped, and covered with chicken manure. Her face was bruised.

"You need to clean up," said Carfelli.

"No!" she screamed. "Don't take me in there!"

Black winced. "Of course not. You can wash up in the barn. We'll bring out a washtub and some hot water."

Her face was tragic. "They're all dead, ain't they— aren't they?" she corrected herself.

"Yes. Let me get the tub. You and Mr. Carfelli find a private spot in the barn where you'll feel safe washing up." Black left for the house.

Carfelli put the rifle away. "What's your name, missy?" he asked, as they walked to the barn.

"My name's Mary Enfield."

"How old are you, Mary?"

"I'm fifteen." He would have guessed younger, but she was a country girl.

Black returned with a tin washtub and some clothes. "I guessed this was your drawer," he told Mary. "They look the right size."

"Us girls all share clothes anyway."

Black pumped the cold water. The comb, soap, towel and hot water came from the truck. Carfelli and Black closed the barn door and waited outside while water splashed.

At last she came out, cleaner and calmer. "Is that your truck?"

"Yes."

"Can you take me to Gouverneur? Please?"

"Sure," Black replied. "Do you have family there?"

Mary nodded. "My Aunt Carrie." She followed the last footprints. The men kept pace with her. Beyond the stand of trees, a man's body lay, face down. "That's my Uncle Delbert," said Mary, stone-faced. "He's responsible for this. Aunt Carrie should know."

***

Mary sat between them as the truck trundled onward. "I heard them shooting," she said. "I wasn't in the house. Uncle Delbert was visiting, carrying a big suitcase.

You said it wasn't there, so I bet it was full of money and the gunmen took it."

"What did Uncle Delbert do for a living?" Black asked.

"He worked in a bank," Mary replied. "But he said he was going to live the good life."

"Embezzlement?" Carfelli suggested.

"It's a crime, isn't it? 'Thou shalt not steal.'"

"Exactly right," Carfelli sighed. "But you know, Mary, we're thieves, too."

"Not much, though, right? Or you'd have a newer truck. And you wouldn't've asked which chicken I hated most when you killed one for supper." They had roasted Mary's nastiest rooster over a campfire. Both men smiled ruefully. Despite her simple vocabulary, Mary Enfield was a bright girl.

Black kept his eyes on the road. "Mary—why were you sleeping in the chicken coop?"

Mary's lips trembled, and the tears began. "Pa and Ma kicked me out because they said I lied."

"About what?" Carfelli asked.

"School," said Mary, tight-lipped.

"And hit you," said Black. "Didn't they?"

Mary's jaw clamped.

"Don't speak ill of the dead," Carfelli told Black. "They were her parents."

Apparently Mary needed those few supportive words. "I was walking home from school. It was dark, but I know the road. Somebody knocked me down. He—yanked up my skirt, and—d-did things." She swallowed. "When I told Ma and Pa, Ma said, 'Shut up! Nothin' of the kind ever happened to you.' And Pa hit me."

Carfelli sighed. "You were raped, and your parents called you a liar. Any idea who?"

"Not really. There's so many mean people on our road…" Mary breathed deeply. "My Aunt Carrie is nice, but we're not close. If she hasn't got a place for me, then

I'll … I'll go to work for housekeeping at a hotel. I can't drive, but it'll give me somewhere to live."

"That's a good plan," Black approved.

As darkness fell, Mary began to nod off. Carfelli said, "If you don't mind my stink, lean against me." She rested her head against his shoulder, and fell asleep. Softly, he said, "Jesus, Black, we gotta get her to her Aunt Carrie's."

"I know." Black had mended the holes in the windshield with a transparent mixture he made at the farm. "We should be there tomorrow, if we keep going."

"If we keep going," repeated Carfelli. "We can't. You need rest, too, and I don't know how this flivver is doing for gas."

"The flivver's fine." Black turned down another road. "I admit it's tiresome, driving these back roads, but I don't want to show. If they think we mauled this girl, we won't end up in jail, they'll shoot us."

"I hadn't thought about that."

"Mary says her aunt lives alone. Two men showing up with her niece—she'll assume the worst."

"I'll take that chance." Carfelli was determined. "*She's* got family left." Carfelli tapped his arm. "Here, pull over and catch forty winks."

Black stopped before an empty storefront in the middle of nowhere with a big GOING OUT OF BUSINESS sign in its window. Immediately, he bunched his jacket against his window as a pillow, and fell asleep.

The stillness woke Mary. She sat up, embarrassed, as Carfelli removed his arm from her shoulder. The cigarette he rolled and lit was the only light in the cab. "I thought we just stopped, but Mr. Black is sound asleep."

"We did. He falls asleep fast. We all do."

"The soldiers, you mean?"

"Yeah. Sleep while we can."

"He wasn't—a soldier—like you, though, was he?"

"Naw. I was infantry. Black was a pilot."

"You were both in the Army?"

"I was. Black was in the Royal Flying Corps. Before America got in the war, if you wanted to be a flyboy, you went to England."

"Mr. Black loves machines more than people, doesn't he?"

Carfelli chuckled. "You already figured that out?" He puffed the cigarette and passed it to her. She took a tiny puff and returned it. "Don't hold it against him. The Brits seem pretty cold, and besides, he was shot down over Germany. He was a prisoner of war for a while."

"Is that why he limps?"

Carfelli blinked. "Limps?"

"Just a little."

"Yeah, it is, but I never notice. I must be used to him."

"I bet you are." She glanced at the dashboard. "Whose letters?"

"Black's."

"Do you ever get any?"

"My family is all dead."

"Now," said Mary sadly, "so is mine. How did they die?"

"Someone stole the money I sent home out of my Ma's mailbox. They got evicted, and froze to death in the streets." It seemed easy to tell her that.

"It's a hard life," said Mary.

"Yeah," said Carfelli, "it is."

Black awoke in a while. He broke and entered so they could use the abandoned store's restroom. Cleaner but still cold and tired, they returned to the truck as the sun rose.

Miles later, Mary asked Black, "May I look at your letters?"

"You won't get anything out of them," Carfelli warned.

"Try it," said Black.

Mary opened one envelope. Her eyes widened. "You were a Captain?"

Black almost drove off the road. "You can read Latin?"

"*Ducem Nigri*—that's Captain Black." Mary read slowly. "'Return to our home. Two years. Bad man in Carthage. Evil in Lake Saranac. The lake is not Placid. Beware of Watertown.' Your friend likes puns, doesn't he? And he really wants you to get out of here."

"Where did you learn to read Latin?"

"School. I got an A. Is your friend a priest? He's good at Latin."

Carfelli burst into laughter at the expression on Black's face.

***

Black stopped at the Gouverneur Diner. "I'll wait here with the truck. If we all show up, and your Aunt Carrie is alone, she'll call the Sheriff."

"That's silly," Mary protested. "You rescued me."

"We can't prove we weren't the men who raped you, Mary. Mr. Carfelli's taking a big chance as it is."

Mary thought it through. "That's just not right, Mr. Black."

Black smiled. "I know, honey. But that's the way the world works. You know it, too." He leaned over and kissed her cheek. "Good luck." Black went into the diner.

"At least he has a nickel for a cup of coffee," said Carfelli. "Come on, Mary." Then he looked closer, surprised. "Those aren't tears, are they?"

"I'm going to miss you both so much. You feel more like family than even my family did."

Carfelli felt that old familiar pain. "C'mon. Gotta get you to your aunt's. 'Stiff upper lip, chaps.'" He imitated a Brit.

Mary remembered the way, although she visited only at Christmas. They walked down the street, then turned a corner.

Carfelli's warning senses rang. "Mary—that's an unmarked police car ahead."

"What?"

A plainclothesman stopped them. It was too late to run. Certainly not with Mary.

"Could I see some identification, sir?"

"Sure. My discharge papers are in my pocket," Carfelli answered, trying to sound unconcerned. "That's the only ID I've got, at the moment."

"Is something wrong, sir?" asked Mary.

"We're blocking this road at government request, miss, sorry."

Mary said, "I don't have papers. I can only tell you my name is Mary Enfield, and I live in DeKalb Junction."

"Could you come over to my vehicle to talk? It's warmer inside."

At the car, the agent suddenly turned like lightning. He clamped handcuffs on Carfelli's wrists. Mary gasped as he cuffed her, too. "Now don't struggle, folks. You're coming with me to Watertown." He showed them the gun inside his jacket. He maneuvered Mary, then Carfelli, into the car.

"*Caveat auctor,*" Mary murmured, stunned. "Beware Watertown."

They'd been kidnapped.

***

This Ford was not nearly as fast or comfortable as Black's truck. Carfelli wondered if they had seen the last of Black. He had advised against this; he might give up on them. *Or maybe not.*

Silently, Mary leaned her head on Carfelli's shoulder. Carfelli lifted manacled hands to brush her hair from her eyes.

Three hours later, the car arrived at the Watertown train station. The agent escorted them to the platform. Men waited there, wearing uniforms unlike any Carfelli had ever seen—royal blue, with red and green piping, matching the stripes on the silvery train perfectly.

No black smoke poured from any smokestack along the streamlined roof. The engine seemed silent. There was a locomotive, two passenger cars, a boxcar, a crew van, and

an equally sleek and shiny rear engine. The first car read
Bobby W.

Mary breathed, "This is a luxury train. I read about it
in a magazine at school! This is Barbara Walcott's train!"

The conductor demanded, "They were where you
expected?"

"Yes, sir," the plainclothes agent replied. "The folks at
that farm only had the one relative in the area. The
neighbors were helpful." His tone suggested that some
coaxing had been necessary.

His gaze rested on Mary's delicate wrists. "Remove
the handcuffs, please."

"These are dangerous felons. I escort them," the
agent objected.

"My orders are for *me* to take them aboard," stated
the conductor.

The agent shrugged, and released them. The
conductor escorted Mary and Carfelli up the steps and left
the agent behind. Immediately, the train started moving.
In the compartment, it was indeed the famous hotel
heiress who looked up at them. She had a ladylike French-
Provincial-looking desk with the obligatory African violet
and posh desk accessories, but there were papers spread
out; she had been working. A thin man stood near her.
"Who are these people, Hammond?"

"Miss Barbara Walcott, Dr. Henry Schmidt, allow me
to introduce Miss Mary Enfield and Mr. Victor Carfelli."

Barbara became alert. "But no sign of Mr. Walcott?"

"No, miss."

Carfelli felt a chill.

Mary spoke, charmed. "You really are Barbara
Walcott, aren't you? You look like your pictures. I've seen
so many pictures of people who don't measure up to their
photographs, it's nice to see someone who does."

Surprised, Miss Walcott answered, "Thanks—Mary,
is it?"

"Yes, I'm Mary."

"Well, come over and sit down, Mary. You, too, Mr. Carfelli."

"You know what?" Mary disagreed. "We'd get this nice furniture all grubby."

Barbara Walcott actually laughed, and stood. "You look about my size, Mary. Let's see if my clothes fit you."

Hammond and Carfelli followed them down the corridor, to the compartment beyond Barbara's. "Wash and change here, Carfelli."

"Thanks," Carfelli replied, "but why don't you think I'll just take off?"

Hammond smiled slightly. "The windows are sealed. I'm armed. You're worried about the girl. And we're moving."

"All good reasons. So," Carfelli asked, as he stripped, washed, and shaved, "who's the Doctor? Medical or Professor?"

"Medical, but he's an inventor, too." The conductor handed Carfelli a fresh change of clothes, in his size, from a closet. "Like the late Mr. Walcott."

"Barbara's father?"

"No, brother. Killed in the war, they say."

Carfelli felt the chill again. "Have you always worked for the family?"

"Yes," Hammond replied quietly, "for generations. They're fine people."

The girls had spent time dressing and making up. Mary looked downright pretty, as well as comfortable in her surroundings. Another woman sat with them. Her tightly-bound auburn hair and competent hazel eyes proclaimed her profession: Nurse Rose Creighton. Mary remarked, "Mr. Carfelli, you really look handsome."

"Well, thanks, but being clean isn't the same as being handsome."

"Miss Walcott showed me around, but I didn't even know you were on the train, Miss Creighton," said Mary. "Do you live in Car Three?"

"Yes, I'm residential."

"That's what my sister wanted to do." Mary swallowed. "Maybe Trudeau Sanitarium."

"That's a good place," said Nurse Rose. "I trained at Pilgrim State Hospital, myself."

"You're a psychiatric nurse, then," said Mary. "I thought you might be."

Carfelli spoke. "Now can I ask? Why are we here?"

"Hammond says you have some idea," Barbara Walcott replied.

"I'd rather be told I'm wrong," Carfelli answered.

"That private investigator really thought he was turning criminals over to the Feds. I knew you weren't criminals, but I'm happy to help our government. For him."

Dr. Schmidt objected, "We have not achieved our goal. We are not certain he's following us."

"Oh, he'll follow us, I guarantee it. He's as stubborn as I am." Barbara looked up, past Carfelli's shoulder. "What do you think of your train?"

"Not quite as I imagined it would look."

Henderson Black stood there.

"But you did a nice job, anyway, with my plans," he continued.

"You shouldn't have come, Black," sighed Carfelli.

"I wouldn't ditch you, buddy." Black looked grim. "Nor Mary."

Barbara Walcott stood to face him. The resemblance between them was striking. "All our childhood summers at Henderson Harbor, Robert Nigro Walcott—Henderson Black."

"Pretty simple, wasn't it?"

"You're not well, big brother. Your war experiences broke you down. Let the doctor help you. Please, Bobby. I love you. I want you back."

"I didn't have a nervous breakdown, little sister." Black's gaze traveled to the doctor. "I take it you haven't told her why you've been hunting me down, Schmidt."

"*Hunting* you? *I've* been hunting you, Bobby, not him."

"Babbie, I love you, but you've been stupid. How much have you paid Schmidt?"

"Not a cent," she shot back.

"That's my point. Who do you think *is* paying him?"

"He's a trained psychiatrist, Bobby. I've given him every facility—"

Dr. Schmidt cut in. "True, I might not have found you without her." He regarded Black, head to toe. "The work you have done is marvelous, Captain. Far better than anything I accomplished."

Barbara Walcott realized something was wrong. "Hammond!"

The conductor reached inside his jacket.

"Hammond," Carfelli cautioned, "stop. If Schmidt hired the guards, you don't stand a chance."

"Yes, sir, he did." Hammond left the gun in its holster, and stepped back. "I'm sorry, Miss Barbara, Master Ro- Mister Walcott."

"Understood, Hammond." As if there had been any doubt of Black's identity.

"You will accompany Nurse Creighton, Mr. Walcott," Schmidt ordered.

"Not without my vehicle."

"Where did you leave it?"

"In Watertown."

The doctor suggested outrageously, "Bid it come to you, then."

"No. We'll go there."

***

Hammond radioed to clear the track. The train's alternate engine reversed their direction. It was smoother than anything imaginable, a cutting-edge twentieth-century maneuver worthy of Henderson Black.

The only disturbance came from within. "I want to talk with my brother," Barbara stated.

"I am sorry, but I cannot allow that. It would be a monumental intelligence risk." Schmidt never said whose intelligence. "Nurse, accompany Mr. Walcott to Car Three." After they left, the doctor warned Carfelli, "Soldier, I cannot overstate the confidentiality of this work. Among our rivals is the government of Italy. With a name like Carfelli, you cannot afford to excite suspicion that you may be involved in espionage."

"Certainly I understand," said Carfelli. "The U.S. Government couldn't tell *Italianos* apart when I was in the trenches, either." Bitterly, Carfelli realized that Schmidt knew his man. Black, as wild a fighter as Carfelli had ever seen, was hog-tied while they remained hostages for his good behavior. Wordlessly, Black accompanied Schmidt to Car Three.

Barbara Walcott was stunned and angry. "He won't let me talk to my own brother, after all I've done!"

"That's not surprising. They got what they wanted." Carfelli stared out the window at telegraph pole after pole after pole. At last the grey scenery devolved into Watertown Station.

"Mr. Carfelli." Nurse Rose appeared, looking harassed. "Would you come with me, please?"

"What's wrong?" Carfelli stood.

"Dr. Schmidt refuses to allow me to sedate my patient, so I suggested your presence might calm Mr. Walcott. You and Miss Mary. Will you come?"

Barbara rose. "I'm coming, too."

"I'd advise against that, Miss Walcott. My patient has very strong feelings—

"I'm coming." Barbara slid on a jacket, and handed one to Mary. Hammond trailed them from the car onto the platform.

Schmidt, Black, and guards stood around the truck. "Such an ordinary-looking vehicle," Schmidt marveled. He opened the door and peered inside. "A thousand just like it in appearance. Simply amazing. Synchronized control. My dear fellow!"

"Where do you want it?" Black asked shortly.

The doctor indicated the train. The boxcar door was open. The guards lined up planks to load the truck aboard. "I want to see the radio-synchronicity. Can you load it from here?"

Grim-faced, Black gazed at the loading ramp, and breathed. He lifted his right hand and twitched his fingers.

The truck started.

Black's right hand and foot moved slightly.

The truck shifted into first gear. Black's fingers twitched.

The truck drove slowly up the ramp and into the boxcar. The guards moved back superstitiously.

Black's fingers twitched again. The engine silenced.

Dr. Schmidt's face shone. "What have you done for neurological switches? You must need thousands!"

"No. I've been in the woods, Schmidt, not a laboratory."

"You circumvented your implants. I must learn how, Captain." He motioned to the guards. "Take him to the laboratory, and stand by while the nurse restrains him."

"Doctor," Rose protested, "we can easily confine—"

"We cannot afford to take chances, particularly with the vehicle aboard. No, Nurse. Restrain him."

"I won't escape if you treat Carfelli and the women well," said Black.

"Thanks to the Pater, I know your promises mean nothing," said Schmidt. "I suppose you know where that traitor is now, too."

Canada, thought Carfelli. *Still urging Black to a British Commonwealth country, to safety not possible in a neutral like the U.S.A.*

Carfelli, Mary, and Barbara returned to Car Two. The train moved. Hammond had the good sense to provide them all with liquor, including himself, damn the Prohibition. Barbara finished her first drink in one gulp. "I don't understand. But I think I've been suckered."

"You have," Carfelli agreed. "Your brother was seriously injured and used in a scientific experiment. He escaped, thanks to a friendly priest. But the scientists weren't finished with him."

"If we run away," asked Mary, "can Mr. Black escape?"

"No, honey. Because Schmidt knows everything about us, thanks to Baby Sister here. He'd track us down again in a minute." Carfelli drank whiskey. "They know about you, me, your Aunt Carrie, everybody."

"Was this phony psychiatrist the one who experimented on my brother?" Barbara demanded.

"Judging by how happy he was to see Hend Black's 'improvements,' I would say yes."

Barbara stared out the window. The only justice Carfelli felt in the world was watching her get her nose pushed in, too.

Rose entered. Carfelli had no sympathy for her, either, but Mary seemed oddly unprejudiced. *Of course, her sister had planned to become a nurse,* he thought. Mary fussed over Rose, seating her with a drink. The nurse's face was haggard. "I'm sorry, Miss Walcott. I thought as you did—that we were searching for a shell-shocked serviceman. I had no idea." Rose shook her head. "He—he's removing his artificial limbs. Without anesthesia. Because he wants to measure the neurological connectivity. I've never heard a man scream like that. I had to leave."

Carfelli swore helplessly.

Barbara was on her second drink. "I never believed Bobby died. Our parents were so busy with their big important lives. Bobby was the one who was always there for me. I thought—for a change—I could be there for him." She stared into her glass.

Carfelli wished he'd been able to reach the rifle when they loaded the truck. But they would have noticed. And maybe he would have been tempted to use it on Black now, to put him out of his misery.

The Car Three gangway door slammed open. Schmidt strode in, carrying the tool box. "Got it," he announced jubilantly. "And you knew it, too, didn't you, soldier?" He slammed the toolbox down on the elegant salon desk. "*Mercury.*"

Carfelli stared at him blankly.

"Mercury!" Schmidt elaborated. "A fluid metallic conductor, allowing him to open multiple electrical synapse ports at once, smoothly and sequentially. The reason for broken thermometers and equipment wherever you appeared—he tapped them to fill his appliances after every modification!" He pulled out Black's glass bottle triumphantly. "The reserve supply of a mercury vampire. The angles at which he holds his limbs, electrical impulses to hidden radio controls—that's how he works the vehicle. Imagine useless brains and bodies like Walcott's, returned to combat. A mechanical army created from the detritus of the Great War!"

You're a mad scientist straight from the movies, Carfelli thought, and wished again for the rifle.

Schmidt lifted the top rack from the toolbox and pulled out a human-looking foot and forearm. "I'm taking these units to the boxcar, to test them with the vehicle. These innovative mercury switches are just what I need. Nurse, scrub down the laboratory. There's a body bag beneath the table." He dashed out.

"Body bag!" Rose exclaimed, aghast.

"Run, run!" cried Mary, jumping up.

Carfelli sprinted behind them, through the cars' gangway doors. He halted, stunned.

Car Three's main compartment was the full width of the train, windowless. Bright light came from a translucent ceiling and a system of electrical lamps. It reeked of hospital alcohol. Equipment lined wall counters. On a central white slab, strapped in place, were the remains of a body.

Carfelli remembered bomb explosions—staring eyes, litters of body parts. Here, the room shone in silver and white. There was no blood or stink. But, atop the main table were the same body parts. And, in the midst of it all, Black.

Henderson Black had no limbs.

His face was wet with tears. Rows of tiny wires and connectors dangled from four stumps. Carfelli stared in horror at the living remains of the man he had known for years.

Rose's voice trembled. "I didn't realize what he was doing until we were well into it—that this had become a torture chamber, not a surgical suite. I'm sorry, I'm sorry."

Mary's voice sharpened. "Did you see how he took him apart?"

"Yes."

"Can you put him back together?"

"I don't know how," the nurse choked. "That was why he ordered me to discard the remains."

"Well, you're going to put him back together, anyway," Mary Enfield stated firmly. "Wash up. Now." She turned to Carfelli. "Mr. Carfelli, Rose will need your help. Wash up." Mary climbed up onto the slab, and lifted Black's head into her lap.

"Mary," Black said weakly, "let me die. Please."

"No," said Mary. "You're in great pain, Mr. Black, but we're going to fix you. Don't give up. Here's what you need to do—deep breath in, through your teeth. Then out, puff puff puff. Can you do that?" She demonstrated.

Rose's lips twitched in a ghastly smile. "I won't let Mary down, Mr. Carfelli. Ready to help?"

"I'm on," Carfelli confirmed. They washed, and donned cotton aprons.

Breathe—puff puff puff.

Left leg to attach at the knee. With Carfelli's help, Rose hurriedly untangled tiny electrical wires extruding from the knee and the stump, male and female connections, in order. As she began re-attaching them, Black cried out.

"Nerves are still good," Rose observed feverishly. "Here, get this one."

Breathe—puff puff puff.

"Hurry, hurry. She's doing great—it's self-hypnosis —she's got his full attention —"

Breathe—puff puff puff.

After an eternity, Rose said, "I hope that's done it."

Black glanced down. And moved his ankle. "Left hand," he panted.

Mary overrode, "Breathe, puff puff puff."

Left arm. "I never thought—" Rose sorted arm wires —"that I would assist a man being coached through labor pains."

Carfelli grinned, and kept pushing tiny color-coded connectors together. Of course Mary, as the oldest daughter, assisted in all the family births. "Pain is pain."

Black heard them. "I will never live this down."

"Breathe, puff puff puff," Mary insisted.

They reconnected wires, shoved the limb base in place, and prayed. Black's fingers twitched. He made a fist, and released it.

"My right hand itches," Black groaned.

"Phantom limb syndrome," Rose muttered. "We don't have your right arm or foot. Dr. Schmidt does."

"Carfelli," gasped Black. "I'm right-handed. I need that hand."

The boxcar would be well guarded. Black was asking him to risk his life. Not the first time for either of them. Carfelli stepped past Barbara, standing in the doorway, Hammond behind her. Carfelli tapped Hammond's shoulder and motioned him to Car Two.

Once the doors closed, Carfelli demanded, "Do I have to knock you down to get the passkey to the other cars?"

Hammond handed over his key. "Must be what you did, because I wouldn't give it up voluntarily."

Carfelli re-entered Car Three, passed the slab, continued to the rear prep compartment, and unlocked the supply hatch. The roar of the train buffeted him. He eased out the hatch.

Carfelli evaded lines of sight along the train exterior, knowing guards would spot him. As he pressed against the swaying boxcar, he thought fiercely, *Don't look down, Black needs you.* Carfelli sidled along the trim until he found the boxcar hatch, unlocked it, and pushed it open.

As he expected, crates hid the hatch from sight within. Carfelli crept forward cautiously until he lifted himself onto the truck's flatbed.

The truck was chained in the dark as securely as Black was tethered in the bright white compartment. Two guards stood in the personnel door, smoking cigarettes and pitching butts into the valley below. Schmidt had left.

Carfelli found cartridges. Then he checked the magazine on the M1917, aimed, and fired.

One guard tumbled off. Carfelli's second shot also found its mark; another body hurtled into the river. Carfelli waited for a third guard, in case anyone saw the action. No one appeared. He slid into the cab.

Knife and duffle bag, good. Carfelli opened the shipping crate on the truck seat. He extracted Hend Black's arm and leg and stuffed them in the bag. He crept back to the hatch, rifle and bag over his shoulder.

Returning seemed deceitfully easier, which kept him cautious. At last he entered the lab's hatch, and stored his acquisitions, including the rifle, out of sight in a prep-room drawer.

To his alarm, Schmidt stood with Rose in the lab. The body bag lay atop the slab, filled. "Feeling better, Mr. Carfelli?"

Had Rose lied to cover them, or not? "Black was my buddy once."

"Dissociate yourself from this experiment," the scientist advised, "and keep the personal element out of it. Robert N. Walcott died years ago. These are mere remains."

"Thanks. I'll keep that in mind," said Carfelli. The scientist patted his shoulder and left. The tween-doors slammed.

Only then did Rose slip the "remains" from the bag. Black's eyes opened. Mary slid from beneath the slab. "Have you got them?"

"Yeah. What if he comes back?"

"He won't," Rose stated. "Barbara told him they'd celebrate. We'll see him when his hangover lets up." She pulled out fresh surgical aprons from an apparently unending supply.

Carfelli retrieved his bag. Then, dressed and washed for surgery, they wiped down the limbs with alcohol, and began the arduous task of reconnecting the tiny wires. Black gasped an occasional, "Ow, goddammit," as they reconnected his right arm. "Because I was right-handed," Black explained as they worked, "the main locomotor controls are in my right arm and hand."

"England lost twelve planes a day, I read somewhere."

"Yes. The RFC were expendable. No one expected to retrieve a body, so no one looked for mine."

Mary understood. "That's why Barbara inherited the money."

"If Robert Nigro Walcott came back to life, old wounds would open, his sister's business deals would be invalidated, he'd be in Schmidt's line of sight, and they'd both be blackmailed by anyone who caught on. Bobby had to stay dead."

Rose placed her hand on his bare shoulder. "I see an unethical trend right now in the medical field, to use the weak and helpless for scientific experimentation."

Carfelli scowled, but Black nodded. "No one believes it's happening. I was finished, until the Catholic priest interpreting my Latin found out what they were doing to me. He gave me the strength to get us both out of Germany." Then Black grinned. "When I bought the truck in New York and somebody recognized me, I ran for open country. But I knew I needed another fighter to keep me sane."

Carfelli returned the grin. "And found me hitching by the roadside."

"Yep, sorry." Black's left hand smoothed the artificial skin in place over his right wrist. Then, he winced, took a deep breath—and sat up by himself.

"Come on," Carfelli breathed, relieved. "One more leg to go."

Black helped them re-attach it. "What's our situation?" This could have been a military briefing.

"If Schmidt's getting romantic, his guard'll be off drinking with Hammond."

"Hammond will keep him down."

"There's three asleep in Car Six. I thought there was a cook, too, but Mary says no. Hammond cooks. Don't know anything about the engineers."

"If they're mercenaries," Rose suggested, helping Black dress, "they might reconsider if Miss Walcott stops their paychecks."

"Babbie's enough like me that, once she gets solid evidence of Schmidt's treachery, she'll drop him in a deep hole and hammer on the lid."

"Your arm and leg were in a box labeled for Tubingen, Germany," Carfelli replied. "That oughta do it."

Black turned to Nurse Rose. "Your paycheck won't be covered, either."

"I'm not worried about the money. When you've waited your whole life for something, you recognize it when you see it. We'll be fine." Calmly, Rose buttoned the last button on his shirt.

"I know you're recovering," said Carfelli, "and you'd like to sleep, but hell, so would I. We'd better strike now, before they start counting heads."

***

"You comfortable sneaking around here?" Carfelli muttered.

"This train is *mine*." They stood at the tween-doors between Car Three and the boxcar. There was a glint in Black's eye. "Usually you're trying to calm me *down*." Carfelli grinned.

Black jimmied the lock on the personnel door and entered, Carfelli behind him.

One bored guard leaned against the chained truck, smoking a cigarette. The noise of the train wheels covered the sounds as a wrathful form rose from the darkness to break his neck.

Black broke the lock on the van door, startling two guards in a card game. Carfelli saw the third reach for his gun, and shot him dead. The guards raised their hands.

"Doesn't take much to switch your patriotism from Germany to America, does it?" snarled Carfelli.

They stared. "*Germany?*"

"What the hell did you think Schmidt was, Swedish?"

They herded the guards into a compartment and jammed the lock. Black opened the last personnel door.

The engineer turned and shot.

Carfelli dodged and returned fire. The engineer staggered.

Black, enraged, leaped to the control platform, grabbed the engineer, and threw him bodily from the train.

Carfelli followed. "Who's going to run this now?"

Black twisted knobs and wheels, examined gauges, and applied levers. Slowly, the train came to a standstill. Then, Black competently reversed direction.

"*Kessel, was ist los?*" a radio speaker crackled.

"*Nichts.*" Carfelli knew Schmidt would not recognize his voice amid the noise. He turned off the radio. "Suppose we hit another train?"

"We just passed a crew. They'll alert the line."

"And if they don't?"

"Hammond can call it in."

"If we can reach Hammond."

"You worry too much."

"Don't act like a goddamn flyboy!"

Black grinned. "I'll put the train on one of the Oswego sidings."

Carfelli stayed with him, sweating. This train was small, light, and beautiful, a moth among elephants. A heavy freight train could mash them into the rails. If they didn't get onto a siding soon, something would either run them over, or smash into them.

Black slowed down to nothing as they approached parallel rails. "Bottom notch. I'll jump off to switch us onto this siding."

Carfelli pointed. "No. You won't."

Hammond trotted by, followed by Mary. They threw their weight against a lever. Carfelli jumped down to help. Together, they wrenched the track from the main rails to the siding. Black moved ahead slowly, putting the four cars and two engines on the siding. With a hiss of brakes, the train grew still.

"Are the others disposed of, sir?" asked Hammond.

"Yes," Black replied, "according to Mr. Carfelli's count."

"Then there is only Dr. Schmidt left, sir."

"How about the other engineer?" Carfelli asked.

Hammond's eyes glinted. "MacAdam? I paid him out of my own pocket. I wanted *one* man on this train I could trust."

"Don't ever change, Hammond," said Black appreciatively.

"I hope not, sir. If I may speak freely, sir, it's bad enough listening to Miss Barbara compliment Dr. Schmidt. We are in a false position, sir, both of us."

"It's still a mess," agreed Carfelli. "The government can't prosecute crimes from the last war. They'll just turn Schmidt over to the German Embassy and let him go."

Mary's mind was elsewhere. "I wish *I* still had sisters. She loves you, Mr. Black, and she tried so hard to help you. How was she to know?"

In the Car Two salon, Barbara sat alone, smoking. "So you're back."

"Yes," Black replied. "Where's Schmidt?"

"In bed. The cocktails seem to have made him ill. And we can't even check the dregs, since we threw the glasses off the train as we celebrated."

Carfelli caught his breath. "Mercury doesn't work like that."

"Vi-O-Let-Grow plant food does." Coldly, she indicated the African violet on her desk. Barbara Walcott had taken the law into her own hands. She chose to save her brother, to her own cost.

As if it was still wartime, Black touched Carfelli's shoulder and murmured, "Take care of my sister."

Carfelli nodded and patted his hand.

And Black was gone.

AUTHOR'S NOTE

Linda Tiernan Kepner's previous books include two science-fiction novels (*Planting Walnuts, Play the Game*), two fantasy-fiction novels, two romance novels, and two paranormal novels. Her short stories have been published in *Absolute Magnitude, Reality's Escape, Sorcerer's Apprentice, Fantastic Stories,* and *Dreams of Decadence*. She lives in New Hampshire. Linda's website is www.lindatkepner.com.

And Every Pebble a Soldier

Sarah Smith

He had been a builder's apprentice, in love with stone. He liked clockwork; he had fixed his friend Felix's pocket watch. He liked order. He dreamed of neat rows of stone houses, sunny streets, and young men walking the streets.

When he limped back from the war, his town was in ruins. Every young man of the town had gone for a soldier and every young man but himself was dead. Shadows stumbled through the streets with barrows of money, looking for food. Shadows clubbed each other to steal bread.

When you look back at it afterward, everything he did was inevitable.

He went to the churchyard, which had spread out past its old walls to cover the town square where the market had been. Only the earliest dead had gravestones. The latest names were only painted on the paving stones and already fading. He found his friend Fritz painted at the entrance to an alley. It seemed to him that everything that was missing from the town was there.

From Fritz's paving stone he chipped a bit of rock.

His car was still parked in front of his parents' house, beginning to go bloody with rust. He limped inside (the front door was broken), blinked at the looted rooms, and found paper and pencil. He sat down at the kitchen table, polished his eyeglasses, and began to draw a clockwork man.

He was insane, of course.

What does a man of gears and tin look like? Two legs, two strong arms to haul rubble, a torso to hold it all together. A heart to remember the old well-ordered days. Not much of a head. A tin man needs only to know order.

How does a tin man move? He pried off the back of his dented watch with his fingernail and looked at the moving gears.

He burned furniture, down to the last bed in the house, for light to work by. He begged the works of smashed clocks, stole scribers and calipers. He went to the one-legged clocksmith and the half-blind locksmith and begged knowledge. They laughed at him but they told him what he was doing wrong. He bent over his worktable, which had been the kitchen table, and drew and filed and wound springs until his eyes filled with tears.

The pastor came to see him. "We are cursed for our sins," the pastor said.

"I am building," the builder's apprentice said.

"Building a tin man to repair the corpse of a town! We have no food. The town must die."

"But I build," the builder's apprentice said.

"You do evil."

The builder's apprentice placed the pebble he had chipped from Fritz's grave into a bag made of an old sock, and tied the sock around the tin man's neck, to keep the pebble safe. A bit of rock in a worn bag on a leather cord, a chipped bit of name. Fritz's pebble. Fritz's man.

That first tin man marched into the town square on a cold Friday morning. By then a few old women had started to sell food, half-frozen turnips with wilted greens, spread out on blankets among the fading names, over the piles of rubble. The beggars had reinvented themselves as thieves. The builder began to clear rubble from a corner of the square; the tin man followed his motions. The women screamed.

But the thieves laughed. And when the clockwork ran out and the tin man froze in place, the thieves stole its lamplit eyes and its strong pincer hands.

The builder was insane, of course, but he saw nothing but the pile of rubble the tin man had moved before it wound down.

A tin man is no good alone, the builder decided. You need two of them, wound in series, one to wind the other's gears. He worked all through the winter, while the town shivered and starved around him.

The pastor came to see him again and looked at the half-finished second tin man. "You create abominations in the shape of men! Let what is dead die."

"I do what I can do," the builder's apprentice said. "I build."

"You do evil."

The builder's apprentice's hands were cut and covered with sores, and his vision faded even with his glasses. But he finished the second clockwork man.

He wound them up and fell asleep exhausted, and woke to find a fire on the hearth, the sun shining through clean windows, everything in order, and the two tin men moving about with a great purring like contented cats. They had kept each other wound.

He led them to the town square. And this time the thieves were as astonished as the old women. The locksmith and the clocksmith came out of their shops.

"What is the name of the second one?" the one-legged clocksmith asked.

"He has no name yet."

"Name him after my son." The clocksmith limped into his shop and brought out the watch he would have given his son on his wedding day. "Let him wear this around his neck, and let his name be Resurrection."

"Make me a tin man," said the locksmith, "and let his name be Opened Doors, and let him have lockpicks for hands."

"We are starving," said the old women. "Make farmers for us, and let their names be Give Us Food."

From then on, no clock chimed in the village; every clock-spring, every gear, beat in the chest of a tin man. Old swords and rusty pails, faded tin signs, and the fenders of the mayor's new red car were beaten into arms and legs. The seamstress traded in her scissors for tin snips. Thieves filed gears and old men fit arms and legs to torsos, and new tin farmers ploughed the fields.

The cabbages came up crisp and fresh; there were gleaming carrots like shafts of sunrise and fat dimpled potatoes like babies.

The town began to revive with each tin man they made. Each one they led to the marketplace, and to each one they gave a name. They chipped bits of pebble from the paving stones and the stones of the graveyard. "This is my son, who died in the war." "My husband, dead in the war." "My fiancé, starved on the march to the war." The one-armed blacksmith, with a blow of his hammer, fixed a chip of rock in his son's tin chest like a heart. The little seamstress sewed a silk heart.

With each shining new tin man, a part of the village came home, and with each man came more of the village's pride.

The pastor had secretly rejoiced at the sorrow and death in the town. Sorrow and death were the bitter earth from which redemption grew; sorrow and death would lead his village to Heaven; sorrow and death were more powerful than Heaven itself, and when the tin men strode around the town with tall shining bodies like angels, the pastor raised his hands and cursed them.

"Abomination!" he said. "Things like men, that walk on their own!"

"Next Sunday," said the builder to the townspeople, "come to church with all your sons."

The next Sunday, rather than scattering through the half-empty church as they usually did, all the villagers sat in front, and when the preacher began his sermon, the doors opened and all the tin men marched in too and filled the pews and, with a shriek of metal, they sat down. The church rang with the groan and thump of it, and the church was full.

"They are not human," the pastor said. "You do evil."

The builder's apprentice looked round the church.

"No," he said. "They are not human." He got up and walked to the lectern where the pastor was standing, and pushed him away, and stood there himself. And it seemed to him that he was surrounded, not by the men of his village alone, but immortal men strong as houses and graceful as airplanes. "They are not human. They are better."

For what is human dies, but a rock-hearted man is perfection; the glory of his metal skin burns like lightning.

The next village wanted men too, and the next, and the next. Mayors came with petitions and proclamations; widows came with a chip from their husbands' graves.

And with every new man, a family revived; a village took pride. Towns gave every bit of metal they had, their pots and pans, the metal posts of their fences, until every dead man of the war was alive again, every victim of bombing and sickness was whole, and every starved child grown up.

When you look back at it afterward, it all was inevitable. The cure for loneliness was a tin man; and a tin man could not work alone, he needed more tin men. Through all the region, the sound of hammers and the purring of gears made a proud country; and the louder the sound, the greater the pride.

"Master Builder," the villagers were calling him that now, "there are not enough of us to build our men. More hands!"

"Teach them to build themselves."

"Leader," they were calling him that too. "We do not have enough tin or steel for bodies, or brass for gears. We do not have coal for fires!"

"We must find tin and steel and coal." For we must build, that was all the builder knew; building is our order and our perfection. "Where shall we find them?"

And the old women and the one-legged old soldiers, the seamstresses and the farmers, and all the great lamplit eyes of the tin men, turned and looked West.

What had the war been about? No one in the village

could have said, not even the builder's apprentice, who had been a soldier. It had been about the snap of a bullet past his head, bodies trodden into mud, cold rain in the winter, starving, marching. Somewhere far over his head, someone who never wore a helmet had decided that to end the war, some part of the country would be taken away, all the coal mines, the tin mines, the steelworks of the West.

The war had not been about that, until now.

The leader, who had been the builder's apprentice, gathered them on the westward road, and when all the region had formed a great multitude together, he knelt down and from the side of the road, he picked up a pebble and held it high. "From now on," he said, "we will not name ourselves after men! From now on, our hearts will be the stones of the road, the rocks of the very land!"

The ticking of the multitude of tin men was like thunder.

"All land is yours!" he preached to them. "Your heart is the land, the rock itself! Your land fights for you! Take it apart and make hearts for yourselves!"

And so the tin men marched westward until they reached the enemy's city. They took the pebbles of the road and pounded the pebbles into their breasts, and took the enemy's city apart until it was bits of rock and dust and pounded the rocks into their breasts, and they moved westward, westward, westward over the world, every steel bridge a body to come, every stone building pebbles to come, and every pebble a soldier.

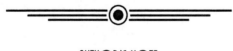

AUTHOR'S NOTE

Sarah Smith's historical mysteries have reached bestseller lists here and abroad and are published in 14 languages. Her most recent book, *The Other Side of Dark,* won the Agatha Award for best mystery and the Massachusetts Book Award for best book in the YA category. She has just finished a mystery about the *Titanic*. About her story, she says "At the Boston convention Arisia, Judith Dial mentioned the connection between Art Deco and Nazism. That was all I needed...."

BERNICE BOBS YOUR HAIR
WILLIAM RACICOT

This is a portrait of Bernice, a young woman 20 years of age, strolling with unaccustomed confidence around a corner past the bank, a monstrous brick hatbox of a building, not at all modern, on her way to open, for the first time, her very own shop, a storefront beauty salon her father has secured in her name.

Despite her coal-black Gibson-coiffed hair, elaborately piled and tucked into itself, a few stray locks writhing down her forehead, Bernice is not, herself, beautiful. Compared to her more fashionable acquaintances, her jaw is too heavy and her eyes rather widely placed around her nose, which is a little too flat; although she is not what one would call swarthy, she can only dream of the fair complexion idealized among the girls in her set. Overall, the effect is more mule than kitten. And if the pictures in the fashion papers may be trusted, even her hair, her one truly striking feature, a cherished bequest from her departed mother, will soon be desperately out of style among women her age.

Worse yet, she is not wealthy, not really. Bernice's father, the indulgent widower of an islander woman politely described as French by the more conservative elements of society, works. He is the supervisor of a team of machinists in a factory that makes neon lights, and Bernice has often had to scrape to find nickels for pinochle with the other girls. At the last cards party, a small affair comprising two tables of women for pinochle followed by dancing with several charming and well-off young men, Esther and Gertrude Collins had bragged of a trip to

Havana. Their father owns the factory, so the expense had been nothing to them. Of course the Collins sisters had no idea Bernice's father works for theirs. Sometimes Bernice has found needing to dissemble about her circumstances to be exhausting, but if the other girls knew, they would be even more horrible to her.

"Bernice, darling, don't you just *adore* Cuba?" said one of the sisters, at the cards party. "Oh, that's right. Of course you've never *been*. Isn't it just dreadful being poor, dear? You must thank your stars every morning that you have wealthy friends like us to guide you in the correct fashions." At this, Esther and Gertrude together took a moment to look Bernice up and down, and clucked quietly in their throats.

Worse luck, although she had been to Haiti several times to visit her departed mother's relations, Bernice never had been to Cuba. She had read about it in magazines, and of course everyone knows the song. Rather than admit her inexperience and validate the ill behavior of the Collins sisters, she sang, in a sultry voice such as might radiate from a lustrous muse in a low cut dress, bewitching young wastrels and romantics in a torch club, *"Cuba, where wine is flowing! Where all those dark-eyed Stellas light their fellas' Panatell—"*

"Oh no, dear, don't sing!" said Esther Collins, quite unfairly, for Bernice is possessed of a lovely voice, and Gertrude contributed, "Heaven knows you're no Billy Murray. *Hee! Haw! Cuba! Heeeeeehaw!*" Lulu, who was Bernice's partner for pinochle, had smiled quietly and looked at her cards. Lulu is generally nicer than Esther and Gertrude; she is a harmless, biddable girl with pretty auburn curls and a bit of angle in the bridge of her slender nose. She is not very bright, but she should have known better than to smile at Bernice's humiliation. No matter— she would learn. They all would.

As Bernice struggled to hide her face, which she was sure had gone thoroughly pale with rage, girls at both card tables began to whisper their fondness for Billy Murray, whose song celebrating Cuban vacations was very fashionable that week, and their indulgent, condescending scorn for Bernice herself. She was certain everyone had stared at her, but she didn't see; she was hiding her face behind her cards. When was her turn? Surely her strong meld would place everyone's attention back on the game, double pinochles and jacks around, and with such a good hand at least her pinochle partner would feel gently toward her.

After the cards, when the boys finally arrived for dancing and cigarettes and gin, distracting the Collins girls for a moment from their predation, the subject of our portrait had breathed a visible sigh of relief. She devoted herself gamely to a series of lurching Charlestons and quicksteps around the ballroom, in the hands of a series of young men with tidily slicked hair and short evening jackets and breath that smelled of Collins gin, with narrow waists and strong, fast legs. During a slow song, she confided in one such beau, Henry, a dark-haired bravo with a waxed and curling moustache.

"I know it's dreadful of me to criticize my hosts, but really, those Collins sisters! You should have heard how they abused me at pinochle today, as though it were my fault Papa has to work to keep me in party gowns. Heaven forbid they should learn he works for Collins Industries! Each girl is dreadful, and together they rival Pharaoh in their persecutions. Imagine the river of blood that would flow from my reputation if they got their hands on that bit of news."

"I dare say!" opined the young man, his moustache rising and falling.

"In any case, those days will end soon, when I open my beauty salon. I shall earn my own money for gin and party clothes by cutting bobs. A working woman! I shall be thoroughly modern. And so I have named my shop. You must come see me for your next trim."

"Oh, I shall," Henry had agreed. "I shall indeed, and I shall tell all the men."

Bernice had rewarded him with a kiss. He gleamed openly, even though she had ravaged his moustache.

Later, during a pause in the music, she overheard him doing just as he'd promised.

"Our Bernice is going to be a barber," he said jovially, twisting his maimed whiskers in a vain attempt to recover from the kiss, to a ginger fellow home on holiday from Annapolis and splendid in the dress uniform of a student sailor.

The sailor said "You lie! How grand! We must bring her all our business, the bold girl."

Unfortunately, Esther had overheard this exchange and turning to Lulu wondered aloud how Bernice would ever pay the lease on a fashionable shopfront.

"Why surely her father borrowed the money from yours, against his wages," said Lulu. Bernice had confided her circumstances to the simple girl at the beginning of their acquaintance, and Lulu had sworn an oath of secrecy. The poor girl, wide-eyed, realizing her error too late, clapped both hands over her mouth. Too late, of course. Her fate was sealed.

The Collins sisters looked to one another and away in a coordinated, Vaudeville gesture that would have made Laurel and Hardy jealous for its precision. "Oh *really,*" Esther had said, and Gertrude had said "Yes, that is surely what happened." The treacherous sisters had turned their hawk-like attention to Bernice, and the social bloodbath that followed does not bear description.

Bernice had done her best to keep an even temper, but she broke under the weight of the taunting levelled by Esther and Gertrude and their toadies. "Why must you be so horrible?" she had shrieked, hurling her cocktail at Gertrude, and then she had fled to the washroom to compose herself.

Suffice it to say that she lost at more than cards that day. Bernice is a mediocre card player in any case, so she seldom wins, but she rationalizes her losses, preferring to believe that money goes to money. At least she hadn't needed to pay for her gin. The Collins girls have a bathtub still in the washroom, and thank God for Prohibition!

At gentle Lulu's urging, Bernice calmed herself and emerged, but the damage had been done. When the party ended and she had put on her shawl (fine crochet lace, but her late mother had made it—it had not come from a boutique), her head spinning slightly with homebrew liquor, Bernice stroked a hand over the Apollonian, geometric carvings that adorned the great double doors out of the Collins mansion, bas relief mythological beasts rendered in bold concentric lines, carved from marble and trimmed in chrome. She idly ran a finger in one groove, as though stroking Pegasus' wing, and kissed the air beside Esther's cheek, a gesture of peacemaking. Had the Collins girl rolled her eyes? Bernice kissed Gertrude goodbye without comment, and then left.

***

All that is in the past, now, surely. Since graduating from the Institute of Art and Sculpture, Bernice has completed, in secret, a course in hairdressing, and her father—darling Papa!—has managed to rent her shop. With the coming changes in hair fashion, lots of girls will be after a new look, and Bernice specialized in bobbed hairstyles at the academy. Best of all, if she earns enough on her own, the shop has room for an additional girl. Bernice feels strongly that after all she has endured, she deserves an underling, or, that is, an *employee,* to do her bidding. Lulu seems a likely candidate, with her normally docile nature. How much sweeter if it were one or even both of the Collins girls! She laughs low in her breast, imagining the haughty Collinses cleaning the silver shears and dusting her shop. Nothing is impossible, no matter how unlikely, if one is truly creative and determined. There will be no more scraping after nickels for Bernice, in any case, and no more submitting to the sneering, sarcastic treatment of her so-called friends. She will soon have the means to complete her social ascent.

In the shop, watch Bernice as she hangs her shawl

carefully around the shoulders of a bust, in the modern style, of Nefertiti. She takes a moment to admire the sleek lines of the ancient queen, one eye watching over the boutique, one looking into the next world. She rolls a long stitch of her shawl between two slender fingers, thinking of her mother, another woman of spirit and strength. Bernice lacks her late mother's skill with crochet hook and thread—she had tried to learn, but the squinting detail of it had always thwarted her. Even so, she learned other, more practical skills at mama's foot, and at the feet of mama's many sisters with their thick not-quite-French accents, their many-bangled wrists clinking and jiggling throughout each lesson, skills they had in turn learned from their own mother, Bernice's tiny, wizened *Memere*, a shrunken apple of a woman whose eyes gleamed from her gray-brown face.

She indulges in a sense memory: softened tallow squeezing slowly between her tiny, little-girl fingers as she fashioned a crude manikin, the slickness of the oily medium beneath her sharp fingernails as she sculpted its eyes and mouth, the salty smell of the work. She had trimmed it with a tiny nightshirt fashioned from a handkerchief and a tiny moustache of real human hair. Her aunts had proudly demanded she "show *Memere* the cunning poppet she has made, how it resembles *Pepere*, and how well she can say the words"—how her *Memere* had praised her inexperienced and accented French. How her aunts had swelled with pride at their wise mother's praise for their niece, their pupil. And how *Pepere* had moaned in his sickbed.

***

After nodding with satisfaction at a crate of sculptor's clay delivered ahead of schedule to her shop, Bernice flips a switch, hidden on the wall behind Nefertiti, lighting a neon sign, an extravagant gift bestowed by her father's employer, burning the name of the shop in angular cursive letters, liquid fire tracing a sleek upward diagonal across the shop-front window: *Thoroughly*

Modern! She takes a moment to appreciate the marble and chrome of her shop. *Her* shop, and only the first step on her path to independence and respect.

Soon, as Bernice knew would happen, Lulu timidly enters the salon, accompanied by the tinkling of a tiny bell installed above the door. "Sweet Lulu!" Bernice cried, "You are my very first customer, and I could not have hoped for a better one!"

Lulu gives her a dimpling smile. "How could I resist, dear? How exciting! How modern…" She touches the bust of Nefertiti and gestures to the neon.

"Shall I bob your hair, darling?"

"Oh! I don't dare. Daddy would absolutely *panic!*" Lulu giggles.

"All the girls will be doing it soon enough," urges Bernice, "but if you fear being too modern too quickly, perhaps just a trim and style. You shall make Gibson himself weep in his grave when we are through."

This nearly-necromantic reference makes Lulu tighten her belly and gasp. "You're so wicked! But you are right—there is no sense fearing progress, and even Daddy can't disagree with that. Let's bob my hair! Gertrude and Esther will be *furious* to miss being the first of us girls!"

"Oh, Lulu, you've no idea how proud you make me." Bernice leads the other girl to a stool, and drapes a tightly-woven linen smock about her friend's shoulders. "No doubt they'll come running once they see how glamorous you look."

"I'm afraid they won't, Bernice. They are quite vexed with you. They've told all the girls you spoiled their last cards party."

"Have they?! How rude. Well, one must forgive one's friends, and we shall all soon be reconciled. You must be my agent."

"I couldn't! I hope you won't be too angry, but I don't want them to shun me as well…"

Bernice just brushes Lulu's hair for several minutes, appreciating the sheen and sleek texture of the curls, then sets aside her brush and reaches for a gleaming, new set of shears. Soon enough, Lulu is the height of fashion, and her fallen auburn tresses litter the salon floor.

At the tinkling sound of the shop door, Bernice hands a small hand-held mirror to Lulu and turns to see her moustachioed party champion casting a slender, flickering shadow from the neon in her window. "Henry! Please have a seat and keep dear Lulu company while I clean up. I'll be with you ever so soon."

She sweeps Lulu's hair into a dust tray and carries it and the carton of clay into a small storage room in the back of the shop. She carefully pours the hair into a canvas pouch marked "Lulu," one of several similar pouches marked with other names, "Esther" and "Gertrude" prominent among them. She opens the carton and softens a block of clay.

She is a fast worker, but still her task takes time, squeezing and rolling the clay until, when she hears Henry clearing his throat impatiently, she has sculpted a fair likeness of Lulu in her best Deco style. "I'm nearly done, sweet Henry!" she calls. She reaches into Lulu's pouch, and pinches several auburn curls into the clay doll's head. She says the words her aunts taught her, and taps the poppet on its tiny arm. When she hears Lulu exclaim "Oh!" she nods with satisfaction and sets her sculpture on a shelf.

As Bernice returns to her friends, Henry says, with admiration in his voice. "Darling, I didn't know you could speak French."

"I learned so *many* useful things from Mama and her sisters," she says. "Come over and sit on my stool and we'll have you trimmed and dashing before you know. Lulu, be a dear and bring the Collins girls. They'll look cunning in bobs, don't you think?"

Lulu nods, dazed, still rubbing her arm as though she's been struck. "Yes, of course."

AUTHOR'S NOTE

Bill Racicot lives near Boston, and he doesn't write as many stories as he'd like. "Bernice" was inspired by, but cannot hope to compete with Fitzgerald's more realistic story of another socially unsuccessful girl by the same name.

Airboy and Vooda Visit the Jungles of the Moon
Paul Di Filippo

1.

A Guest from the Sky

Airboy and Birdie were enjoying the splendid May sunlight and the warm fragrant air of the upper reaches of New York City on the sturdy and expansive duralumin landing deck jutting from the Nelson penthouse in midtown. From the polished wooden cabinet of a large Zenith radio big as a gasoline filling pump, the sweet coronet stylings of King Oliver's jazz wafted gently out of the cloth-covered speakers.

Clad in a simple dun mechanic's coverall, and not his crime-fighting uniform of aviator's goggles, red tunic with yellow blazon, leather gauntlets, blue leggings and sturdy knee-high boots, young Davy "Airboy" Nelson was lovingly applying a coat of special aerothane dope to the miracle fabric that comprised Birdie's fuselage and wings. The semi-intelligent craft—evocative of a grey bullet-nosed bat, possessor of the one and only existing Martier Deductive Engine, and capable of astounding metamorphic changes to its flexible structure—practically wriggled in delight at the attention.

The intent and capable adolescent lad addressed his plane with familiar bonhomie as he worked the gel into the magic fabric. "Well, Birdie, we came out of that latest scrap with the Valkyrie pretty darn well. The G-men have those engraved counterfeit plates in their possession, old Doc Whentel is back with his niece Peggy, and while we didn't manage to cage the Valkyrie herself, her base of operations on Punishment Plateau is effectively kaput."

Airboy paused in his loving buffing of the plane's skin. "Gee, it's a shame that Valkyrie won't go straight and fly right. She's a mighty smart and talented and brave lady, but she's all mixed-up in the head."

Birdie twitched her ailerons in annoyance at mention of the adventuress's name, making obvious without words her disdainful opinion of the arch-criminal.

Resuming both his tender treatment of Birdie and his dialogue with the sensitive craft, Airboy said, "When I compare Valkyrie to someone like Doc Whentel's Peggy, it's obvious which gal a feller should go for. Peggy's so sweet and good-natured and affectionate. I can just picture her in an apron in the kitchen, rolling out pie crust. But I truly can't figure out why I can't get Valkyrie off my mind…"

At that exact moment, as if summoned by Airboy's musings on the nature of distinctions amongst the fairer sex, a majestic female figure dropped as if from the naked sky, landing on the platform in a graceful three-pointed crouch.

Here in all her titanic, muscled, graceful, tanned flesh, completely unannounced, was Vooda, South Seas Jungle Princess, Mistress of Vanishing Island!

Vooda's most striking feature, on first glance, consisted of her copious tresses, a veritable waterfall of dense ebony wavelets barely constrained with a rawhide tie. Her hair trailed behind her like a black cloud of glory. Having assimilated these abundant curls, any observer would certainly have next noted with favor Vooda's dynamic countenance, a beautifully consorted arrangement of finely hewn features: sparkling eyes, flaring nostrils, full lips. And then, of course, one registered with undeniable impact her lithe, Junoesque body. Clad only in an abbreviated, ragged-hemmed, magenta-colored sarong festooned with lemon starbursts, Vooda displayed an abundance of bare skin that had a most disconcerting effect on any red-blooded male. Her allure had more than once distracted an enemy at just the crucial moment and saved the day.

Vooda's strong bare feet had thumped to the duralumin terrace with a solid resonance as her legs bent to accommodate her landing. Her empty hand, so recently clutching a rope that now swung back into space, rested on the floor in a supportive gesture, making her look like the female equivalent of some husky football player ready for a "hike." In her other hand she clutched her omnipresent spear, whose wicked razor edges had tasted the blood of many an evildoer.

Coming erect now with catlike fluidity, Vooda hailed Airboy in her charmingly accented English. "Young Davy Nelson, I bid you fair seas and calm skies!"

Airboy narrowed his eyes at the departing rope that had vanished back toward some unseen anchor point. "I wish I knew how the heck you do that, Vooda. This terrace is the highest place in the whole darn block! Where did you swing in from?"

Vooda smiled with Sphinx-like slyness. "The ways of Vanishing Island are not to be disclosed to any person not of the royal lineage, Davy Nelson. Not even to such a staunch ally as yourself."

Airboy shrugged away the enigma. "Well, it's good to see you Vooda. How's Cheetah?"

By that cognomen, Airboy referenced the giant leopard ally of Vooda, whose spotted thews, dagger-like claws and icepick fangs had been influential in the demise of many a bad man. Cheetah accepted few humans as his friends, and Airboy felt proud to be numbered among that elite. Why, once, he recalled, he had even shared Birdie's tight cockpit with the big cat. That had been some adventure! Shed fur and dried saliva had decorated Birdie's instrument panel—much to the craft's visible displeasure—for weeks afterwards.

"As ever, Davy Nelson, you intuitively strike to the heart of my mission. I have learned through Cheetah of an impending war, one which I wish to halt, if I can. But to reach the scene of the conflict, I must have the assistance of you and your unique craft."

"Why, sure, Vooda, Birdie and I would be happy to ferry you wherever you want to go. Just name the place, and we'll set off right away."

Vooda grinned with unsettling battle-zest. "Our departure will not be as imminent nor as easy as you imagine, Davy Nelson, for we are heading to the Moon!"

2.
White Apes and Black Leopards of Luna

The Moon! What wild adventure lay in store now?

Airboy listened with fascination to Vooda's account of the races and politics and environment of Earth's satellite, esoteric knowledge that he had never been privy to before.

"The first thing you must realize," said the Princess of Vanishing Island, as she sat incongruously in a chromium and leather lounge chair inside the Nelson penthouse, sipping on a glass of cold punch, "is that the seemingly lifeless Moon is hollow, and filled with organic matter. This fact was first hinted at some thirty years ago, in a novel by Mr. Wells. But he chose to obscure the true facts of the matter, for reasons of his own.

"Inside the Moon—a vast natural chamber with a complex topography, and illuminated by a ball of cold radiance at its center—we find no insectoid Selenites, but rather two intelligent races vying for dominance of the inner sphere, a lush terrain of thick jungles and deep lakes, of arid tablelands and sinuous rivers. Eternally at odds, these rivals are the White Apes and the Black Leopards.

"The White Apes, whose spectrum of coloration implies grades of status, ranging from the most gorgeous platinum to the dingiest of ivory, are smart and ruthless and the aggressors in this conflict. They are ruled by General Barch in feudal fashion.

"The Black Leopards being trespassed upon are, to the contrary, a gentle folk, serene and beautiful, who seek to extend their range only by peaceful migration. And how absolutely gorgeous they are! Instead of tawny with black spots, like our terrestrial breed, they are ebony with gold maculations. Their social order is a kind of cooperative individualism."

Airboy contemplated all this startling information for a moment, sipping at his own fruity punch. "I have to assume that Cheetah is your conduit to these Moon doings."

"Yes, Davy Nelson, quite astute! Cheetah is partly Black Leopard by inheritance, for long ago both the White Apes and the Black Leopards would visit Earth and mate with their counterparts on our world—although they have lost that capacity for interplanetary travel over the centuries."

Airboy felt himself blushing at the notion of these ancient conjugal cohabitations, and took another swig of his drink to cover his flustered condition.

"Cheetah's ancestry allows him to remain in telepathic communication with Queen Zemzem of the Black Leopards, and so my furry friend has served as my information pipeline to the lunar sphere."

"Well, it seems that our course of action is clear, Vooda, if what you say is accurate. We've got to help Cheetah's relatives resist the onslaught of the White Apes. But it's going to take some heavy-duty upgrades to Birdie to make her capable of undertaking the journey through space. I think we'll have to visit Ann Martier."

Brother Francis Martier, the genius Franciscan monk who had invented and perfected Birdie, endowing her with a mind and soul in the form of the Martier Deductive Engine, had unfortunately perished during one of the early test runs of the plane, having neglected to fasten his seat belt during a barrel roll with an open canopy. But his skills and knowledge had not died with him, having descended to his cousin, Ann Martier, who now ran the Martier Aviation Company in California.

"Agreed. I left Cheetah in my room at the Waldorf

Astoria. We'll pick him up and be off. But first, let us consecrate our noble intentions with a toast."

Vooda set her empty flagon down on a glass-topped Lalique table—one of the cherished mementos of Airboy's departed mother, whose residual fortune allowed Airboy his complete freedom—and the youthful aviator did likewise.

"I'll get the pitcher of punch from the icebox."

When Airboy returned with the frosty Fiestaware pitcher, he noted that Vooda was crumpling up a small sachet and tossing it into the fireplace. Possibly some regular daily tonic from her native isle, he conjectured. He filled their glasses and they toasted the success of their mission.

Talk turned to less consequential topics. After a while, Airboy found himself feeling rather lightheaded, yet not unpleasantly so. Vooda too seemed slightly tipsy and uninhibited.

"Davy," said Vooda with a purr, "did that nasty old Valkyrie ever succeed in having her way with you when you were in her power?"

"How do you mean?"

"Oh, you know. Like this."

Suddenly Vooda was in Airboy's lap. The Princess weighed twice as much as the lad, and her sinuous limbs seem to stretch for yards in all directions. Her hair smelled like brine and frangipani, and her skin was as hot as day-old lava flow.

Airboy quickly slithered out from under Vooda, but she ensnared him in her embrace and he found himself sitting unwillingly on Vooda's lap. While somewhat more harmonious a composition, the arrangement was no less disconcerting in its extensive tactility.

Vooda ran her deft fingers through Airboy's hair. "Daaay-vee, did Valkyrie ever kiss you?"

"Crimenettlies, Vooda, lay off, will you? What's come over you? Jeepers, you'd think we had nothing better to do with our time than play post office. There's a whole world waiting for us to save it!"

With a sigh, Vooda ceased her teasing blandishments. Airboy stood up, and she did also, smoothing her silky sarong. "Yes, the hero's lot is full of duty and sacrifice. I suppose we had best get going."

Outside the sliding glass doors leading to the landing dock, Birdie ceased to creep forward on her landing gear. Airboy thought she looked as if she had actually been intent on entering the apartment.

3.
Into the Moon!

Pert and saucy Ann Martier stood at the hanger door in the field where Martier Aviation had its Golden State facilities. Rather tomboyish in appearance, including a brushcut hairstyle, and clad in grease-stained khakis and a denim shirt with rolled sleeves, she regarded her handiwork with satisfaction. On one side of the girl engineering whiz stood Airboy, and on the other, Vooda. The recumbent form of Cheetah occupied the ground at his mistress's feet like a bundle of compressed lightning.

"Well," said Ann proudly, wrapping one arm around Vooda's waist in an excess of enthusiasm, "what do you think of the improvements?"

From Birdie's streamlined tail projected a set of stubby baffle-choked tubes that focused the Martier Inertialess Impellors. Reliant for power on a deep physics which Airboy did not pretend to understand, the new drive mechanism did not even require a fuel source. Thus it had been unnecessary to disfigure the sleek lines of Birdie with additional tanks to supplement her internal chambers.

However, one new exterior feature was an aerodynamic nacelle with viewing window securely slung atop Birdie. In this compartment, Cheetah would ride into space.

Only by flying low and slow, and by making frequent

stops, had the extended trip from New York to California been barely possible for the three of them, with Vooda and Airboy cramped in the cockpit and Cheetah constrained in some makeshift basketwork outside the cabin, exposed to all weathers. But such an arrangement would not do for the rigors of the vacuum.

"I think they're mighty keen, Ann," said Airboy. "And I suspect Birdie does too."

Indeed, the smart plane seemed to stand a tad taller even as they praised her, making little pawing motions with her wheels in the dirt of the yard.

"You understand how to use the new sanitary hookups, don't you?" asked Ann.

The trip to the Moon would take a fraction over three days. A special diet of ultra-efficient spaceman rations would eliminate the need for the passengers to void solid wastes. But certain bodily functions could not be foregone. Thus a kind of intimate plumbing apparatus had been installed, a feature even Lindbergh had not enjoyed on his famous trans-Atlantic voyage.

Airboy nodded seriously to affirm his comprehension of the sanitary hookups. Ann said, "Great! Well, I guess it's time to say farewell then. I know you're eager to get off!"

Still clasping Vooda's waist, Ann turned and extended her other hand to shake Airboy's. Removing one gauntlet, Airboy took the mechanic's calloused palm in his and pumped it whole-heartedly. After relinquishing her tight grip, honed by many hours of heavy-duty labor, Ann spontaneously embraced Vooda and, standing on tiptoe, planted a hearty kiss square on the Princess's lips. Vooda returned the token of friendship with genuine sisterly camaraderie. Cheetah twitched his tail and let out a low growl at the spontaneous physical bonding.

Before even another few minutes could elapse, the big cat was safely stowed in his heated and rug-strewn compartment, and Vooda was ensconced in her comfortably cushioned seat. Airboy waited tactfully until his companion had fitted herself with the sanitary coupling under her sarong, then climbed onboard.

"Please look away a moment, Vooda, if you don't mind."

Vooda sighed and complied, and Airboy maneuvered his male organ into the suction tube, then draped a blanket over his lap.

"Okay, eyes forward again!"

"Don't forget to use conventional power until you're well into the mesosphere," reminded Ann. "I can't predict what the inertialess drive will do if you turn it on within fifty miles of the surface."

"Gotcha!" Airboy pulled their canopy into place, dogging it securely down, activated the flow from the oxygen generators, and gripped Birdie's yoke. But his posture of control was a mere formality, given Birdie's self-directed intelligence.

"Take off, Birdie!"

The eager plane leaped into the sky as if catapulted, and they were on their way!

"Luna, here we come!" exclaimed the excited lad. Airboy relished the new challenges he and Birdie would face. A pensive Vooda, however, did not second his utterance.

As they neared the one-hundred-mile mark, the blue skies turned black and the stars appeared in all their polychromatic glory. At this doubly safe altitude Airboy finally gave the command to ignite the Inertialess Impellors. Birdie received a boost as if from the hand of God shoving her from behind. Soon Airboy and Vooda were free of Earth's gravity. Over the intercom from the nacelle came a whine of discomfort as Cheetah experienced weightlessness. A word or two of comfort from Vooda, and the feline settled down peaceably. He would probably sleep most of the journey, as all cats, large and small, liked to do, and Airboy envied his repose. He himself was too excited by this foray into the starry unknown to contemplate any interval of drowsiness.

For the next several hours Vooda and Airboy conversed on a variety of subjects. Vooda sought to explain conditions on the Moon in further detail, including the history and contrasting social structures and cultures of the Black Leopards and the White Apes. Airboy listened carefully, interposing several intelligent questions. Elbow to elbow with the Junoesque Vooda, whose taut yet in places pneumatic body seemed to fill more than her half of the cabin, radiating that heady scent, Airboy at first harbored a vague unease that she would attempt some unwanted familiarities such as she had back in New York. Not that the tight cockpit would permit much in the way of hanky-panky. But Vooda maintained a businesslike demeanor that seemed to honor their altruistic mission.

After they had exhausted the subject of lunar conditions, Airboy reminisced a bit about his personal life, and how his parents had met their untimely separate demises: his father from the machinations of The Starry Alliance; and his mother at the hands of Captain Morgue.

"I had to grow up mighty fast, Vooda. It seems like I never had a real childhood."

"I too had to mature early in my adolescence, after the Volcano God of Vanishing Island wiped out my village, in order to aid the survivors of my tribe. For many years I felt all alone. I recall our initial meeting, Davy Nelson, as our paths intersected during the 'Affair of the Sharktooth Mob,' when I knew for the first time I had met a kindred spirit in you."

"Gosh, Vooda, you say the nicest things. I like you too—a lot!"

Vooda seemed inclined for a second to demonstrate her affections, but then held back.

"After this expedition, perhaps much will have changed between us, Davy Nelson."

"Only for the better, Vooda! Count on it!"

Eventually, of course, fatigue overtook them as they soared on through the uncharted cosmos. Vooda was the first to drop off to sleep, emitting demure snores.

Airboy was glad she had finally gone to sleep, as the pressure in his bladder was becoming uncomfortable. He had not wished to utilize the automatic micturation device in a blatant fashion.

"Birdie," whispered the young pilot, "activate the sanitary hookup."

Airboy experienced a primal relief, but then something in the apparatus seemed to malfunction! The sleeve-like unit attached to his male organ began to manifest a kind of peristalsis, producing novel lubricious sensations. Before he could communicate the trouble to Birdie, he experienced a kind of unprecedented climax of pleasure and swooned away.

When Airboy had recovered his senses, he said, "Birdie, please check out the specs on that drainage amplitude. It seems over-powered."

Able after all these years to interpret Birdie's wordless "body language," Airboy sensed a kind of shy winsomeness from the plane, rather at odds with his request to repair a simple malfunctioning.

No further such incidents marred the trip, however, and at the appointed hour the explorers were fast approaching the Moon.

"Aim for the Clavius region," Vooda said. "That's the entrance closest to the land of the Black Leopards."

"I still can't quite picture how we get inside the Moon."

"You'll see. Just follow my directions."

And so, with some small trepidation, Airboy switched off the impellors and aimed his faithful plane with its residual momentum straight at the lunar surface.

"Full speed ahead, Birdie!"

The crater below them stood half in shadows, and it was only when they seemed ready to impact solid rock that Airboy realized that a portion of the crater represented the mouth of a tunnel into the Moon. Activating her forward searchlights, Birdie disclosed the long, wide, jagged passage down whose centerline they now flew.

Up ahead, a kind of curtain manifested, and Airboy instinctively slowed their speed.

"No," said Vooda, "keep going! It's safe. This is merely the living barrier that prevents the atmosphere from leaking out of the interior. You'll see."

Sure enough, the curtain proved to be comprised of innumerable overlapping green frond-like strips which parted readily at Birdie's thrust, admitting the plane into the realm of air.

Then, suddenly, instead of descending *down* a tunnel, reality flipped one-hundred-and-eighty degrees and they were ascending *up out of* a tunnel. Free of the passage, they soared above the jungle-clotted landscape, all lit by the unchanging cold radiance of the central orb. Airboy halted their ascent and began to cruise above the treetops.

The expedition from Earth was inside the Moon!

4.

Audience with Queen Zemzem, and a Tumultuous Feast

Airboy had adapted more quickly than he would have predicted to a race of talking leopards. Hearing guttural yet recognizable human speech emerge from the furry throats had disconcerted him for just about half a day. Then he took the ability of the Black Leopards to fashion intelligible syllables for granted. Perhaps if he had not previously encountered the Crocodile Men of the Blue Nile, he would have been more resistant to the concept.

Now, as Airboy and Vooda and the regal, ebony Queen Zemzem strolled light-footedly abreast down a wide dirt path that constituted the main avenue of the jungle-shrouded imperial capital, Challapuri, with Cheetah trailing behind, past handsome lodges and elaborate temples, all fashioned from exotic native materials, Airboy found he was able to regard Queen

Zemzem's words with the attention they deserved, rather than focus on the unlikeliness of their origin.

"So again, my Terran friends," said the queenly feline, "I cannot thank you enough for your help. Our forces have been beaten back time and again by the White Apes, for we have no skills in combat, nor in strategy. But if only you two can penetrate to the center of Saffirio, the main city of the White Apes, and capture General Barch as a hostage, returning here with your prize, then I believe we will finally be able to negotiate an end to this conflict."

"Count on us, Queen," Airboy responded. "Birdie is so silent and maneuverable that we can sneak right up to the outskirts of Saffirio. Then Vooda and I will proceed on foot while the Apes are sleeping, snatch the General from the midst of his cronies, stash him in Cheetah's nacelle, and be back here before you can say 'Hello, Joe, what do you know?'"

The party had come up to the comfortable albeit simple guest quarters where Airboy and company were housed. They halted, and Queen Zemzem spoke.

"We will have a banquet tonight, my friends, to consecrate your daring mission and honor your prowess. Rest now, for the festivities will be long and perhaps a bit riotous. We Black Leopards may not be fighters, but we are assuredly lovers of life."

Taking their leave of the Queen, Airboy, Vooda and Cheetah entered their lodge. Bamboo shades on the unglassed windows cut the eternal illumination in a welcome fashion, and they were able to fall upon their cots padded with fragrant grasses and enjoy some sleep, relishing the conditions of light gravity.

They awoke when a servant of the Queen scratched at their doorway and called out their names. Airboy was at first somewhat disoriented by the perpetual bluish "sunlight," feeling he had been in the arms of Morpheus for only minutes. But his faithful Longines 13ZN Fly Back Chronograph informed him that several hours had passed, and he was able to reestablish a sense of the progress of the "day." Sleeping patterns inside the Moon, while regular, paid no heed to ambient conditions.

Escorted to a large clearing—where a woven reed canopy, emplaced at a height of about twelve feet above the ground, afforded shade from the ever-burning luminary—the guests from Earth took seats of honor on mats to either side of Queen Zemzem.

"Let the banquet commence!" bade the Queen.

A kind of constant *a cappella* contrapuntal music was provided by a chorus of Black Leopards performing wordless and intricate vocal harmonies. Airboy thought the symphony resembled back-alley caterwaulings, or perhaps the mad sonatas of the eccentric Russian Scriabin, but refrained from saying so.

Into the clearing trotted Black Leopard servants bearing wicker panniers holding steaming foodstuffs: mostly roasted meats and fishes wrapped in leaves, but also some strange lunar root vegetables that had been grilled. Each celebrant among the scores of big cats retrieved a portion from the wide-mouthed panniers with teeth or, in the case of the humans, their hands. Next came a large open wooden tub pulled on a wheeled cart, a milky liquid sloshing within. Before the Black Leopards began to take turns drinking communally from the tub, Vooda and Airboy were invited to dip large mugs of the stuff for themselves.

Sampling the beverage, Airboy found it to be a refreshing and stimulating drink tasting much like coconut water, with some subtle under-flavors. Along with savory mouthfuls of food, he happily downed his first portion, then, with a determinedly nondiscriminatory embrace of the somewhat unhygienic shared barrel, went back for more.

At about the time the dancing commenced, Airboy, sated with the repast, was feeling pleasurably at ease and without a care in the two worlds, or any trepidation about the upcoming bold foray into the Apes' stronghold. Somehow he had gone supine, his head in Vooda's lap. His comrade-in-arms stroked his brow with strong yet delicate fingers, a hypnotic sensation.

The feline style of dancing involved high leaps, mock battles, slinking crawls and frenzied tail chasings. All the cats, including the Queen, were performing now, and the resulting scrum was a blur of shapes. Airboy could make out the unique form of Cheetah participating as well, and the Earth cat's coloration recalled to Airboy's daydreaming brain the fable of the tiger who had raced around in a loop so fast he turned to butter.

Suddenly the majority of the cats ceased dancing and formed a ring of observers. Airboy sat up to see better, and noted that Queen Zemzem and Cheetah were the sole occupants at the center of the circle. Tails flicking, they maneuvered like prizefighters around each other, and then suddenly Cheetah leaped atop Queen Zemzem from the rear. The other Black Leopards sent up a soul-chilling mass howl.

"Cheetah's not going to hurt the Queen, is he? That would definitely prejudice our status here."

Vooda guided Airboy's head back down to rest on one muscular yet feminine thigh. He did not contest her maneuver.

"No, Davy Nelson, there is no hurting involved."

"That's good..." said Airboy, before passing straight into a bottomless sleep.

5.
Apeland, and Beyond

Airboy could never hope to equal Vooda's silent, ghostlike transit through the jungly suburbs surrounding Saffirio, the redoubt of the White Apes, but he managed a certain amount of stealth. Although his limbs did still feel queerly disconnected after the banquet of last "night." But emerging from a long interval of dreamless unconsciousness, he had awakened curiously refreshed and ready to embark on the kidnapping of General Barch.

Reaching the final border of foliage, Vooda indicated by handsigns that they should stop and assess their next move. She hefted her ever-present spear with an air of competent menace. Cheetah, however, had been forced to remain home, freeing up his nacelle for their captive.

Airboy hoped they could complete their mission with a minimum of bloodshed, and return swiftly to where Birdie awaited in a small clearing that had been chosen to afford the miracle craft enough room for a near-vertical takeoff. He did not relish inflicting mortal wounds on even so reprehensible a set of foes as the White Apes.

Peering cautiously through the leaves, on one of which perched a grotesque but apparently harmless lunar bug, all eyes and antennae, Airboy expected to see ranks of White Ape soldiers. The city of Saffirio had been presented to him as a fortress, a completely militarized place akin to Mussolini's Italy, where the simian *Il Duce* ruled by fear and mailed fist. But instead, he saw naught but a couple of idle unarmed White Apes—a dingy milk of magnesia color, actually—standing by a gate in a stockade and chatting.

Queen Zemzem had assured the Terrans that this period represented the sleep time of the White Apes, and so manifested the best opportunity for an easy assault. The lack of activity seemed to bear out the Queen's intelligence.

Satisfied with what she saw, Vooda signalled "Go!" and then bounded forward. In the slight lunar gravity, her mighty Terran muscles brought her in one jump to the sentries. And before they could even straighten up from their slouch, she had rendered them unconscious with the blunt end of her spear.

Airboy caught up just a bit behind Vooda. "All right," said the Island Princess quietly, "you know what to look for. Let's go."

Through the empty streets of the city they sped, until they came to the impressive multi-storey structure that occupied the center of the complex: General Barch's residence and HQ. Another pair of guards stationed at the front door saw the Earthlings, but again were too slow to avoid Vooda's blows.

General Barch's private quarters were reputed to be on the top floor, and thence they raced, through what seemed to Airboy like miles of spartan corridors.

Factoring in the slight time remaining before an alert was sounded and reinforcements arrived, they checked all the rooms swiftly and without stealth, waking up several possible retainers and family members of the General. Leaving the flustered apes to gather their wits, they eventually came upon the leader himself.

General Barch's lustrous thick fur shone like the purest white opals. Standing by the end of his bed, he reared a head higher even than Vooda, and bulked twice as big. His gleaming fangs showed like a set of chef's cutlery. His voice seemed to emanate from a deep cavern.

"What is the meaning of this intrusion?"

Airboy had expected bluster and crudity from the General, but was surprised with his seeming civility and sensibility.

"Don't let him call for help!" Vooda yelled.

So Airboy unholstered his gun and shot the General.

The big White Ape crumpled to the tiles, much like King Kong in the recent Hollywood spectacular.

Caching on his belt the bulbous-snouted weapon with its big gas cartridge, Airboy said, "I owe Wesley Dodds a favor for loaning me one of his sleep pistols."

Vooda stooped and hoisted the sleeping General to her shoulders, her Terran muscles and the minor lunar gravity allowing her to accomplish easily what she would have strained to do back on Earth.

"To the roof!" Vooda shouted, as sounds of pursuit forced her to alter their escape plans.

Atop the flat, turreted roof, Airboy employed the radio transceiver built into his jacket lapel. Within sixty seconds, Birdie had screeched to a landing atop the palace. Banging sounded from below, against the braced exit door from the palace, but rescue was futile. Stashed in the nacelle, General Barch was their prize!

The flight back to Challapuri occupied hardly any time at all, thanks to Birdie's speed and unerring direction-finding abilities. Even the strange topology of the lunar interior failed to disorient the sapient craft.

The triumphant commandos were greeted with yowling mass acclaim by the Black Leopard populace. The big cats bounded all around them as they carried the still-gassed General to his prison quarters.

In the somewhat fetid hut, the General was laid out on his back atop a stout table, then secured by strong cords at the wrists and ankles.

They left him alone to awaken, and went to refresh themselves, Airboy and Vooda separating.

By now, Airboy had begun to pine a bit for Earth. Helping the Black Leopards and visiting the Moon had been a splendid, noble adventure, one to record with pride in his scrapbook. But he longed to return to his penthouse, where he and Birdie could commune in their domestic fashion. He expected Vooda might like to see her native island again soon too.

So after his ablutions, with this impetus, Airboy went alone to see Queen Zemzem. The regal ruler received him in her private quarters.

"Are you going to open up negotiations with the General now, Queen?"

"Not right away. I want him to stew awhile, to become anxious and eager to capitulate."

Airboy could understand this strategy, but still chafed at delay. So, when he left the Queen, fancying himself a talented and dispassionate negotiator, he impulsively yet cautiously circled around to the back of the cabin that held the General and let himself inside, unseen, through a window.

The great White Ape was awake and alone, staring up at the thatched ceiling in a rather pitiable fashion. He caught Airboy's movements out of the corner of his eye and said, "What do you want, Terran? Are you here to torture me, as the Black Leopards torture all our race? I would not have expected such cruelty from one with whom I share my bloodline."

"Golly, Mister Barch, it's nothing like that. You've got me all wrong. The Leopards too! We just want to make sure you and your kind don't decimate the Black Leopards any more."

General Barch gave out a tired, haunted, cynical laugh. "I don't know what you've been told, son, but you have it all backwards. The Black Leopards enslave us for our thumbs. They are merciless raiders, taking our citizens down with their teeth and claws if we stray outside the stockade to work our farms or hunt for game, and then marching their abused captives back to Challapuri."

"Huh?"

"These cats have no ability to use tools with their clumsy paws. How do you think all their buildings arose? How do they cook and carry and brew? It's all done by White Ape slaves, worked hard until they die. Now, with your help, they intend to save themselves some effort and danger by ransoming me for a huge number of my fellows. They never could have captured me without your assistance. Why, a simple doorhandle is enough to thwart them from entering my palace on one of their raids."

Airboy was stunned. "No, that's—that's impossible! It's a lie!"

"Just go look for yourself. You should be able to find the slave barracks by stench alone."

Airboy clambered out the window and began to follow his nose.

When he returned to the prison cabin, his face was as blanched as General Barch's coat, and his shoulders seemed caved in upon his slender boyish frame. Without announcing himself, he simply bulled past the lone Black Leopard guard posted outside and entered the jail. He planned a quick employment of his knife on the binding ropes, and he would have the General free, ready for transport back to his people.

Airboy's eyes at first refused to acknowledge the scene inside the shadowy cell. But then it all crystallized into an undeniable horror.

A naked Vooda straddled the supine White Ape, her loins mated to his, her palms pressing into Barch's massive chest. With her magnificent tanned breasts lolloping, she teasingly rose and fell upon his forcibly tumescent apehood.

"Now you'll be in my power, Barch! No male can resist Vooda, once she's made love to him!"

Airboy felt the gorge rise in his throat. Here then was the sordid fate he himself had so narrowly escaped. To become the Love Zombie of the Princess of Vanishing Island!

Only inside Birdie's cockpit did Airboy regain his full awareness. Looking past the canopy's reinforced glass, he saw an army of Black Leopards racing toward him to stymie his escape.

"Take off, Birdie! Take off!"

The Black Leopards boiled below him like angry ants. Against such forces, he knew, any recompense for his deluded crimes lay beyond his powers. For one brief moment Airboy almost considered employing Birdie's dual cannons to slaughter as many of the treacherous cats as he could. But his angry heart quailed at the thought of more useless bloodshed. As for marooning Vooda here—well, it was a merciful fate, and no more than she deserved. So instead of taking revenge, he told Birdie, "Head for the exit cavern, old gal."

Birdie waggled her wings exultantly, radiating distinct waves of pleasure at their unaccompanied reunion, and shot off for the tunnel mouth back to the lunar surface and home.

As the craft raced over the variegated jade greenery, Airboy fitted the gently pulsating urine-disposal sheath to his member. He shuddered at the memory of Vooda's abuse of General Barch, and thanked his lucky stars that his narrow escape had left him, forever, just a boy and his plane.

AUTHOR'S NOTE

My love of Golden Age comics has been intensified by the easy availability of online scans. Thus I came better to know my two protagonists, Airboy and Vooda, who, while they never met in known continuity, I deemed perfect partners for their opposing takes on life. Airboy was formerly employed by Howard Waldrop in the *Wild Cards* series under the alternate name of Jetlad. But Amazonian Jungle Queens have fallen out of general use in fiction, and I thought Vooda, as representative of her species, deserved some page time as well.

THE WOLLART NYMPHS
MELISSA SCOTT

The rain had stopped at last, but the streets were still slick, the lights from the docks reflecting like flares in the puddles. The stevedores were still working, of course, and I could hear their shouts over the steady thump of the donkey engines that powered the cranes, and then the clatter of chain as someone on the liner took up the slack and the emptied cargo net floated into the air to be hauled aboard and filled again. This was the transatlantic cargo, goods loaded in Le Havre and Plymouth for consignees in New York, and when it was off, the cargo for New Orleans was piled ready for loading. After that would come the passengers' luggage, tomorrow morning when the sun was up and *Naiade* was gleaming, ready to sail. I had spent all my life around the Wollart Lines; their schedules were as instinctive as breathing. I clutched my drab black coat tighter at the neck, hunching my shoulders against the spreading chill. Black coat, black cloche to shadow my face, black shoes and stockings and gloves: I'd done just as Peter told me, and so far I'd been invisible in the shadows.

It had seemed like a good idea sitting in the automat with a stack of nickels between us and a good cup of coffee and Peter to fetch us each a slice of pie. Here at the head of Pier 54, the late night traffic on Eleventh Avenue at my back, rats busy among the piles of anonymous crates that lay between me and the ship—I wished Peter would hurry. He had promised to bring me to meet someone else who was interested in the fate of the Wollart Nymphs, the three fast liners my father had designed for Wollart, lean and elegant and unlucky. *Dryade* had been captured during the War and converted to a commerce raider, only to be sunk on her first cruise. *Nereiade* had survived the War, but in 1922 she'd passed the Hatteras lightship and disappeared into a fog bank, never to be seen again. Only her ghost remained, a wavering shape seen perhaps a dozen times, and always presaging disaster. Only *Naiade* remained, the last of the Nymphs, just marginally too profitable to abandon, and yet a source of rumor. The line was careless, people whispered, and crews were let go; there was something wrong with the design, they said, and my father lost work, sickened, and died.

I had come to New York to settle the last of his estate, but also to talk to Peter Gagne, who was also from Bath and had grown up in the Wollart Lines. His uncle had disappeared on *Nereiade*, and he'd written to me when Father died, to say that he'd finally found someone who might be interested in helping clear the Nymphs. He'd been close-mouthed about it, not wanting to say more until he was sure, but he'd promised that tonight he would introduce me. I edged a little closer, peering out into the loading lights from the shadows of the terminal wall. Surely he would be here soon.

A steam whistle blew on *Naiade*, and I flattened my back against the damp boards as a gang of stevedores moved toward the next pile of cargo. It was getting busier at this end of the dock, and the least that would happen was an unpleasant set of explanations. I couldn't really wait any longer. I took three careful steps backward, my eyes still on the anonymous crates and the men hauling them toward the waiting nets.

Something turned under my foot, and I barely caught myself on the rough wall. I froze in the shadows as one of the stevedores glanced my way. I hadn't made any more noise than a rat, and after a moment he looked away again. I sagged in relief, still holding onto the wall, and looked down.

I had stepped on someone's leg. A man's leg, in dark pants and scuffed shoes, the cuff pulled up to show a sagging sock and a flash of skin. I tasted bile, but I followed the leg into the darker shadows, already sure of what I would find. The body lay on its back, one arm twisted unnaturally under it; his face was turned away, but I recognized Peter's ear, the line of his jaw. He'd shaved before he'd come to meet me, the skin barber-smooth, a fleck of blood on the edge of his chin.

I went to my knees beside him, heedless of the wet ground, felt along the cord of his neck for some hint of a pulse. His skin was cold and slack under my fingers, and tears stung my eyes as I tried to turn him so that his face wasn't ground against the muddy platform. The bones of his skull gave under my fingers, and it was all I could do not to cry out.

I sat back on my heels, my breath short, wondering what to do. Peter was dead, murdered, almost certainly: I should fetch the police, but then I'd have to explain what I was doing here, and that would be complicated. I touched his cheek again, hoping somehow to feel some fugitive warmth, but there was nothing. I spread my fingers, a last apologetic farewell to a friend and neighbor, and pushed myself to my feet. There would be a phone booth somewhere, in an all-night diner or a hotel lobby; I could call the police from there and not have to give my name.

I backed away, my eyes on the stevedores busy under the lights. I wanted to run, but that was sure to draw attention; I would have to leave as quietly as I'd come. I took another step, and another, and collided abruptly with someone's chest. Hands grabbed my shoulders, and I made a panicked sound, but a voice spoke in my ear.

"Quiet, unless you want the police down on us."

"Maybe I do. There's a dead man ther —"

"Did you kill him?" The stranger's voice was politely curious, as though he was asking if I'd torn my stocking.

"I did not!" I just managed to keep my voice to a near-whisper. "Did you?"

I don't know what I expected him to say, or what I would have done if he'd said yes, but he just shook his head. "I just got here. And I think it would behoove us both to make ourselves scarce."

I looked back down the pier. The stevedores were coming closer, and several of them were heading for the shed that housed the nearest of the donkey engines. "Probably. And if you'd just let me go—"

"I'd like a word with you," he said, and didn't release my arm. "But not here."

I let him draw me down the pier toward Eleventh Avenue. If I cooperated now, seemed docile and cowed, I'd have a better chance of jerking free once we reached the street. I thought I could lose him there.

"Quickly, though," he said. "Was that Peter Gagne?"

He said it the way Mainers did, pronouncing each letter, and irrationally that inclined me to trust him. "Yes."

"Damn."

"You're the one he was meeting?"

We were at the end of the pier, where the streetlights cast circles duller than the bright lights of the docks. It had begun to rain again, a slow drizzle that promised a harder rain to come. In the shifting light, I got a better look at the stranger, a tall man in a dark overcoat buttoned high to hide his shirtfront. His hat was pulled low over his eyes; I could make out a strong chin and not much more.

"I was. He said he would introduce me to—you must be Nicholas Wright's daughter. Thomasina."

I stuck my chin out. "What if I am?"

"I would like very much to talk to you," he said. "All the more so if Gagne's dead. But this is hardly the place."

"It's as good as any." The rain was getting heavier, dripping from my cloche and from the brim of his fedora.

"I'd prefer not to court pneumonia." He paused. "I take it Gagne didn't mention me."

"He said he wanted me to meet someone," I answered. "He didn't say who. And I'm not going anywhere with you—not anywhere private, anyway."

The stranger sighed. "There's an all-night diner on West Sixteenth. It's not very respectable, but it's dry. Will that do?"

"Yes." It was worth the risk, if only to find out why Peter had wanted me to meet him—assuming he was telling the truth, of course. But I had to know.

The diner was what he'd described, brightly lit and smelling of grease and burnt toast. There was a surprising number of people there, mostly men who looked like sailors or stevedores, plus a handful of women in shabby evening dresses and too much makeup. A couple of them were sitting at the end of the counter, trolling for business, but the rest either had clients and were trying to get enough food down them to get them back to their rooms, or were taking a break for the night. The stranger chose a booth, and the waitress slouched over to take our orders.

"Two bits minimum after midnight. And the pie's off."

I glanced at the board with the chalked specials, and heard the stranger sigh again. "Coffee to start, please. With cream?"

I nodded, and the waitress said, "That's a nickel extra."

"That's fine."

He handed me a menu, and I realized with some embarrassment that in spite of everything I was hungry. I had two dollars in my purse, and another dime for the subway in my shoe, and I really didn't care what he thought. "I'll have a grilled cheese sandwich. With the tomato."

"That's extra."

"Fine."

She scribbled on her notepad, and cocked her head at the stranger. "You?"

"Poached eggs and corned beef hash," he said. "And a side of toast—I know, it's extra, that's fine."

"Suit yourself," she said, and flounced off. She came back with our coffee and a very small pitcher of cream.

"So. Who are you, and why did Peter want me to meet you?" When I said his name, I could see the body lying on the pier, feel the curve of his skull giving way under my fingers. I shivered and stripped off my gloves, reaching for the sugar and the cream. The wadded-up gloves left a rusty mark on the tabletop; I winced, and rolled them up with the fingers on the inside.

The stranger unbuttoned his overcoat and shrugged himself out of it, revealing a tailcoat and white tie. "My name's Max Cullinane."

The evening clothes told me where I'd heard the name. "The magician?" I gulped at my coffee, grateful for the sugar and the scalding heat. I had heard of him—who hadn't? He'd been headliner at every major club on both coasts, and had even starred in his own radio serial. There were all sorts of stories about him, that he'd studied mystic arts in Tibet, that he found lost things and people, and that not all his tricks were done with mirrors. I didn't believe that, of course, but he had a look to him that made it plausible.

He nodded. "You may have heard that I sometimes do—favors—for friends. Look into things discreetly. These rumors about *Nereiade* were brought to my attention."

"What rumors—you mean the stories that people saw her before other disappearances?" I shook my head. "I don't believe it, and neither did Peter."

"Oh?"

My eyes fell. We'd argued about that the last time we'd met, eating apple pie at the automat—I was glad, suddenly, that pie was off the menu here. *Nereiade* had supposedly been seen again, trailing other ships that never came home again: no, I didn't believe that. "Sailors can be superstitious, that's all."

"Is that what your father told you?"

I blinked. "Yes, as a matter of fact."

Cullinane gave me a lop-sided smile. "I've been doing some research on your father. He seems to have done some remarkable things in a too-short life. I'd hoped you might be able to help me understand some things about his work."

"I don't know anything about it." The practiced answer came out firm and clear and frank, and I met Cullinane's eyes squarely. "I'm not any kind of engineer— any kind of sailor at all."

"And yet Miss Thomasine Wright—Tommy to her friends—not only won the Portland Ladies' Cup two years running, but struck rather a shrewd bargain for the bulk of her father's designs after his death."

"That doesn't mean I understand them," I protested. "I just knew who was likely to be interested."

"But you didn't sell the Nymphs."

"Wollart Lines owns all the rights."

I could see that he didn't believe me, and I was relieved to see the waitress returning with our plates. She slapped them down in front of us, and I readied another lie, but Cullinane forestalled me.

"Miss Wright, let me be frank with you. Gagne's death is not the first connected to these ships' disappearance, and it's unlikely to be the last. Will you at least hear me out?"

"Of course."

"I know that your father studied mathematics in Berlin before the war, and that he was involved with a small group who had developed some radical theories about wave formation and mapping. I also know that he used those theories when he designed the hulls of the three Wollart liners known as the Nymphs, intending to make them significantly faster than their peers without a corresponding increase in fuel consumption."

I took a huge bite of my sandwich, hardly caring that I burned my mouth on the hot cheese. These were the things Father had told me never to talk about, never to share with anyone; I had been supposed to burn his original designs, though I had never been able to bring myself to do it. *Sailors are superstitious*, he had said. *If they find out there's anything odd about the hull, they'll refuse to sail on any of them...* For the first time, I wondered if there was more to the story than he had told me.

"*Dryade* was, I think, pure bad luck: her engines were out of order when *Zeeadler* —the raider—spotted her or she never would have been taken. As it was, the prize captain was an ambitious young officer who realized there was something special about the ship. She was faster than she should be, and yet burned less coal than he expected, and he persuaded the Imperial Navy to refit her as another commerce raider, hoping to make his name. But somehow the refit didn't work. Whatever they did to her—adding guns, changing her configuration—cancelled out her special qualities, and she was caught and sunk by a British Q-ship before she'd left the North Sea. Erfurt was killed in that action, but he had given a detailed report to his superiors. It was largely ignored, but in the chaos of the mutinies, someone seems to have taken it seriously. The original file on the Wollart Nymphs was stolen from the Imperial Navy's offices in Kiel, and subsequently the abstract of the report—all that was left—disappeared from the archives as well. A friend of mine in the British War Office received an unofficial inquiry from a German compatriot, one who supports the new Republican government, and in attempting a little international cooperation, my British friend discovered that there had been considerable interest in the surviving Nymphs, culminating in the disappearance of *Nereiade*. My friend suspects that *Nereiade* was taken to be the core of a new privateer fleet, supporting itself by piracy, and ultimately available to the highest bidder, not merely among the Great Powers, but among those countries that would like to make their mark on the world."

"You think someone took *Nereiade*," I said, and was proud that my voice was steady. "Captured her and killed everyone who wouldn't cooperate and now they're using her as a pirate ship?"

"More than that," Cullinane said, "I think they want *Naiade*, too."

"We have to stop them." I had no idea how one

might go about such a thing, but it couldn't be allowed to continue. *Nereiade* had two hundred passengers as well as her crew, and there was Peter, too, lying dead on the docks... "What can I do?"

Cullinane eyed me thoughtfully. "If you mean that —"

"I have my father's plans for all the Nymphs." It was a leap of faith, but Peter had trusted him. And I had to do something.

"That could be very useful." Cullinane leaned forward, his elbows on the table, lean face intent. "I have tickets on *Naiade*'s next sailing. I believe that an attempt will be made to take her then, and that this will be the best chance to save her, and perhaps to find out what's really going on. Are you game?"

"I'm in," I said, and we shook hands over the dirty plates.

And that was how I found myself following Cullinane up the gangplank to *Naiade*'s main deck, dressed in a hastily-altered man's suit and carrying a briefcase. That wasn't so much to protect my reputation as that Cullinane didn't want anyone to connect me to my father and the Nymphs, and a secretary was much less conspicuous than a girlfriend. I'd spent most of my childhood in pants, sailing my own skiff or crewing for my friends and their brothers, and played all the boys' parts at Miss Cutler's Day School when we'd studied drama. I felt sure I could pass.

Cullinane had booked one of the medium suites on C Deck, with a large sitting room and two small bedrooms, more luxury than I was used to, and more than adequate privacy. The steward had everything well in hand, and I made my way down to the promenade to watch the departure. We cast off in a flurry of steam and sirens, passengers laughing and shouting farewells and throwing streamers to friends on the dock. I stayed at the rail as the tugs shepherded us through the bustling harbor and out to the open sea, then made my way to the stern to watch the city sink below the horizon. I'd forgotten, or maybe I'd never truly known, how lovely the Wollart Nymphs were. *Naiade* had been designed to echo the lines of a racing yacht, with a rounded schooner's stern and a sharp bow that mimicked a clipper's—she even had the stub of a bowsprit, though old Mr. Wollart had nixed the idea of an actual figurehead. A statue was on display in the First Class Saloon instead, a sleek, half-naked woman with a flapper's face and close-cut hair emerging from stylized waves, and I had to admit she looked better there than she would have on *Naiade*'s bow. There were naiads everywhere in the first class section—holding the light sconces, woven into the curtains, back-to-back on the gilded panels, even sitting on the ashtrays in the Smoking Lounge—and when we went in to dinner the centerpiece on our table was a silver-plated miniature of the figurehead.

The table was full even on the first night: the weather was good, Wollart Lines had a reputation for hiring excellent chefs, and our table boasted not only Cullinane but a second celebrity. Lottie Lowe Davis was a nightclub singer who'd made a name for herself in Paris after the War, and was on her way home to New Orleans, she said, before a trip to Hollywood. Her voice was softly southern, her skin pale as porcelain above her ivory and gold dress, her hair a vivid red-gold that owed nothing to peroxide. Her figure was a little rounder than was fashionable, and I had to admire the way her dress was cut to flatter. She was cheerful and charming and even the older women who had been inclined to mark her off as a mere singer—and a divorcée, no better than she should be—had thawed to her by the end of the meal. I'd had two glasses of wine myself, as well as the chance to chat, and I was feeling quite content.

"There's a pianist in the First Class Saloon," I said to Cullinane, as we strolled sternward along the promenade. "I thought I'd stop in for a while."

"I'd rather you went back to the suite," he said, and

my good humor vanished. This was no pleasure cruise, not for us, and I was foolish to forget it even for an instant.

"Of course."

"I'll join you in a bit," he said. "Set up a drinks table, if you would."

I did as I was told, setting out the bottles and the fancy crystal that had come with the suite, and it wasn't long before Cullinane returned. With him was a sandy-haired man about his own age in the blue serge of *Naiade*'s crew. Even without the uniform, anyone could have told he was a sailor, and Cullinane introduced him as Stefan Mab, *Naiade*'s second engineer.

"And this is my new secretary, Tommy Wright," Cullinane said. Mab seemed to be looking at me more closely that I liked, and I retreated, dropping my eyes.

"May I get you a drink, sir?"

"Brandy and soda, yes, thank you."

His voice was lightly accented: Scandinavian, I thought, or maybe German. If Cullinane was working with the Germans... I killed that thought, and busied myself with the siphon. "And for you, Mr. Cullinane?"

"The same." Cullinane looked back at Mab, an odd half-smile on his face. "Tommy is Nicholas Wright's daughter."

"Daughter?" Mab blinked, then smiled in turn. "Ah. Better to be in disguise, yes."

"I thought it might be kinder to mention," Cullinane said.

"Just so."

I brought them each their drinks, and mixed a lighter gin and tonic for myself. "Are you helping us, Mr. Mab?"

"He is," Cullinane said. "But let's wait a bit. We've one more coming, and I don't want to have to say everything twice."

Even as he said it, there was a knock on the stateroom door. I opened it, and stepped back, blinking myself as I saw Miss Davis in the corridor.

"Come on in, Lottie," Cullinane said, and she gave a tired smile.

"So it's for real," she said, and I closed the door behind her.

"It is." Cullinane handed her to a seat, and she looked up at me.

"If that's a gin and tonic, honey, I'd love one."

"Of course, Miss Davis." I busied myself at the drinks tray, brought her the glass and was rewarded with a nod.

"Thanks, honey. That's perfect."

I perched on the arm of a chair with my own drink, doing my best to look boyish. Cullinane took a swallow of his brandy and soda, and set the glass aside.

"All right. Introductions first, and then a plan." He smiled. "You all know me. I'm here to fix this if I can."

"And I would still like to know at whose behest," Mab said.

"I can't tell you," Cullinane answered. "There is of course interest in high places, but nothing official."

"There never is." Mab slumped back against the sofa cushions.

"Mab is here because he is familiar with the conversion of *Dryade* during —"

"I served on the *Zeeadler* that captured her," Mab interrupted, "and I was in line to be her chief engineer when she was lost. I hope that doesn't make you too uncomfortable, Miss Wright."

I shook my head, aware of Miss Davis's sudden sharp look, and Cullinane went on.

"Miss Wright—who I think we should all call Tommy for the duration of this exploit—is Nicholas Wright's daughter and friend of any number of people who have disappeared on the missing Nymphs. Miss Davis —"

"My daughter was traveling on *Nereiade* when she disappeared," Miss Davis said. "With my ex-husband. I want to know what happened."

"And I think we can find some answers for you," Cullinane said. "For all of us. Tommy, would you fetch the plans? And, Stefan, did you find anything in the engines?"

I did as I was told, and Mab shook his head. "The engines are perfectly ordinary. I have been over every inch of the machinery, and there's nothing that didn't come straight from the builder. And yet we are still using nearly a third less fuel than I would expect, and making better speed."

I unfolded the plans and laid them on the little table, the drawing of *Naiade* on top. In the cabin's lights, the lines of the hull swept down from the bowsprit and back up to the rounded stern. It was hard to follow the curves precisely; they seemed to shift and twist, changing perspective like one of those drawings that shows a young lady at her mirror until you blink and it becomes a glaring skull. Miss Davis whistled between her teeth.

"I don't know much about boats, but there's sure something funny there."

"Yes, indeed," Mab said. He used his finger to trace one of the lines. I'd done that myself any number of times, and waited for the moment when he shook his head, blinking hard. He looked at Cullinane. "What are we looking at, then? Is this why she's so fast?"

Cullinane nodded. "I believe—and correct me if I'm wrong, Tommy, please—Nicholas Wright used the Duplessis-Albericht transformation to calculate hull shape that would slip most efficiently through air and water. Through matter in general, in fact, but the relatively low density of air and water is what lets the Nymphs move so freely."

"It does more than that," I said. "Father said—it slips through time more efficiently, too, so it gets a little ahead of itself. Not by much, only fractions of a second, but over the course of a voyage it adds up to savings."

Mab swore under his breath, but Cullinane merely nodded again. "Of course. Efficiency in more than three dimensions. Brilliant."

"He called it a variation on Schatten-Theorie," I said. "Shadow Theory? I saw the math once, the equations were enormous, at least two full pages, but after he died I couldn't find that notebook."

"Damn," Cullinane said, but Mab shrugged, still trying to trace the lines of the hull.

"If we know that much, the work can be recreated. With this to help."

"But that's not the point," Miss Davis said. "The point is to find *Nereiade*."

"She'll come," Cullinane said, "and I'll remind you that puts us all in grave danger."

"But if they have *Nereiade*, why do they want *Naiade*, too?" I asked.

"She was the first built," Mab said. "The closest to your father's original plans. All the others had alterations to make them easier to build, easier to handle, but *Naiade* is the original. The one that will be the fastest, the best."

Miss Davis looked around the room. "No offense, Max, but there's only four of us. How are we supposed to stand up to a ship full of pirates?"

"All the reports mention a distant light, and then *Nereiade*'s ghostly shape," Cullinane said. "I believe I know what that light is—it's the key to the whole operation, and if we can nullify its effects, I believe Captain Turner's men can deal with the attack."

"It would be helpful if you gave us a few more details," Mab said.

"And I will." Cullinane spread his hands with a disarming grin. "Just as soon as I have them."

Mab laughed, but his eyes were on the plans again. "This is an amazing design. An amazing ship."

"What do you want us to do?" Miss Davis asked.

"I took the liberty of sending some anonymous messages to Wollart Lines before we left," Cullinane answered, "warning that pirates might attempt an attack. I also mailed the same warning to Captain Turner. I believe he has taken them seriously."

"We were told there might be trouble," Mab agreed. "Though my Chief was worried about Wobblies and Bolsheviks."

"I may have mentioned such things," Cullinane said.

Old Man Wollart believed in capitalism and the American Way: those were words guaranteed to get him on your side in a pinch.

"Turner has posted extra lookouts, and is determined to steer clear of any ships encountered in fog or poor visibility," Cullinane went on. "As for us—I think the captain's precautions are good, but we may need a bit more." He crossed to the sideboard, opened a drawer, and pulled out four silver whistles thicker than my forefinger. He put one to his lips and blew softly, and I winced at the shrill sound. Even muted and in the cabin, it seemed unnaturally piercing. "That's our signal. If any of you see anything strange—particularly a light on the horizon, but really anything at all—I want you to sound off good and loud. Oh, and if you do see such a light, for God's sake, don't look at it."

I took my whistle, turning it curiously in my hand. It felt heavy for its size, and rattled softly when I shook it. After a moment's thought, I hooked it on my borrowed watch chain the way I'd seen the boys do it. Mab stuffed his in his pocket, and Miss Davis tucked hers into her beaded purse.

"All right, we'll do it your way." She rose to her feet, and Mab hurried to open the door. "Max—do you think there's any chance Bella might be alive?"

Cullinane winced. "There's always a chance," he said, but I could tell he didn't believe it.

We ran south all the next day, following the Gulf Stream south toward Florida. The weather was good, and *Naiade* ran easily through the gentle swells. I was getting used to my suit and my new persona: I could wander where I willed, and no one would question me, or try to shepherd me back to more respectable pursuits. I climbed down to the engine room, and stared in awe at the massive pistons; I made my way to the very point of the bow, where the bowsprit jutted into the spray, and no one told me to take care, or cautioned me that I would ruin my dress. I lunched with Miss Davis in the smaller dining room—Cullinane was nowhere to be found—and afterwards we made our way around the circuit of the Promenade, her hand on my arm in the most natural way while we chatted. I was falling into a schoolgirl's crush, I knew, but I'd survived those before.

She had been unlucky in her marriage, she said. She'd married young hoping to create a stable life for herself, but by the time her daughter was a toddler, she'd known she couldn't have a singer's life and a family. It had been terribly hard, but she'd chosen her art, and permitted her husband to divorce her and to keep the child. It was only fair, she said, and anyway the clubs and the travel was no life for a baby. But then he had planned a trip to visit cousins in New York (and, I suspected, to see her) and taken ship on *Nereiade*, and the ship had disappeared into a fog bank and never been seen again. Her daughter Bella had been five then; she'd be almost seven now, and Miss Davis spoke wistfully of how big she'd be, but I could tell she didn't truly believe Bella was alive any more than Cullinane did. I closed my hand over hers where it rested in the crook of my elbow, not knowing what else to say, and she glanced up with a watery smile.

"I have to have an answer, you see."

I nodded.

"But let's talk about something else." She drew a deep breath, her bosom rising and falling sharply. "Where do you think we are?"

The horizon was out of sight, but by the time we'd traveled… "Coming up on the Carolina coast." Coming up on Hatteras, I meant, but didn't want to say it out loud. The air was growing damp, too, and the sky ahead was blurred with haze. Fog off Hatteras: I suspected that was what Cullinane was counting on, to lure the pirate in, and my eyes strayed nervously to the silvered horizons.

By late afternoon, the fog had thickened, and Captain Turner had started our own foghorn, blasting at steady intervals. In the intervening silences, I could hear another foghorn answering. Diamond Shoals or another ship? I strained my eyes as I leaned against the rail, and gave a sigh of relief as the fog thinned abruptly. Yes, there in the distance was the Diamond Shoals lightship, and for just a second I caught a glimpse of the coastline behind it, a shadow in the wavering light. Then it was gone, and the lightship wavered as a curtain of fog passed between us. *Naiade* held her course, aiming, I thought, to pass close enough alongside for the lightship's crew to mark our passage. The lightship appeared again, rust-red sides rising high out of the waves, and vanished, then reappeared, closer still. I could see someone on the deck, a tiny shape that raised an arm in a broad wave of greeting. I waved back, and the lightship slipped astern.

The air was damp and chilly now, and I remembered the pullover Cullinane had insisted I bring. Unnecessary, I'd thought, going south in the early summer, but it looked as though I'd be glad of it after all. The main Saloon was crowded, probably because of the lightship; I wormed my way through the crowd and let myself into the cabin. I'd just pulled the sweater over my head when I heard the shrill blast of one of Cullinane's whistles. To stern and to port, I thought, and a light flashed outside the porthole, flat and blinding as lightning. There was no sound, just a heavy smell of lilacs, and against my will my eyes closed.

I woke folded into an uncomfortable shape, my neck bent awkwardly against a old bulkhead. The lights were stark, and there was a hand over my mouth. I promptly bit it, and Stefan Mab swallowed a curse.

"Quiet," Cullinane said. "I told you she'd do that."

"So you did." Mab shook his hand unhappily.

"Sorry," I said, and dragged myself into a more comfortable position. "What happened?"

"I miscalculated," Cullinane said. He looked thoroughly annoyed with himself.

"The pirates have taken the ship," Mab said.

"So where are we?"

"E Deck, starboard crew quarters," Mab said. "They've already searched here."

"Max." Miss Davis came around the corner. She was still in the dress she'd worn at lunch, but she'd changed her court shoes for a practical pair of pumps. "They've moved on."

"Good." Cullinane held out his hand, and I let him pull me to my feet.

"Who are 'they,' anyway?"

"I don't know who," Cullinane answered, "but, yes, they took the ship. They came alongside in the fog before anyone spotted them, and used the light and then gas to put the ship to sleep. The only good news is that they've only got about a dozen men all told, and some of them are back on *Nereiade*."

"Anyone who was in his cabin has been locked in," Mab said. "I'm worried about the others, Max."

"I know." Cullinane pressed his palms together hard. "We need to take the bridge. If we get control of the ship, they'll have to try to take it back."

"They will have hostages," Mab said.

"They're dead anyway," Cullinane answered, and I shuddered. Certainly it was true, there was no reason for the pirates to keep anyone alive if all they wanted was the ship itself, but to hear it said aloud was somehow worse.

"Then we'd better hurry," Miss Davis said. "Tommy, do you have a gun?"

"No." I looked around, saw a fire axe hanging on the wall beside a coil of hose. I grabbed that, testing the weight. I'd used heavier axes at our camp back home, and anyway, fear was giving me extra strength. "Just don't call me Lizzie."

Mab lifted his eyebrows, but Cullinane grinned briefly. "All right. Let's go."

He pulled a blackjack from his pocket, and Mab drew a broomhandle Mauser that surely dated from the

War. Miss Davis dipped her hand into her purse and came up with a dainty pistol not much bigger than her palm, all silver scrollwork and mother of pearl, but from the way she held it I had no doubt she knew how to use it. Cullinane led the way through the corridor and up the crew's stairs to B Deck. From there, we'd have to go forward, past the Smoking Lounge, to reach the stairs that led to the bridge.

Cullinane paused long enough at the top of the stairs to be sure the coast was clear, then led us down the port corridor. As I brought up the rear, I could see why. *Nereiade* was standing off the starboard side, just barely keeping a safe distance. In that quick glance, I couldn't make out anyone on deck, but there had to be watchers on the bridge, and even if they didn't have loudhailers they were close enough to hear shouting.

As we came to the entrance to the Ladies Saloon, I could hear voices, and Cullinane waved us back against the wall.

"They'll do anything you tell them," a man said. "Walk right overboard if you want them to."

"Yeah, sure," a second voice answered, and I suppressed a curse. At least two of them, then, and we had to pass both the open door and the broad windows.

"They will," the first voice insisted. "Go ahead, tell her."

"Won't the boss be upset?"

"He's going to get rid of them anyway."

In the silence, I saw Cullinane and Mab exchange glances, and then the second voice spoke again.

"Ok, lady. Go outside and jump over the rail."

I braced myself, not sure yet for what, and a moment later an older woman in a lilac afternoon dress emerged from the door. Her face was slack beneath her disheveled white hair, her eyes as empty as a dead woman's as she started toward the rail.

"She's going to do it," the second voice said, and giggled.

"If she can get over it," the first man said. "You might have to help her."

Miss Davis moved then, grabbing the older woman and twisting her away from the rail to pin her against the saloon's wall. I saw the first of the men emerge from the doorway, frowning as though he didn't believe what he'd seen, and Cullinane dropped him with a single stroke of the blackjack. Mab charged past him, and I heard a muffled pistol shot, came up with my axe raised to see a second body on the floor, a curl of smoke rising from his singed vest. Nearly a dozen people stood in the room's center, passengers and a couple of stewardesses, their faces as blank as the other woman's had been.

"Come inside," Miss Davis said, to the other woman, her voice trembling only slightly, and the older woman obeyed.

Mab looked up from hogtying the man Cullinane had downed, using a cord he'd stripped from the nearest curtain. "Do you think they heard?"

Cullinane shook his head. "Not unless they were right on top of us."

"Max, you have to do something about them," Miss Davis said.

"I can't—" He stopped, shaking his head. "All right. Ladies, listen. Go back to your cabins at once and lock yourselves inside. All of you. Go back to your cabins."

His voice was low and compelling, and the women turned as one, began making their way toward the doors.

"It's all I can do," he said, to Miss Davis. He looked around the room, frowning, and reached for one of the mirrors that hung on the forward bulkhead. It was bolted in place, of course, and he looked at me. "Tommy, can you get this loose?"

"Not without a wrench."

"I need a mirror."

I looked at it for a moment, studying the possibilities, then turned the axe backward in my hand. "Stand clear," I said, and hit it sharply in one corner. The glass crazed, a spiderweb of cracks spreading over its surface, and I sighed with relief to see that one of the pieces was almost a quarter of the original.

"Good work," Cullinane said, and together we pried it out of the frame. "Let's go."

There was no one in the main saloon as we wedged past, and the doors of the dining room were closed, the curtains drawn. We paused at the bottom of the stairs, listening, and I thought I could hear the muffled sounds of at least three people moving around on the bridge above us. Cullinane took a careful step up, and then another, his head cocked to listen, and Mab lifted his pistol to cover him.

"We have to take them fast," he said, so softly that it was like hearing his thoughts. "Stefan and me first, then Tommy. You cover us, Lottie."

We all nodded, and he peered up the stairs again. "All right. Ready—go!"

He and Mab charged up the stairs, and I hauled myself up after them, Miss Davis at my heels. Before I was quite at the top, I heard someone cry out, and then a shot, and a man lunged toward me, whether to attack or push past me down the stairs I didn't know. I swung the axe at him and missed, and Cullinane swung his blackjack expertly. The man collapsed, and slithered past me to stop at Miss Davis's feet. She stepped over him and hurried on up the stairs. Cullinane and Mab had secured the others, one more out cold and the other two tied back to back in a corner. Both of them looked only half conscious, as though Cullinane or Mab had hit them hard. Captain Turner stood by the far window, the helmsman at his side, both their faces as blank as the women in the Saloon below. Mab stepped to the wheel, studying the controls, and Cullinane said, "Can you move us away from *Nereiade*?"

Mab tested the wheel, then looked at the engine room telegraph. "Only if they're answering bells in the engine room. Can't you wake them?"

"I don't know." Cullinane propped the mirror against the bulkhead, and studied Turner. He touched the man's arm, got no response, and finally took his shoulders in both hands, turning him to face him. "Tommy, take a look at *Nereiade*, but make sure you're not seen. See if there's a searchlight anywhere on the bridge deck. Lottie, if anybody tries to come up the stairs, or if any of these boys try anything—shoot them."

"With pleasure." Miss Davis pressed herself against the bulkhead by the head of the stair where she had a clear shot, and I peered cautiously out the starboard windows. *Nereiade* was still alongside, a sudden puff of smoke rising from her single stack as she adjusted her engines to keep station. The fog seemed to be thinning, and it was easier to see her through the haze. There still wasn't anyone visible on deck, but when I grabbed a pair of binoculars off the chart table, I could make out shapes behind the glass of the bridge. And—yes, it looked like a searchlight, or more like a signal lamp, and I turned to tell Cullinane.

He had Captain Turner by the shoulders, and was repeating something in a soft voice, words that I couldn't quite understand, but that somehow tugged at my hearing as though I ought to be able to grasp them, if only I listened a little harder. He waved his hand in front of Turner's face, then snapped his fingers, but nothing happened.

"Max," Mab said. He was keeping *Naiade* turned into the sluggish swells, his hands moving easily on the wheel.

"I need more time," Cullinane said.

"I can see the searchlight," I said, and he turned toward me.

"Where?"

"There," I said, pointing, and handed him the glasses. He took them, studying *Nereiade*'s side, and I saw his mouth tighten.

"It's a hell of a chance, but—" He handed me back the binoculars, and crossed the bridge to pick up the piece of mirror. "Tommy, does that window open?"

"Yes." I eased the catches back, and he held up his free hand.

"Wait, not yet. Stefan, on my word, I want you to signal full power—I want *Nereiade* to think we're trying to get away."

"They'll hit us again," Mab said.

"That's what I want." Cullinane stooped to take another look at *Nereiade*, still keeping station as neatly as a Navy cutter.

"What is that light?" I asked.

"It doesn't have a name," Cullinane said. "It projects a special frequency of light that stuns the eyes and mind. Some hypnotists use it to put subjects into a trance, which is how I know about it, and why I thought of it when I heard the stories. But I've never seen it used on this scale."

"If they hit us again, we'll all be under," Mab pointed out, and Cullinane shook his head.

"Trust me, Stefan."

Mab sighed. "I do."

"Full ahead."

"Full ahead aye," Mab answered automatically, and reached across to move the lever of the engine room telegraph to full ahead. The warning bell sounded, kept sounding, and Cullinane nodded to me.

"Open the window."

I slid back the heavy pane, and he raised the mirror, keeping it just below the opening. The bell stopped, the needle finally moving on the repeater, and the deck lurched under my feet as the engines came up to full power. The vibrations slowed as abruptly as they'd begun, and I saw figures moving on *Nereiade's* bridge.

"Get down!" Cullinane shouted, and in the same moment raised the mirror. I ducked, but not before I saw the light's projector swing toward us, shutters opening. I could see the flash through my closed lids, but it was somehow behind me, and when I bobbed up again, the man at the light stood frozen, and there was no movement on *Nereiade's* bridge.

"You turned it back on them!"

"So far." Cullinane let the mirror slide to the deck. "We're not out of the woods yet—"

He stopped, and I lifted my axe, only to realize what he'd seen. Captain Turner was moving, shaking his head, the helmsman blinking to life beside him.

"What the devil?"

"Pirates," Cullinane said. "As I warned you, sir. You and your men have been knocked out, and the pirates may still have the engine room—"

"That's her," the helmsman said. "That's *Nereiade*."

"She's out of commission at the moment," Cullinane said, and one of the speaking tubes whistled.

Turner grabbed it from the bulkhead. "Bridge here."

"Captain! Thank God." It was impossible to recognize the voice, and Turner frowned.

"Identify yourself, man."

"It's Martin, sir. We've just broken out of the forward crew's quarters. I don't know how we got there—"

"Stow that for now." Turner looked at Cullinane. "Can you hold the bridge? I intend to take back my ship."

"We can do that, sir," Cullinane answered, and Turner turned back to the speaking tube.

"Martin! Bring the men aft to D Deck, the crew stairs. If you meet anyone who isn't crew or passenger, put them out of action."

"With pleasure, sir," Martin answered, and Turner glanced again at *Nereiade*, now falling away to starboard under the pressure of wind and waves.

"Do we have steering way, Mr. Mab?"

"Aye, sir."

"Then hold her steady. We'll take care of things from here."

I leaned against the bulkhead, not quite daring to put down the axe, though I let its head rest on the deck. "What about *Nereiade*?"

"With luck, we'll have a chance to take boats over," Cullinane answered, but I could see she was already starting to drift away into the fog.

Miss Davis gave a soft cry. "Max, we can't just do nothing—"

"What would you have me do, Lottie? We don't even have control of our own engines yet."

She put her hand to her mouth, muffling her words. "I know. God, I do know."

After a moment, I held out my hand, and she took it, moving close so that we stood shoulder to shoulder against the bulkhead. "I'll find her," she whispered, after a moment. "I'll find my little girl."

I put my arm around her shoulders, wishing I had something more I could do, and we settled ourselves to wait.

It took Captain Turner a good hour to winkle the pirates out of the engine room, and then they damaged the condensers, so that we had to heave to for repairs. That lasted well into the night, and by then *Nereiade* was long gone. Miss Davis huddled dry-eyed in our cabin, a cup of coffee laced with brandy cooling in her hands, and I sat with her, silent, not knowing what to say. Cullinane came and went, sometimes with Mab, sometimes alone, and finally as the naiad clock struck midnight, they returned together, disheveled and, in Mab's case, grease-stained, but with a certain air of satisfaction about them. I moved to mix them drinks, and Miss Davis fixed them with a stare.

"Well?"

"*Nereiade's* well away," Cullinane said bluntly. "Turner put out a general radio call, and the Diamond Shoals Light spotted her heading south."

"Damn it, Max!"

"But there's some good news." Cullinane took a swallow of his drink, working his shoulders as though they were sore. "We have a name."

"The pirates talked," Mab said, with a dark smile.

Cullinane nodded. "Howell Hall, supposedly based in New Orleans. Mind you, it's probably an alias, but it's more than we had before. And—Lottie, when *Nereiade* was taken, Bella was spared. They don't know why, maybe just because she was a child, but Hall had her taken onto the tender with him when they parted company with *Nereiade*, and presumably took her back to New Orleans with him."

Miss Davis wept then, hard and nearly silent, a storm that shook her like a giant hand. I put my arm around her, half afraid she'd push me away, but she clung closer, her head on my shoulder, until at least she could master herself and sit up again. "Oh, God, Max, are you sure?"

"The men were sure," Mab said, and Cullinane nodded again.

"It's still a long shot, but—better than nothing."

"Yes," she said fiercely. "Yes, indeed. You'll help me—keep helping me?"

"You know I will," Cullinane said.

"Let me help, too," I said. "I know a lot about my father's work, and I've been around the waterfront all my life. I can be useful."

"It's dangerous," Cullinane said, but I wasn't looking at him.

"Are you sure you know what you're asking?" Miss Davis said.

"I'm sure." I took her hand in both of mine. "Please."

She nodded slowly, and I heard Cullinane sigh. "All right. For now. When we get to New Orleans—"

"I'll be ready," I said. "We'll find her."

Miss Davis set her other hand on top of mine. "I believe we will."

AUTHOR'S NOTE

Melissa Scott is from Little Rock, Arkansas, and studied history at Harvard College and Brandeis University, where she earned her Ph.D. in the Comparative

History program. She is the author of more than thirty science fiction and fantasy novels, and has won Lambda Literary Awards for *Trouble and Her Friends, Shadow Man*, and *Point of Dreams* (written with her late partner, Lisa A. Barnett), and *Death By Silver*, with Amy Griswold. She has also won Spectrum Awards for *Shadow Man* and again in 2010 for the short story "The Rocky Side of the Sky" (Periphery, Lethe Press) as well as the John W. Campbell Award for Best New Writer. Her most recent short story "Finders" (*The Other Half of the Sky*) was selected for the 2013 Year's Best SF. "The Wollart Nymphs" is her homage to the golden age of the transatlantic liner, and to the pulp stories that found tremendous possibilities in both the burgeoning technology and the uncharted psychic frontiers of the period. Scott can be found on LiveJournal at mescott.livejournal.com and on Twitter as @blueterraplane.

Judy Garland Saves the World (And I Don't Mean Oz)

Edward M. Lerner

Okay, it *wasn't* Judy who did it. Except in an archetypal sense. Never mind that, when all this began, I couldn't have said what an archetype was. Regardless, from the movie, Judy Garland was the archetype of *The Harvey Girls*.

But it's because Grandma was once a Harvey Girl that all this happened. We'll leave it at Judy because Grandma was a very private person.

That doesn't make her story any less important.

I was, near the end, staying in a motel in Flagstaff, visiting daily at the nursing home. I checked in remotely when I could, alert for any work fires that *had* to be fought. But mostly even the crises piled up. I was the only family Grandma had left. I'd long since given up on moving her near me, knowing that nothing less than a bulldozer could have gotten her out of Arizona.

Like Grandma, my memory was once pretty good. So: I'll begin with her story, having had the good sense to transcribe everything while it was fresh in my mind.

To be clear: *we* didn't talk, not really. *She* talked. Sure, I asked questions. I commented. But I knew upfront she wouldn't hear much of anything I said, much less hear it correctly, because it had been years since she had. Getting Grandma fitted with hearing aids, like getting her to move, was a battle I could never win.

That mostly she guessed wrong, answering the questions she thought she had heard? Or perhaps the questions she thought needed to be answered? Maybe that worked out for the best.

I'll tell Grandma's story just as she did, except that I've rearranged and condensed things from the disjointed, repetitious manner in which, over several days, she reminisced.

It all began (Grandma said) with Judy Garland....

**

Who is Judy Garland? Jeez-oh-Pete, how can anyone not know Judy Garland? Oh, don't open your laptop thingie. Surely you've seen *The Wizard of Oz.* You remember the Dorothy character? That was Judy.

The other night, watching a movie on the TV in the lounge, I got to thinking about the old days. A 1946 movie...however unlikely that might seem to you, it wasn't. The classic movies are standard fare in places like this, I suppose because we don't do well with change. If we residents had had any part in running things, the clock on the DVD thingie (is that what replaced VCRs?) would always flash zeroes, and none of us would know how to run off the movies.

You would think I'd have seen this particular film way back when. But it was playing in the theaters just a few months after VJ Day. Less time than that after ... after I'd learned George wouldn't be coming back from the war.

Sorry, boy. I still get teary remembering. More than fifty years it may be, but it seems like yesterday. You would have liked your grandpa, I know you would. Your Dad would've, too. The shame of it all is, my own son never knew his father. George and I were married in '44, just before he shipped out. He went missing before I even knew I was expecting...

But the point, pardon an old woman's rambling, is that no matter how much I loved the movies, I wasn't going to theaters when this particular movie came out.

Anyway, the other night the movie the staff put into the whatever-it's-called doodad was *The Harvey Girls.*

Who, you ask? A bunch of waitresses. That's what people remember nowadays, if they remember at all. But back in the 1880s, when Mr. Harvey started his hotels, men waited tables.

Don't give me that look, boy! I'm old, but I'm not *that* old.

So, were we just waitresses? Hardly! When Mr. Harvey started his hotels and restaurants out West, the joke was there were "no ladies west of Dodge City and no women west of Albuquerque." Mr. Harvey brought out women by the carload. By the train car, that is. Harvey Houses served train stations across the Southwest. A bunch of young men, no offense, is just so much rowdiness and trouble. Add enough women, and you get civilization.

I'm rambling again, aren't I? Sorry. It goes with the age. Anyway, here's how the movie goes. The Judy Garland character is on a train out West, engaged to a man she knows only from letters, because she had answered his lonely hearts advertisement. Only it turns out he's an old coot. They weren't *his* letters at all, which was another man's idea of a joke. So...

You can stop peeking under the edge of the table at your Blueberry. Blackberry. Whatever. And your cell phone, too. And anything else from your Batman utility belt.

Hah! Well, you shouldn't be surprised. The Batman comic goes back to 1939, just like Judy's version of *The Wizard of Oz.*

Anyway, about *The Harvey Girls.* Judy and the old coot don't get married, but she's far from home. She takes a job at the local Harvey House...

Just like your old grandma did.

∗∗∗

The Great Depression? Hah! There was nothing great about it. Nothing. And in 1930, with jobs few and far between in Chicago—heck, everywhere across the country —I was in a pickle. Clerical jobs in libraries were expendable enough, and mine had been expended.

Well, not quite *everywhere.* Hollywood followed

rules all its own, and the worse off the rest of us became, the more we flocked to theaters for respite. For a nickel, back then, you got a double feature, and newsreels or an episode of a serial, and a big chocolate bar.

Sad to say, even nickels were hard to come by.

I was twenty-six, younger than you. You'd never guess it now to look at me, but back then I was tall, with blond hair down to my shoulders and twinkling blue eyes. And quite the chassis, too—not that, in a shapeless Harvey Girl uniform, *anyone* looked womanly. With my money running out, I piled what few things I owned into the old car and headed down Route 66 for Hollywood.

The car? A five-year-old Model T, and it was about my only asset. After the fire, after settling Mom and Dad's debts, Dad's car was all I had left.

I never told you about the fire? (She had. Often.) Twenty-two died that night at the Study Club, not that much studying had ever gone on there. Prohibition, you know? It was a speakeasy. Mother and Father had gone to Detroit, to celebrate there with old friends. Celebrating what, exactly? That, I don't remember anymore, only that the fire wasn't much of a celebration.

About a month after they died, the market crashed. Everything went…

Well, *depression* is right enough, even though *great* doesn't hardly apply. But I guess I repeat myself.

Anyway, a few months after that, once their affairs were settled, as soon as the weather allowed, I left Chicago. A woman driving, much less alone? Much less across the country? Mother would have been scandalized. Father, red in the face, would have been forecasting doom.

And he would have been vindicated when, on the edge of Winslow, the car broke down.

***

The last I heard, Winslow is a shadow of its former self. But in 1930? Another story, boy. Route 66—America's Main Street, everyone called it—ran straight through downtown Winslow.

Where? Here in Arizona! Don't they teach *anything* in school anymore?

Route 66. The railroad, the Santa Fe. And Lucky Lindy, Charles Lindbergh to you, had just designed the town's new airfield. Transcontinental air service was only beginning. Back then that meant a bunch of short flights, and Winslow offered the only all-weather airfield between Los Angeles and Albuquerque. People didn't fly at night in those days. The airline scheduled a flight to land in Winslow before dark. Anyone in a hurry hopped on the train, to travel through the wee hours.

Planes, trains, and automobiles (just why are you grinning at me, boy?), they all stopped in Winslow. That's why Fred Harvey built La Posada, The Inn, and the jewel of his hotel chain, right there. Pueblo Deco, the architect called La Posada: geometrics and sand painting and fantasy hacienda all rolled into one. Seventy guest rooms. Three restaurants. Three private dining rooms. The great lounge. Lovely gardens, all around. Smack dab on Route 66 La Posada sat, and just across the tracks from the train depot. Call it a mile from the airport.

There I was, with a broken-down car, and no money to get it fixed. But I was pretty, not yet thirty years old, and, at least I so asserted, of good moral character. That, and being white—this was another era—was what they were looking for at La Posada.

That's how I went to work as a Harvey Girl.

***

No one used the phrase yet, they wouldn't for decades, but I was star-struck. I admit it. How not, when a big Hollywood star or three was at the hotel every single day. Mary Pickford. Shirley Temple. Gary Cooper. Clark *Gable*.

Oh, spare me that look. You surely know who Gable was, without Googling him. Whatever that means.

But my thoughts are wandering about even more than usual. Sure, it was usually the Hollywood folks who caught my eye. But it wasn't just them and, anyway, so many years later, it was other guests who seem to have mattered.

Who? Funny thing, at the time I didn't always know.

Oh, I knew Charles Lindbergh! It had only been three years since he had flown solo across the Atlantic. And Howard Hughes, though, truth be told, I knew him as a movie producer more than anything else. I hung on every word from his table, waiting for all the talk of aviation and starting an airline and whatnot to give way to Hollywood gossip.

But that wild-haired German man, who seemed never to be without his pipe? Or the reserved fellow who sometimes came by train to huddle with Mr. Hughes? If not for Mr. Hughes's questions, I would never have guessed the colleague with the Boston accent was shooting off rockets in Roswell. Or the pilot who went on and on about using instruments to fly, about how cockpit gauges of some sort were more reliable than the eyes in one's own head? I didn't come to know *his* name till during the war, when I read it beneath his photo in the newspapers. Jimmy Doolittle.

Jeez-oh-Pete. The Doolittle Raid, 1942. *Thirty Seconds Over Tokyo.* Google that.

At first, I mostly worked in the finest of the hotel's restaurants, the Turquoise Room. Let me tell you, that was one elegant place. Heavy linen tablecloths, fine china, lovely candle fixtures, sprays of flowers all around. Lovely Navajo blankets, hung like tapestries. And the tips were … let's just say if I hadn't been on a six-month contract, I still would have stayed.

Anyway, the Turquoise Room was ever abuzz with conversation. I was a sponge for it all. I lived for the Hollywood gossip, I admit it, but I didn't miss out on other things. Once the Indian Detours started—

I know that look. Indian Detours were another Fred Harvey innovation. Beyond serving people who *had* to travel, Mr. Harvey hoped to make the Southwest someplace people *wanted* to travel. So his star hotels, like

La Posada, offered guided excursions. To the Petrified Forest. The Grand Canyon. And the pit not nearly as grand, but much closer, that the locals called Franklin's Hole.

I'd not ever managed to see these sights, but every day, as I bustled among the tables, I'd hear—well, overhear —guests marveling about them. And I talked with the girls who were couriers. You'd call them guides, but on the Detours they were called couriers. They were college graduates, and they all studied up on things like southwestern art, geology, and history.

Anyway, I asked the couriers a lot about what all they'd seen. I borrowed some of the notebooks from which they studied. I suppose the hotel manager noticed my interest because one day, when a girl was under the weather, he asked me to fill in on a Detour. Or maybe he was just desperate. Lord knows I was no college graduate like those girls.

Back then, my memory didn't leak like a sieve, not like nowadays, at least about anything that's happened, well, in recent years. Recent decades. So, despite my nerves, I knew the Petrified Forest spiel well enough. I even had answers for most of the group's questions.

Two days later, I was promoted to courier.

***

Have I ever told you about Terrence? Terrence Smith? Back in the old days, I'd have remembered a detail like that. No matter. And while I hope to tell you I loved your grandfather, that I miss him still, every day, well, that movie the other night brought another era, and another man, back to my mind. Someone I'd known years earlier. Someone I hadn't thought of in ages.

Oh, but that Terrence was the handsome one! I noticed him almost as soon as I started at La Posada. He was too gorgeous not to have noticed. Oh, my, yes. He was much taller than average, with the most striking cobalt-blue eyes. He had straight black, slicked-back hair. Chiseled features. A strong jaw, a Roman nose, and thin, straight lips. No matter the hour of day or night, Terrence was always clean shaven. He didn't seem to tan, no matter how much of the day he spent working under the desert sun.

Hollywood handsome he was, except that, well, it took me a dog's age to put my finger on it. His features were too, too...what's that word? Even? No. Smooth? Smooth? No. Symmetric. That's it. His face was unusually symmetric. And his speech was a bit different. A bit... mechanical, maybe.

Anyway, Terrence did odd jobs at La Posada. He was good with his hands, fixing all manner of things that got broken. And that doodad in your hand that you're don't think I see you peeking at? Terrence had something similar, I think. I asked once what he called it, and he told me it didn't have a name. Just something he said he'd put together.

Oh, how he flirted with all us girls. Terrence was as fascinated as anyone with celebrity, but in his case, it wasn't the stars, but politicians and professors and business folk. One morning Terrence might ask what this one or that one had talked about the night before as we were serving the dinner. Or, after a Detour returned to the hotel, he might be curious what comments the guests had made. More than once he said that La Posada, not New York City, was the crossroads of the world.

He seemed more interested in me once I became a courier. But for all that, he was altogether too...respectful. Especially for someone otherwise so good with his hands.

Oh, that shocked look is priceless! I wasn't always a crone, you know. And this was less than a year after the Crash. If I had never been a flapper, well, I came of age (do people still say that, I wonder?) in the Roaring Twenties.

Still, it did nothing for a girl's self-confidence that Terrence would sooner talk about Howard Hughes—the aviation stuff, not his movies or his latest starlet—than about *us*.

***

The scientist guests gave me the heebie-jeebies. Oh, not them personally. They were mostly nice enough. But the questions they would ask on the Detours? Oh, lordy, how I dreaded those. And when I drew a scientist type for my first outing to Franklin's Hole? Jeez-oh-Pete.

Well, let me tell you, I had the shakes for the entire fifty-five mile outbound drive. I did my best to hide it but my nerves must have showed, because all three guests in the touring car were determined to jolly me out of it.

When we arrived, when I *saw* this enormous, gaping hole, I was more anxious still.

I went into my memorized spiel. Franklin had been a scout for General Custer—yes, *that* Custer—and the first white man to report on the hole. The hole was about 4000 feet wide and 600 feet deep. The experts, I recited, said it was almost certainly a volcanic crater.

"I think not," the German man said. He was the scientist of the group.

In waitressing as much as in retail, the customer is always right, so I was leery about correcting him. My notes, fortunately, gave me something to fall back upon. "Some people believe," I remember beginning cautiously, "that this crater was the result of an impact. By a meteor or comet of some sort."

These days, that *is* what they think. That big hole in the ground is Meteor Crater, no two ways about it.

Anyway, I told the three men on the tour that a Philadelphia geologist named Barringer had staked a claim to this area, hoping to mine meteor iron from beneath the crater floor. I remember I pointed out to them, *way* at the bottom of that gigantic bowl, a little dot: the mine shaft Barringer's company had sunk. They never did find any metal.

Would Barringer have found anything if he had kept drilling? If his backers hadn't pulled out? I don't know. After the Crash, no one had the money for any such hare-brained scheme.

"Ja, ja," the German told us. "I have also heard that.

But the energies involved?" His eyes glazed over, as if lost in his thoughts. "To have made such a large hole? The meteor would have weighed many thousands of tons. Or…"

"Or what, Albert?" another guest prompted.

Albert Einstein: he was another visitor I only recognized later. I only knew he was on a visit to America, making his way to a meeting in California. Back then, I doubt anyone but other scientists would have recognized him. So, as he chewed on his pipe, I went back to the history of Franklin's Hole, things the Indians had had to say about it. Well-memorized material.

"Or a very much smaller mass, converted into energy," Albert finally continued.

"That can happen?" a second passenger asked.

"Ja, ja," Albert agreed. Fussing with his pipe. "That is how the sun works."

"Something small enough to be dropped from a plane?" the final passenger asked. A pilot. We often had pilots passing through. Maybe this was Jimmy Doolittle. I can't picture anymore what Jimmy looked like, only the young Spencer Tracy cast in the movie as Jimmy.

"A bomb?" After much puffing on his pipe, Albert had decided, "Perhaps, I think."

***

I found the whole day exhausting. When we finally got back to La Posada, all I wanted was a cold drink, a light dinner, and a long, hot bath. But Terrence found me first, and *he* wanted to talk. And talk. And *talk*.

He thought my day had been fascinating.

"Matter converted into energy?" he prompted me, more than once. "You're sure?"

"*Yes*," I answered. Again. The third time, I added something else I'd heard that day. No matter that I was speaking by rote, I used the tone of voice that says: doesn't *everyone* know this stuff? "E equals em cee squared."

Terrence's eyes went round. "Do you understand what that means?"

I managed to keep a straight face, pleased to have made such an impression.

"Why else would I say it?" Remembering the pilot's question that afternoon, I came up with a wrinkle all my own. Mr. Hughes's colleague, as far as I knew, the one working in Roswell, was still making holes in the desert. Combined with Albert's idea, couldn't Mr. Goddard blast much bigger holes? And so I tossed off, almost flippantly, "Soon enough we'll be seeing devices like that on a rocket."

Smug from seeing Terrence shocked speechless, I went off for that cold drink.

***

The day after my Franklin's Hole adventure, Terrence didn't show up for work. Nor, when the chief handyman went looking, was Terrence in his room. All Terrence's stuff, the clothes and books and whatnot, were there, but I didn't see any of his personal projects, the gadgets he tinkered with.

One of our maids, thinking back on it, remembered she'd seen a bright light in the distance from her third-story window, gazing out toward the desert. A few of us not on shift that morning trudged out the direction she pointed us. Apart from a scorched area maybe thirty feet across, about a half mile from the hotel, we saw nothing unusual. Certainly, we didn't find Terrence. But on our return, about halfway back to La Posada, I spotted something familiar. It was standing on end, peeking out from within a clump of mesquite grass, behind a knee-high stand of buffelgrass.

Terrence's favorite doodad.

That and a stained photograph are all I had to remember the man by. Somehow, don't ask me to explain, I knew that something I'd said the evening before is why Terrence left.

I never saw him again.

***

And that was the last time I spoke with Grandma.

She passed away quietly in the night, propped up

with pillows in her bed, hours after she had finished her rambling story.

She had never made it to California, never gotten any closer than Flagstaff. I had; that's why I kept checking for messages, for my job in LA. Remembering stolen glances at my gadgets made me feel rotten.

Okay, more rotten.

Grandma's room looked as if the reminiscing had set her to looking for...something. The battered old steamer trunk at the foot of her bed—the steamer trunk I couldn't recall having ever seen open—stood agape. All but empty. Surrounded by ancient crocheted tablecloths, embroidered dresser scarves, and hand-sewn quilts.

Had she found what she sought? I wanted to think so. Clutched in her hand, in a tarnished brass frame, was a faded black-and-white photograph, a greasy thumbprint in its lower left corner, of a young man.

I didn't know then that it was important—only that, there at the end, finding it had mattered to Grandma. That *made* it important. I made myself a promise to understand what it meant.

After the funeral...

***

The funeral was hard. I had been so focused the past several days (barring the occasional guilty email lapse) on being there for Grandma, that it hadn't struck me: she was all the family I had.

Had had.

And so, it was three days till I got back to the nursing home to sort through Grandma's belongings. Where, within the folds of an old tablecloth, inside a paper bag crumbling with age, I encountered a gray, plastic-and-glass rectangular slab. It was similar in area to my Blackberry, but thinner, and it had no keyboard. Terrence's "doodad"?

Opening my laptop, I wikied *plastic.* There were no plastics, apart from Bakelite, in 1930, and this—well, *doodad* would serve—wasn't Bakelite.

Grandma didn't have much of an estate to process. The antique handicrafts I offered to the staff, to share among the residents as they saw fit. Ditto, her clothes and the few sticks of furniture. I packed up her photos and the doodad.

Then unsealed the box to look again at the photo that had been found in Grandma's hand.

Was this Terrence? Slicked-back hair was the style back then; I couldn't go by that. The image was too small to decide if the man's face was "unusually" symmetric. But, I decided, his eyes were more widely spaced than average. Maybe *they* were what made the face seem just a little... different.

Then—because I was the one-man IT department for a small accounting firm, this was high tax season, *and* the Y2K deadline loomed—I drove home through the night to LA.

***

Now and again I would study the doodad and the photo. And then put them away, none the wiser. The latest time seemed no different.

My Blackberry and brick-like first cell alike were long since retired, replaced by a modern phone with a touch screen. Terrence's doodad *still* looked slicker. Not that I saw how that could be an electronic device. It had no power switch that I could see, nor any port to accept a charger plug. Not that a smart phone in 1930 could have made *any* sense.

But nothing would keep me from musing...

Over the years, a suspicion had taken hold: Terrence had been a spy. If he were foreign, that would explain his speech being a little mechanical and his features subtly unusual. It would explain a handyman's curiosity about certain of the hotel guests and his disinterest in the usual celebrities. A bit of Googling had long since confirmed that in the Thirties La Posada *was* a crossroads and a vacation stop, someplace where people might speak more unguardedly than in Washington, New York, and Los

Angeles. That a hostile foreign power—which? I had no idea—might put an agent at La Posada to eavesdrop on the unwary made a strange kind of sense.

Grandma had found the doodad off the path to the scorched area. In my mind's eye, I saw the device accidentally dropped in the dark as Terrence toted his papers and other incriminating stuff to the desert to be torched. Scrub grass and bushes had caught fire, the blaze reaching out several feet before burning itself out. All the pieces fit.

Except for why Terrence had picked *that* night to flee. Except for the doodad itself.

All I could come up with was that the doodad was some kind of recording device. I pictured Terrence dictating into it each night the juicy tidbits reported by his unsuspecting Harvey Girl accomplices. Only I had trouble reconciling a recording device with Terrence taking enough paper notes that he had needed a desert bonfire to destroy them—

Or the notion that in 1930 any voice recorder could be as compact as an early iPod.

***

There matters remained until Apple released another generation of iPhone.

That's when (as Grandma would have said) the penny dropped....

***

The doodad's glass surface had, centered just above one of its narrow edges, an oval that suddenly struck me as a possible fingerprint sensor.

Uh-huh. In 1930. And if it were such a sensor?

Ridiculous. Right?

Except that removing the old photo from its tarnished frame, holding the greasy thumbprint near that oval, I found I had brought brightly colored symbols up onto the glass. Onto the *screen.*

App icons of some kind? Pictographs? Characters from an unfamiliar alphabet? Spider doodles?

I muttered, "What the hell?"

And the doodad responded aloud in...I don't know what. It was half glottal stops, half sibilants. Wholly unintelligible.

"English, damn it," I said in frustration.

"Yes, Commander," the device responded. The swirl of cryptic symbols vanished, replaced with short lines of text:

> EMERGENCY POWER AT 0.02 PERCENT.
> REPLACE FUSOR IMMEDIATELY.

"Status!" I demanded, wondering:

Commander of *what?*

And: speech recognition in a handheld device? Real-time translation? In *1930?*

And: could a fusor possibly be what it sounded like: a fusion power source?

And: could any source *but* fusion have maintained any power for 84 years?

And: could a fusion mechanism possibly fit into a handheld device?

And: never mind compactness, did anyone on Earth have *any* fusion technology apart from really big bombs?

And, finally forming a practical thought: how long till the last power bled away?

"Commander," the device said. "Your directives are confirmed. The courier ship relayed your latest report; the outbound transmission will almost certainly reach the fleet before it passes the commit point. The cold-sleep pod, as requested, has been prepped. As for your lander, at last report it had just left orbit en route to the extraction point."

No, the lander had come and gone, leaving behind only a scorch mark in the desert. Just as the courier ship had long ago departed orbit. Otherwise, some astronaut, astronomer, or military radar would surely have spotted it.

I had been more right in my speculations than I

could have believed—and Terrence was a lot more foreign than I had ever imagined. Only I still didn't understand why he had run.

Or maybe I just didn't want to know. The mention of an alien fleet had shivers racing up and down my spine.

"Commander?" the device said tentatively. "I sense an anomaly. According to my internal clock, the date is—"

"Play back the report," I ordered.

The device reverted to hisses and clicks, and I interrupted. "In *English*."

"Yes, Commander." Its voice quality changed subtly, as though to denote recitation. "The natives have progressed unexpectedly, beyond both the level Conclave analysts had extrapolated from Earth broadcasts and even my most recent findings. They are experimenting with rockets and, I have just determined, matter-to-energy conversion. The potential of these technologies is familiar even to the menials. We must assume that these capabilities, and perhaps additional weaponry, will be mastered during the years of the fleet's final approach.

"It is imperative that you recall the invasion fleet immedia—"

Mid-word, the last dregs of emergency power had dribbled out.

***

Eighty-four years have passed since Terrence vanished—all without an alien onslaught. It would appear he succeeded in waving off the invasion fleet in time ....

And so (I say to everyone on the Internet), that's how —although she never knew it—"Judy Garland" saved the world.

If Grandma were still with us, I'm guessing she would say, "You're welcome."

But do you know what I'm *certain* she would say? Well, do you?

She'd say, "Menial? Hardly! I was a Harvey Girl."

AUTHOR'S NOTE

Edward M. Lerner, by training a physicist and computer engineer, worked in high tech and aerospace for thirty years as everything from engineer to senior vice president. His employers have included Bell Labs, Honeywell, Hughes Aircraft, and Northrop Grumman—and a few companies you've likely never heard of. For seven of those years, he was a NASA contractor. For a larger part of that time he wrote science fiction as a hobby.

Since 2004 Lerner has written full-time. His meticulously researched solo novels include near-future technothrillers like *Fools' Experiments* (artificial life and artificial intelligence), *Small Miracles* (medical nanotech), and *Energized* (solar power satellites and near-Earth space exploitation).

About "Judy Garland Saves the World," he says: My wife and I recently had occasion to pass through Winslow. We spent the night at the newly restored La Posada, where we enjoyed an excellent dinner in the Turquoise Room.

Admiring this masterpiece of Pueblo Deco architecture; touring Meteor Crater and the Petrified Forest, both nearby; discovering Albert Einstein, Howard Hughes, and Jimmy Doolittle among the famous guests of La Posada ... pretty quickly, a story for this anthology began to write itself.

Serendipity happens.

Corn Fed Blues

Catherine Asaro and Kate Dolan

No one believes me when I tell this story. They think I must've been blotto when it happened or else I'm a deranged Jane. I'm writing it down because it was real, and if you think it's hooey, well you don't know from nothing. Besides, crazier things have happened. After all, this is the great state of Ohio, where the law says that if some fella is orating on Decoration Day and you pitch horseshoes anywhere within one mile of where the blowhard is blowing, the police can fine you twenty-five bucks. I mean, honestly. So my story could be true, too.

***

I found out a secret, that Bertie Claxton wanted to hire a girl to sing in his new establishment. He didn't advertise because no one knew about his secret venture. Supposedly. After all, no one went to Claxton's Mercantile and Chow to hear singing. Mostly, he sold livestock feed. He lived upstairs and he had a diner out back, the Chow half of his establishment, but the only drinks he served were sodas and fruit juice, what with Prohibition and all. The news about him looking for a singer came by word of mouth through the gossip mill, all hush-hush. Being a girl of the singing variety and having recently attained the mature age of eighteen, I took myself to Claxton's to see what was up.

Bertie's secret was the most interesting news I'd heard in ages. Not that such a fact meant much. Nothing ever happened here in Gatesburg. That might change, though, what with his new venture, the kind of place where you needed a password just to get past the door.

Only a few hundred people lived in our town, but we weren't far from Mount Vernon, the right proper seat of Knox County, which last I heard had a population of more than nine thousand. News had trickled through the rumor mill that Bertie's joint was bringing in folks from all over these parts.

When I arrived at Claxton's, Bertie was bent over behind the counter on the Mercantile side of the store. His brown hair and worn shirt blended in with the sacks of cornmeal so I didn't see him at first. The cowbell clanged when I closed the front door, and he straightened up with a start, all tall and lanky, his hair flopping into his blue eyes.

"Hi, Willie." He thumped the counter in greeting.

"Good to see you." I went over to him. "I heard you were looking for a singer."

He lowered his voice. "Don't say that so loud."

"Why not? Ain't nothing wrong with singing." My Gran had other ideas, convinced that what I liked was devil's music, the jazz and blues coming out of New Orleans, Chicago, and New York, that smooth whiskey sound curling out of speakeasy lounges where they sold gin juice behind hidden doors. It was another world, one I could only read about in the papers or hear on the radio, in secret, when no one knew I was listening.

Bertie scratched the back of his neck. He just said, "Maybe."

I leaned closer, my elbows in the counter, my hair falling across my arms like a yellow waterfall, if such existed, which quite frankly I'd never seen, but that was how my ex-boyfriend Virgil described my hair when he was trying to be romantic. "I heard you was looking for a girl who could sing like in those New York clubs."

He blinked at me, then grinned and laughed. "What, *you?*"

That wasn't the reaction I'd hoped for. I mean, really, who was he to laugh at me when he ran a speakeasy in a feed store. I straightened up. "It's not funny."

"Listen, Wilhemina Gale," he said, "You're the bee's knees, the cat's meow, a right bearcat of a girl, but I ain't looking for someone to sing hillbilly music."

"I ain't a zoo," I told him. "And where'd you get all that talk? You need to hear me sing before you say I can't perform in your gin joint."

He scowled at me. "I ain't got no gin joint. And if you tell anyone I do, I'll deny I know you."

"I won't tell anyone. You have my word."

"Says you."

"I'm serious. And you know me. I keep my promises."

He considered me. Then he said, "I got a piano downstairs. Let's see what you can do."

***

I'd never realized Claxton's had such a big cellar. Bertie had fixed it up nice, full of round tables topped by candles in mason jars, wooden chairs with scalloped legs, a dance floor, and even an old chandelier with smoky glass drops. No surprise that I didn't see any liquor. I'd known Bertie all my life and we got along fine, but he wasn't ready yet to trust me about his new venture.

Pictures of farms and horses hung on the walls instead of signed portraits of stars like Louise Brooks and Rudolf Valentino. Bertie did have one ducky painting, though, different from anything I'd seen before, a flapper girl in a gold and black dress sitting with her head tilted back, all against a red background. A border surrounded her with bold lines in gold, black, white, blue. You couldn't see details of her face, just an impression of eyes and mouth. It looked like magic.

I pointed at the picture. "That's nice."

Bertie puffed up his chest. "It's called—" He stopped, squinting at the painting. "Art Stucco? Something like that. I got it from a fella who came through Mount Vernon few months back. Spiffs up the place, don't you think?"

"Sure does. If your pa could only see what you've done with his feed store." I couldn't help but smile, Bertie looked so proud of himself. He hardly fit the image of a moonshine mobster. He was too good-natured. His place might do all right, though, if he didn't get raided.

Bertie nudged me toward the front of the dance floor. "Let's hear what you can do."

I went where he pushed, to a stand-up piano with yellowed keys. I didn't have anyone to play, though, so I sang without music. First I did "Can the Circle be Unbroken," because Bertie loved that song. He clapped the same way he did when Fat Joe played bluegrass at the church socials on Sunday. Hardly glamorous for a speakeasy, but then, neither was the cellar of a feed store. As soon as I finished, I launched into "That Thing Called Love," one of the songs I listened to in private, when no one would hear and make me stop.

"Cause nobody knows what that thing called love will do," I finished, "To me and you." I stopped then, watching Bertie, uncertain.

He regarded me warily. "I ain't never heard nothing like that before."

"It's blues," I said, warming to one of my favorite subjects. "Mamie Smith sings it so much better. She made it famous." The more that the naysayers said I shouldn't listen to such music, the more I wanted to know about it. Music seemed like it was breaking down race walls, that someday those walls would crumble in ways we could hardly imagine today. "She did a phonograph record, all songs by a fella named Perry Bradford. It sold more than I'll bet you can ever imagine. Folks say it'll be in the history books." I felt like a fake, doing jazz and blues, but I loved the songs. If he wanted a real speakeasy, he needed a real jazz singer, but given that we were in the middle of rural Ohio, my hick self was probably the best he'd get.

Bertie scratched his chin. "Huh. I never heard the like." Standing up, he stretched his arms. "You've a right nice voice, Willie. And you're a looker, sure enough." He came over, all business now. "So you want to sing here?"

"I'd consider it," I said. "If the pay's good."

"Can't pay you nothing."

I scowled at him. "Then why would I sing for you?"

He considered me. "How about if I give you a sack of chicken feed?"

"It'll take more than that." I thought for a moment. "You still carry that worming medicine?"

"For chickens or goats?"

"Throw in one of each and you've got a deal. The big batches, mind."

"Done."

"Good." Our new worming supply might well outlast his new business. After all, the sheriff's deputy was sweet on the town gossip, so he probably already knew about Bertie's joint. The deputy most as likely would let it go, but only if Bernie stayed quiet and careful about the whole thing.

I motioned around at the cellar. "You've a nice place here."

"You bet. Everything I need."

"Not everything." I told him. "No powder room."

"Why would I need that?"

"Girls come to speakeasies, too."

"I told you this wasn't no gin mill." He tugged a lock of his hair. "It's just for, um...dancing."

"Well, unless you fellas plan on dancing with each other, you still need a powder room."

"With each *other?*" He glared at me. "Go fly in the flue, Willie."

I couldn't help but smile. "I got no idea what that means." Bertie was always trying to sound hip, like a big city fella, and mostly it didn't work. I would never tell him that, though, because he was a sweetheart. Of course I didn't tell him that, either. He might get a swelled head. So I just said, "You want me to spell it out? Water closet, johnette, ladies puff palace. Honestly, Bertie."

"Honestly Willie, you could just say toilet. The word don't bite." He squinted at me. "You going to help me build this pufferoo palace?"

He clearly expected me to say no, which would give him a reason to avoid figuring out where to put a second toilet. So I said, "Sure thing."

***

The cellar had no room we could convert for ladies, but Bertie reckoned he could make a door in the storeroom that let out onto the back stairs of the diner. A secret door, which was pretty nifty. That way, women could go up the back way and use the john upstairs. All he had to do was knock a hole in the storeroom wall and make a door. I'd promised to help, so I put on overalls and old shirt, tied up my hair in a red bandana, and attacked the wall with him. Except it didn't turn out like we expected, because wouldn't you know it, Claxton's had another secret in its cellar.

We stood gaping as plaster dust swirled around us in the dusky light of our kerosene lanterns. Instead of seeing the back stairs to the diner beyond the hole in the storeroom wall, we were staring at a secret room. It was hardly more than three paces across, just big enough for—

A man sitting in a chair.

"What the hell?" Bertie strode forward, holding up his lantern. "Who are you?"

"Bertie," I hissed. "He's dead!" He had to be, because the room had no door and the wall we had just knocked down had surely been here for years.

Bertie froze. I joined him and we stood together while plaster dust settled on our heads and overalls. With the two of us side by side, we were brave enough to step closer to the fellow. He sat quietly, his eyes closed as if he were asleep. He looked healthy. Well, except he wasn't breathing.

"He don't seem dead." Bertie sniffed the air. "Don't smell dead, neither."

I spoke to the man. "Hello?" When he didn't answer, I glanced at Bertie. "Do you recognize him?"

"Can't rightly say that I do."

I went closer, holding my lamp in front of me as if

that could offer protection. The man stayed still. Bertie came with me and after a careful pause, he brushed dust off the man's shoulders. Nothing happened, except that more grit swirled around us, making me cough. Bertie was right, it didn't smell like death down here. It smelled like decades of lost memories.

"He sure has some old clothes," Bertie said. "My gramps dressed like that."

I saw what he meant. The man had on a fancy three-piece suit with a long jacket, striped trousers, and what my pa called a double-breasted waistcoat. Instead of a tie, he had a swath of cloth around his neck. He looked about thirty-five, a spiffy fella dressed in glad rags for a night on the town, but old-fashioned style. Stranger than the style, though, was that his old clothes looked new.

"Maybe he's in a coma," I said. "You know, like what happened to George Smithson last year after he fell out of the loft in his barn and hit his head. He was out for weeks."

"Maybe." Bertie nudged the man's shoulders. The result was odd. The fellow moved as if he were a solid block rather than a person. Bertie tried shaking harder, but the man didn't shake. He stayed exactly the same, all of him, with his hair and clothes unruffled, like a statue.

"Must be a wax figure," Bertie muttered.

The man didn't look like wax. I touched his cheek—and it was *warm*. I jerked back so fast, I dropped my lantern. It broke into pieces on the packed dirt floor, adding shards of glass to the piles of chalky debris. A tongue of flame ran across the dirt floor, carried along by kerosene spilling out of the broken lantern. As the flames reached the man's leg and lapped around his trousers, I yanked off the bandana tied around my hair. Bertie stomped on the runnels of kerosene while I beat at the fire with my scarf.

It didn't take us long to put out the flames, and that was when matters became even stranger. The fellow couldn't be wax, because he hadn't melted one tiny bit.

Nothing. His pants weren't burnt at all. I had seen flames licking his clothes like a cat at her milk, yet here he was, not a singed thread to be seen.

Bertie heaved in a big breath and yelled "HO-YAH!"

I jumped back. "What was that for?"

"See if he'd wake up." Bertie peered at the man. "He didn't."

I shot a glance around the room to see if Bertie's yell had woken up anything else, like the dead. Nothing seemed out of place, except for my broken lantern and the smelly kerosene.

"Okaaaay," I said, just the way I did when my ma went about serious business, like the time she flattened the Beckelhymer's pigsty with our tractor because she was mad at Bertha Beckelhymer. Lord only knew what she would do to Bertie's place if she found out about his cellar.

"This building has been here more'n eighty years," Bertie said. "I've done some work on it, but nothing in this storeroom. It's been the same for decades."

"He's a statue," I said. A warm statue, which made no sense.

"Well, hell," Bertie said. "I can't finish the new door with a statue in the way."

Trust Bertie to stick with the practical. "We could move him. Store him with the sewing mannequins in the back of your store. You know, those ones you put away cause no one wanted to buy the ugly things."

Bertie glared at me. "My merchandise ain't ugly. Anyway, we can't move him up there. What if someone figures out I'm knocking down walls and wants to know why?"

"You could put the new door in the other storeroom." I hesitated. "I mean, it's all right if we leave him here, right? He can't really be alive."

"It's like you said." Bertie rubbed his chin. "He's solid. Not real."

That had to be the answer. If it seemed impossible that a statue could be warm to the touch, well, the world was surely full of strange business that I'd never heard about.

∗∗∗

I sang for the first time at Bertie's the next day, on Friday night. The crowd was a mix of folks, including farmers in dungarees and boots, well-heeled couples from the glassworks in Mount Vernon, and a fella I'd have sworn was a wise-head professor from Kenyon College in Gambier. I did torch songs and folky favorites, with the piano player and a fiddler making music. Sweet in the smoky candlelight, couples danced on the floor, even a few women in dresses with no corsets (scandalous, Gran would say). I pretended I didn't notice the liquor that Ralph, the not-bartender, was serving.

I wore a flapper dress I'd sewn from a pattern I had mail-ordered. The dress was all creamy white and silky. And the fringe! When I twirled on the stage, it swirled around my legs. The hem was daring enough to give Gran vapors, only a few inches below my knees. Even worse (in Gran's view), I had on slinky stockings from Holeproof Hoisery. I had found them through an ad drawn by a local legend, Coles Phillips, who believe it or not, had gone to Kenyon College just a hop, skip, and a jump from here. I hadn't bobbed my hair because it was impossible to hide that from folks in town, and anyways I liked it long. A few of the farmers knew me, but they weren't going to tell what I was doing any more than I was going to promulgate to the heavens that I saw them down here drinking hooch. And yes, promulgate is too a word. I looked it up, special for writing this narrative.

All the time I was singing, I couldn't stop thinking about the man we'd found. Bertie had hidden the room by hanging a quilt over the hole in the wall. We'd been trying all day to wake up the fellow, but he showed no sign of life. He just seemed so *real*, as if someone had frozen him in mid-breath.

When it came time for my break, I acted like I was going to the powder room, bringing a candle in a jar with me, but instead I went to check on our secret. His room was dark and smelled of dust and kerosene. He was just the way we'd left him, doing nothing except being a statue.

I walked around the little room studying the place, holding my light up high, then low. I didn't find a whit more to explain his being here than the last I'd checked. Finally I leaned my back against the wall in front of the man so I could look at him as if we were chatting. Then I just stood, listening to the distant sounds of people talking in the main room. Finally I let out a loud breath and gave the wall behind me a frustrated thump.

A scratchy noise came from wall at my elbow.

"Hey!" I jumped away, keeping a tight hold on my jar so I didn't drop it and start another fire. The candlelight sent shadows chasing each other across the wall. My thump had dislodged a panel, a square about one handspan wide. When I tugged, the panel came loose real easy, as if it had been crumbling for decades. Huh. I'd uncovered a lever. It lay flat against the wall and scrolled around in a S-shaped curlicue. A flattened metal horse with outstretched wings stood on the top, tarnished but intact.

"What're you doing in here?" a voice demanded.

I looked up with a jerk and dropped the panel. Bertie was watching me from the doorway, a lantern held high in his hand. He was a sight, all decked out in his striped coat and vest, high-waisted trousers, and two-toned shoes, with his flat cap set jauntily on his head. The red handkerchief in his breast pocket even matched his necktie. Who would've thought Bertie could cut such a fine figure.

"I found a lever," I told him. "It has wings."

He came over. "You shouldn't be poking around in here. It's not safe."

"I'm okay. Look what I found." I tapped the lever. "It was hidden under a panel."

He peered at the discolored contraption. "What's it do?"

"Can't say that I know."

"Think we should push it?"

That was the question of the hour. Who knew what would happen. Probably nothing, but then why was it hidden?

"No way to find out unless we try," I said.

"Yep." Bertie kept staring at the lever.

I stood next to him, staring too.

"Might not do anything," Bertie said.

"I reckon it's too old." I made no move to touch the lever.

Bertie looked at me. I looked at him. We looked at the lever.

"Okay," I said. "Together?"

"Right." Bertie put his hand on the lever. I put my hand on top of his.

We pushed and the lever scraped down along the wall.

I held my breath. Bertie stood next to me, still as could be, as much like a statue as any real statue. We waited.

Waited.

Waited.

"Well, hell." Bertie took his hand off the lever, letting mine slide off, too. "That's all ishkabibble."

"I guess so." Whatever ishkabibble meant. "You never know. Maybe we just blew up the post office or someone's grain silo."

He slanted me a look. "I ain't heard nothing."

"Can't say I have, either," I allowed. "But in that picture show *The Lost World,* they didn't expect to find dinos alive, and then a volcano erupted and sent the dinos on a wild rampage."

Bertie made an exasperated noise. "Willie, what does that have to do with the price of eggs?"

"You know what I mean. That anything can happen."

"Yeah, well, I don't see nothing happening."

Behind us, a raspy voice said, "Who are you?"

***

I'd known Bertie most of my life. My family had shopped at Claxton's since his father ran the place, back when I was a little girl and Bertie was a gangly boy. In all that time, I'd never seen him look as unsettled as he did when he turned to see who—or what—had spoken to us.

Seemed our corpse hadn't kicked the bucket after all. He sat slouched in the chair now instead of bolt upright, with his face gone pale and sweat on his forehead, staring as if we were the ones raised from the dead instead of him. And he *was* breathing, no doubt about that.

I recovered enough to say, "I'm Wilhelmina Gale." Tilting my head at Bertie, I added, "This is Albert Claxton."

"I own this place," Bertie growled to the man. "And I figure it's you who ought to be saying who you are."

The fellow just kept staring at me, his eyes wide. Well, so maybe my flapper dress was a little out there. This fella, though, he stared as if I was a ghost or else a loose woman, which I didn't like. So I glared back at him.

He wasn't up to a staring contest. With a sigh, he closed his eyes.

I quit glowering, feeling guilty, and spoke more gently. "Are you all right, sir?"

"Sick..." His voice trailed away into nothing.

Bertie kept his distance. "Sick with what?"

The man muttered something that sounded like "Ladders and windpies."

Bertie gave me that scrunched forehead look of his that came when he was puzzled. I lifted my hands and shook my head.

Bertie spoke to our guest again. "Who did you say you are?"

The man's only answer was his labored breathing. He didn't open his eyes.

"Mister, would you like to lie down?" I asked.

"I—yes." His answer came out as a hoarse cough.

I glanced at Bertie. "What about your apartment upstairs? He could rest there."

"Don't know as if I want a sickly fella where I live."

I could see his point, but we didn't want our sickly fella dying again, either. "He needs help. If he stays here, he might get worse."

Bertie raked his hand across his head, knocking off his cap, which fell to the ground. Then he said, "All right. Let's see what we can do."

He hung his lantern on a hook by the door and we helped the fellow up. The man moved so stiffly, it was a wonder he could stand at all. He said something I could barely hear.

"What was that?" Bertie asked him. "Dip or eat?"

"Don't worry," I told the man. "We'll get you some food." I wasn't any more easy about this than Bertie, but neither of us meant to run off and leave this fellow without help.

***

Bertie's bedroom was cramped, but well kept and clean, with yellow throw rugs on the floor and a four-poster bed covered by a blue quilt. The place smelled of the Palmolive soap that he sold downstairs. We closed the blue curtains on the windows against prying stares. As we helped our guest lie on the bed, his lashes drooped over his eyes. I had a million questions, but I didn't want to push. He barely seemed able to breathe.

"Willie, you should get back downstairs," Bernie said. "Ralph is looking after the place for a bit, but one of us should check in with him."

I didn't want to leave without hearing this fellow's story. He seemed as if he were out cold, though, so I said, "All right. I'll be back as soon as I can."

Bertie smiled, which made him look more like the boy next store than a bootlegger. "Go on down and sing like you do so pretty."

Oh, he sure did make me feel all soft when he smiled that way. I headed for the door, trying to put myself back into the mind of a smoky jazz singer.

"Elias Featherstone," a voice creaked behind me.

I spun around. *That* hadn't been Bertie.

The man on the bed had opened his eyes and was watching us with that stare people get when life has thrown more at them than they know how to handle.

"What was that?" Bertie asked him.

"Elias Featherstone," the man whispered. "That's my name."

Bertie blinked. Sooner or later everyone in town came through his door at Claxton's, and I was guessing that he had never heard of an Elias Featherstone. I sure hadn't.

"You must not be from around these parts," Bertie said.

Elias looked him straight in the eye. "I've lived here all my life."

Bertie crossed his arms. He had never cottoned to anyone trying to pull the wool over his eyes, which I know is one of those mixed-up metaphors, but never mind. This Elias fellow was telling tales.

"No Featherstone lives here," Bertie said. "They used to own this building. My gramps bought it seventy years ago, after the last of them passed away."

"Yes...passed away," Elias said. "In 1857." He glanced at my dress, then reddened and looked away. In a low, hoarse voice, he added, "Either a great deal of time has passed for the female fashion, or I've ascended to heaven."

Well, goodness. That was nice. Better than those folks who thought my dress was as wicked as the devil coming to Gatesburg for a tea party. "Mister Featherstone, it's 1928," I said. "Lots of girls dress this way now."

Bertie had the oddest look, as if a ghost had blown cold air on his neck. "If you agree that the last Featherstone died seventy-one years ago," he asked Elias, "how can you be one?" His expression brightened like a light bulb switching on. "Wait a minute. You mean the last one moved away, right? Now you've come back to see the old family homestead. You were looking for a place to stay. That's why you hid in my cellar, because you knew this building." He was warming up to his theory. "You haven't had enough to eat, I'll bet. And you're feeling under the weather, like you said. That's why you couldn't wake up."

I raised my eyebrows at Bertie, glad for the chance to use that action I had read about in my novels. It was perfect for his wacky theory.

"No," Elias whispered. "I didn't mean moved. I meant died."

Bertie had no answer for that. Neither did I.

"Are you saying you really did die?" I finally asked.

Elias inhaled slow and careful, as if he needed a deep breath but had forgotten how to take one. Then he said,

"I went into stasis in 1857."

***

I've never laid claim to any genius. I did well enough in school, but it wasn't as if we had much to learn, what with so few teachers in town. My least favorite teacher, the evil Mrs. Geraldine M. Schlumpberger, told me as how I didn't have extra space for thoughts in my head, an idea she especially liked to declare after those times I fell asleep in her class. Well, she should try getting up before dawn to milk our cows and then stay awake during her oh-so-exciting lectures on Ohio crop production. So okay, I'm not learned. But that's not the same as being dumb. When it comes to common sense, I know my onions. And I can tell you this. What Elias Featherstone told us that night, deep in those quiet hours before the dawn brings hope back to the sky—what he laid out was so far beyond real, you'd have to be even more of a rube than me and Bertie put together to believe him.

And yet...it explained so much.

Elias was the last of his line in these parts. His ma had passed away when he was small and his pa, Jacob Featherstone, worked a farm. Jacob had also built this place, trying to start a feed store. He wanted so much for Elias. He scrimped and saved so his son could be the first in their family to go to college.

Elias did well for himself. He went to Kenyon College

and they even helped pay his way. He graduated right pretty, with all sort of honors. He told us about the books he loved, the classics. Afterward, he went back east and earned another degree, this one from Harvard. I wouldn't have believed his story more than I'd have believed any palooka telling tales, except Elias talked so well and dressed so fine. It didn't take fancy schooling on my part to see that he was a smart man.

In 1853, Elias' father took sick. I swear on my ma's bible, that's the year he gave. 1853. And you should know that me and Bertie, we checked later. We found the Featherstones listed in the town records, their births and deaths just like Elias said. Jacob and his wife were buried in the town cemetery, side by side. But no grave for Elias. No record of his death. He just *vanished.*

That night Elias told us why.

He met a man back east named Zachary Reichert. They were at school together and became good friends, though Elias loved novels and Zachary loved physics. Eventually Elias returned home to teach English at Kenyon. His friend Zachary surprised him. He asked Elias if he could come out and rent the Featherstone farm. He wanted to set up his physics lab in private, in a place where no one would disturb him.

Elias didn't understand Zachary's work. *No one* understood Zachary's cracked ideas. He was a quack, a charlatan, a speaker of phonus balonus. So everyone said. His fiancé left him, he lost his friends, and other scientists scorned him. It reached the point where he just wanted to hide away and pursue his life's work in private, with no one to sneer at him. So Elias, who had always remained his friend, said yes, Zachary could use the farm and this building, too, free of cost.

What Elias told us about Zachary's work made no sense. Quantized energy? Wave functions? Do you know that means? I didn't. I'd never even seen ocean waves, let alone a wave "function." Yet Zachary claimed these wave functions described things, *everything*, including you and me. Atoms made up our bodies, bits of matter so tiny, we couldn't see them, so many that we could never count them. Even I knew about atoms, or at least I'd heard the word. Zachary said a "wave function" could tell you exactly how every atom behaved. A *wave?* No wonder everyone thought he was screwy.

But here's the kicker. Zachary told Elias that if he fixed the wave function that described a person so the function couldn't change, then he fixed the *person,* too. He didn't mean fixing in the sense of repairing something that was broken, but rather, fixing you in place so you couldn't move. That meant Elias, you, me, anyone, we could be made rigid. If our wave function couldn't change, neither could we. Our atoms would go on with whatever they were up to when he fixed the function, shaking or spinning or doing whatever atoms do, but they couldn't do anything *new,* not even the tiniest bit. You can't see anything as small as an atom move, so on the scale as big as a person, we'd be frozen. No breathing, no clothes wrinkling, no aging. No nothing. Which was crazy, of course, except that it described exactly how we had found Elias.

"He called it quasis," Elias said, his voice like sandpaper. "Quantum stasis." The candles on the dresser had burned low until nothing was left except squat, melted columns of wax. Quiet filled the room as if the shadows muted sound and no hint of dawn lightened the curtains. The world seemed to have retreated to another place while we listened to the tale of a man who would have us believe he had lived, loved, and dreamed in a century before we were born.

I glanced at Bernie from where I was sitting on the lower corner of the quilt. He was standing at the front of the bed, leaning against the wall as he listened to Elias. He met my stare and shrugged. Elias had his eyes closed, so he didn't see. Was Elias crazy? He mostly sounded worn out, as if waiting in stasis for so many years had drained his life.

I spoke quietly. "Elias, how'd you end up frozen? Did Zachary try experiments on you?"

Elias opened his eyes. "No. I did it myself."

"Why?" Bertie asked.

"Zachary caught diphtheria. I looked after him. But I —I couldn't stop his illness." His voice cracked. "And so my friend with his great, absurd genius died."

"I'm sorry," I murmured. Whatever else might or might not be true, Elias' grief was real.

Bertie straightened up, all sudden like. "No!"

"What's wrong?" I asked.

"Willie, what he said downstairs—he wasn't saying he wanted to eat." He turned to Elias. "You were trying to tell us that you have diphtheria."

"I caught it from Zachary." Elias sounded so tired. "I was dying alone. So...alone. I thought—if his device worked, maybe I could remain in stasis until...someday...a cure."

"Elias, I think we do have a cure!" I jumped up by the bed, all jittery now, and spoke to Bertie. "We need Doc Maples. He'd know for sure."

Bertie stared at me, his face pale. He paced away from the bed, came back, paced away, then came over to me. He jerked his chin in the direction of his cellar. "We got people down there."

"Send them home." I laid my hand on his arm. "Go for the doc. You can say you have a friend visiting, that he has this sickness."

Bertie raked his hand through his hair. "What, just say, oh sorry, my friend has *diphtheria?*"

I didn't know diphtheria from dip sticks, but Elias needed help. "That way, Doc Mapes'll come right away, won't he?"

Bertie put his hand over mine. He had a stark look as if he was making a decision that could hammer him bad. This much I knew: the more people we brought here, the more chance someone would discover that Bertie had more than canned food in his cellar. But we couldn't let

Elias die.

Bertie took a breath. "All right. I'll warn Ralph and get Doc Maples. You stay here. When I get back, you go down and help Ralph clear the place."

With that, he was off and out the door.

***

Ralph charged over as soon as I showed up downstairs. "Where'e Bertie?" he rumbled, towering over me, as big and husky as a bear. "I got a lollygagger who won't leave. I'm fixing to toss him out, but he's making trouble."

"Maybe he'd git if you let him have one last belt of gin," I said.

"He says the gin tastes like embalming fluid," Ralph growled. "He wants Scotch, and I ain't got no more."

I wondered how this fella knew what embalming fluid tasted like. "Bertie is upstairs with the doc and his, um, sick friend."

"I can't go looking for booze," Ralph said. "I need to get these people *out.*"

He had the right of that. Even after Bertie had told them to leave, people were still standing around, farmers and high hats alike, gabbing with each other. Bertie wanted us to keep quiet about the diphtheria. He was afraid that if folks heard, it would start a panic, but these folks, they needed to *move.* I was tempted to go get a cattle prod.

Instead, I told Ralph, "You keep herding 'emout. I'll find the Scotch."

"Hey, Miss Wil-he-mina," a farmhand called as I hurried across the dance floor. "Sing some more, doll. You're just about the prettiest thing this side of the Tuscarawas River."

Most days, I would've smiled and teased him about being a hick, but tonight I kept going. I didn't want Ralph or anyone else nosing around the storeroom. The more folks found out about Elias, the more trouble we could be in. Who knew what people might think if we claimed a dead man had come to life, besides which, if Elias really had come out of stasis, the diphtheria bugs that made him sick had probably woken up, too.

Bertie's lantern was still hanging in the storeroom, shedding enough light to see by. Crates filled the place, all innocent like. Only Bertie knew where he had stashed the hooch, but it had to be in the boxes he'd already opened. I checked the first I crate saw, throwing its packing straw on the floor behind me. Canned carrots, peas, and condensed milk filled it, but no hidden bottles or jars. The next crate had plenty of jars, but they were all ketchup, mustard, and Phez loganberry jelly.

Outside, feet pounded across the cellar. As I jumped up, Bertie ran into the storeroom. The moment I saw his face, all pulled into strained lines, my pulse skipped.

"It's a damn mess!" He strode over to me. "The doc says it's diphtheria, but he don't got the medicine. He's calling around for a hospital that does. The police found out. They're raiding my place! You have to get out of here."

"A raid?" I spun around to the crates. "We have to dump the booze."

"Willie, listen!" He caught my arm and pulled me back, right up to him, so close that for an instant we stared at each other, him looking down like he was seeing me for the first time. Then he said, "I don't want you here. Get out and get safe."

"You need help getting rid of—"

"We don't have time!" He let go of me, then grabbed the kerosene lantern off its hook and hurled it into the straw I'd left strewn around the place. It landed in a crackle of breaking glass. Flames ran over its lip and danced across floor. The straw popped in big bursts, like fireworks on the fourth of July.

"What are you doing?" I shouted. "You'll burn down your store!"

"Better that than end up in a diphtheria outbreak or the Knox County Jail." He pushed me toward the door. "Trust me. Not everything will burn. It'll be fine. Now

go!"
I took one look at his face, then ran for the door. I knew what I had to do.

***

Elias could barely walk. With my help, he stumbled down the stairs from Bertie's apartment, leaning on me so heavily that I nearly fell over. The doc was off desperately trying to locate the anti-serum he needed to treat the disease.

It was warm outside, beautiful in a sobering sort of way with the fire casting an orange glow over the night. I helped Elias to a lot on the other side of the packed dirt street and eased him down to the cool grass. I sat under a tree and leaned against the trunk while I cradled his head in my lap. Across the street, Claxton's crackled with flame. The volunteer hose company and their bucket brigade had contained the blaze to that one building, but Bertie was going to lose it all. Even if the sheriff or the deputies dug up any of his hooch, I doubted they'd toss him in jail. They all knew Bertie. They knew the price he had paid to protect the town from the diphtheria. That was enough.

The firelight played across Elias's still figure. His throat was swollen. He kept his eyes closed, but his face wasn't slack like a person asleep. He lay tensed in pain, his legs stretched across the grass. His every breath rattled, and he choked in air as if he were strangling. I knew I shouldn't be so close, but I couldn't leave him to die alone.

"I'm sorry." Tears were running down my face. "I'm sorry we woke you up. I'm sorry we didn't have the medicine. I'm so, so sorry."

"Not...your fault," Elias rasped. Flickering light bathed him, reminding me of how my family had gone camping when I was little, how we sat on logs around the campfire and told stories. Tonight, I had no stories for Elias. He had lived to see a new century, but he'd leave it almost as soon as he arrived. I bent my head and my hair brushed his shoulders. One of my tears fell on his cheek.

"You sing, yes?" His cough racked his body. "Sing—

sing me to my final sleep, angel."

Softly, with my tears falling, I sang a lullaby my mother had crooned in my childhood when nightmares had awoken me in the moonless hours.

Sleep my child and peace attend thee
All through the night
Guardian angels, God will send thee
All through the night
Soft the drowsy hours are creeping
Hill and vale in slumber sleeping
I my loving vigil keeping
All through the night

And so Elias Featherstone died in my arms while Claxton's Mercantile and Chow roared in flames.

***

Bertie's place burnt to the ground. If the stasis machine had ever existed, we found no trace of it in the ashes. Bertie lost his mercantile, his diner, his ugly mannequins, and his magical speakeasy. He had only one bit of luck, but it was a huge bit. His building burned in 1928. Not 1929. He got the insurance payment for the fire only months before the stock market crash hit the world like the clang of a giant bell announcing the end of gin joints, flappers, and the roaring, giddy years of the 1920s.

Bertie and I buried Elias in a quiet, respectful ceremony. By then, I understood the decision Bertie had made. He had known full well what would happen if he woke the doc in the middle of the night to say a fellow in his home had diphtheria. He could have let Elias die in secret and protected himself. Elias still would have passed with us by his side instead of dying alone in his own time. In our time, he didn't exist as far as the rest of the world knew. We could have kept a safe distance from him, scrubbed the hidden room, scoured the storeroom, and boiled everything clean of diphtheria bugs. Instead, Bertie made a decision that changed his life and destroyed his business, all in the hopes of saving a man who was already dying and ensuring that the town was safe. People think Bertie's a little shady because of that juice joint business, but I know the truth. The good in him goes deep.

The fire killed whatever germs woke up with Elias. When the anti-serum finally arrived from a big city hospital, no one in town needed it—except me.

I had a rough time for a while there, but I didn't give in. My pa told me I had the constitution of a she-bear. In the end, I recovered fine. And Bertie stayed by my side the whole time. We were married three years ago, in 1930, a year after the stock market crash. We're helping my parents on the family farm now, but it's slow going, what with the Depression and all. Someday, Bertie is going to rebuild Claxton's Mercantile and Chow.

Three big events marked this year, 1933. On December 5, the Twenty-first Amendment became law. No more Prohibition. The second big thing is that experts say the economy is showing an upturn. Maybe, just maybe, we can struggle out from under this crushing Depression. And the third thing? A man named Schrödinger and a man named Dirac won the Nobel Prize in Physics.

Here is why they won.

Schrödinger created an equation that describes how particles act like waves. He figured out their wave functions. Dirac worked out the wave functions that describe particles that spin and go really, really fast. They won the Nobel Prize for their work in quantum theory.

Only four people in the world know that a man named Zachary on a farm in Ohio did all that first, many decades ago. Two of those people, Zachary and Elias, are dead. The third, Bertie, says none of it makes sense to him. It doesn't make sense to me, either, but I'm going to find out more.

We have some money from the insurance payout on Claxton's, enough for me to go to college. Folks around here say it's nuts and they don't understand why Bertie doesn't tell me to stay home. Hah! Bertie knows better.

Anyways, he likes the idea. Me and Bertie, we've never been the type to go by what people expect. It took me a while to work it out, what with my less than top notch schooling, but the College of St. Mary of the Springs accepted me a few weeks ago. I'll take our old jalopy into Columbus for classes. My ma threatened to drive her tractor into the city and flatten the lecture halls, but she was mollified when I told her it was a college for women only. No men to distract us virtuous ladies to unseemly behavior. Though maybe she just likes driving that tractor. It's no secret where I get my ornery streak.

I'm going to study physics. People say it's ridiculous, a waste of time, that a girl can't do that. Well, they're wrong. I have a lifetime to prove it. I'm only twenty-three, and the world is changing more every year. I'm going to learn quantum mechanics, and someday people aren't going to laugh.

I can't tell folks why. The few times I tried, they thought I was crazy before I hardly started. So I'm writing this down and I'm going to leave it in a safe deposit box to be opened by my and Bertie's children after our deaths. If I ever succeed with my plans, I'll show it to people when that happens, and if I don't, our young'ns will find it someday. I'll leave my notes too, so if I don't succeed, someone can carry on my work. Because here is the truth:

I'm going to learn how to make that stasis machine.

AUTHOR'S NOTE

Catherine Asaro is an author of science fiction, fantasy, and thrillers, and has written over twenty-five novels, as well as short stories and non-fiction. Her acclaimed Ruby Dynasty series combines adventure, hard science, math, romance, and fast-paced action. Among her numerous distinctions, she has won the Nebula and

Analog Reader's Choice awards. Her most recent books are the novel *Undercity* (Baen / Simon & Schuster), the anthology she edited, *The Nebula Awards Showcase 2013* (Pyr), and the novel *Lightning Strike, Book I* (Spectrum). All her novels are available in audio form, including most recently the anthology *Aurora in Four Voices*. Her most recent eBook releases are the award-winning works *Primary Inversion*, "The City of Cries," and "The Spacetime Pool."

Kate Dolan began her writing career as a legal editor and then newspaper columnist before she decided she was finally ready to tackle fiction. As the author of more than ten novels and novellas, she writes historical fiction and romance under her own name and contemporary mysteries and children's books under the name K.D. Hays. When not writing, she enjoys volunteering as a living history interpreter and coaching a nationally-ranked precision jump rope team.

The Peculiar Fate of the Infamous Torrance Gang
Duncan Eagleson

The siren wailed, and Fogarty sat forward in the passenger seat, as if shifting his not inconsiderable weight forward could actually make the Packard go faster. He told himself to have faith. Abbot was the best driver the Bureau had; he'd stick to this gang like a tick to a hound dog. The car jounced and juddered along the rough country road, and Fogarty braced himself against the dash.

They'd been too late to prevent the Torrance Gang from robbing the bank, but their lateness turned out to be a blessing. They intercepted the gang on Ptarmigan Lane, ten miles outside the city limits. Torrance had lost the local cops by then, so he'd felt safe enough to drop off the hostages, whose presence on the running boards of his Ford sedan had prevented the locals from shooting. Agent Fogarty could see the former hostages huddling together at the edge of the cornfield as Torrance and his boys sped away. The G-Men had given chase. Carlisle had opened up with his Tommy gun, but Fogarty made him quit until they'd gotten closer. These back roads were so rough; at these speeds, he'd have been lucky to get a bullet anywhere near the yeggs, even with the Tommy throwing dozens of rounds in their general direction. There was no point in wasting ammunition.

Fields and occasional trees flashed by. Torrance must have thought he was home free with his fast Ford V-8 leaving the local cops behind. Fogarty watched the back of Torrance's Ford grow gradually larger—they were gaining. He grinned. He'd had to juggle the books a bit to manage it, but he'd bought two new Packard Twin Sixes for the Columbus office this spring. After losing Dillinger last year when the public enemy's Ford outpaced the Bureau's aging Studebakers, Fogarty had been determined not to let a criminal outrun him again. Torrance's Ford's top speed was 76 miles an hour. The Packard could hit 85. They were within yards of the Ford now; Fogarty could even read the tag. Not that that meant anything. The tags were probably stolen.

"Close enough!" yelled Carlisle, and he leaned out of the backseat window to train his Tommy gun on the car ahead. Fogarty drew his Browning semi-auto, but did not lean out of his window. If he had, he'd have been lucky if Carlisle didn't hit him, with the car jouncing the way it was.

There was a blinding flash of light ahead, a sound like thunder. Abbott stood on the brake. The car fishtailed, and Fogarty was thrown into the dash—it felt like he'd been hit in the ribs with a baseball bat—and he collapsed on the floor as the Packard rocked to a halt. Fogarty was seeing colored blobs, his vision blurry. His ribs ached. He didn't think any were broken, but knew he'd be damned sore tomorrow. He pulled himself up onto the seat, wrenched open the door. There was a smell in the air, sour and acrid. Fogarty stepped out of the car and stared at the road ahead, blinking.

To either side there were fallow fields, the landscape flat and featureless for acres. The road stretched ahead, straight as a surveyor's snap line, to the flat horizon. No Ford.

Fogarty shook his head, blinked, and looked again. Still nothing. There was nowhere for the Torrance gang to have turned off, no building to drive behind and hide, nothing. Emptiness as far as the eye could see. And no speeding Ford. He glanced back at his men. The second Packard had managed to stop just short of ramming the first.

Carlisle was getting out, empty-handed, his Tommy gun torn from his hands by the force of the jackrabbit stop. "Jesus!" he said.

"Yeah, and Mary and Joseph and all the ships at sea," said Fogarty. He resisted the impulse to cross himself.

Carlisle stalked to where his gun had tumbled, picked it up, a sulky look on his face. "Jesus," he said again. He looked up at Fogarty, and down the road. "What the... Where are they? What the hell just happened?"

"Beats the hell out of me," said Fogarty. He never drank on the job, but if he'd had his flask with him now, he'd have taken a snootful. Instead, he brought out his pack of Luckies, lit one up, and began walking down the road. Carlisle and Abbott trailed slowly after him.

When Fogarty had reached about where he thought the Ford had been when the flash-bang came, he stopped, staring. There was a large black spot on the road, as if the gravel of the road itself had been scorched. The shadow was a little bigger than an automobile.

**

Dan Fogarty did not intimidate easily. He was a big, bluff red-headed Irishman—or at least, he had been a redhead before it all turned gray—and previous to his FBI employment had been Chief of Police in Coverton, Illinois, for more than a decade. He'd tracked down the murderous Canfield brothers, had fought running gun battles with bank robbers and bootleggers, apprehended the kidnappers of the heiress Penelope Hartington, and had once given chase (unsuccessfully) to John Dillinger.

Standing on the steps of the Victorian mansion that housed the Seward Agency, however, Fogarty was as nervous and cowed as he ever got. The Seward Agency was generally considered to be the Pinkertons of the supernatural. He suspected Father Connolly would have disapproved, and he was dead certain Mr. Hoover would object, if he'd known.

It was clear the Depression had made minimal impact here. The mansion that housed the agency was well kept up, the marble and brass shining and the walnut paneling glowing. The foyer of the mansion was not huge, but well appointed, with a thick Persian rug on the marble floor and a massive mahogany desk, behind which sat a woman who looked like she'd just stepped off the silver screen. Hair as black as night, a peaches-and-cream complexion, and bee-stung lips to die for. Fogarty wished he could get a look at her legs, but they were hidden behind the desk. He gave his name, and she said, "Oh, yes, you're expected. Go right up." She gestured to the stairs. "First door on your left." Fogarty had been hoping she'd lead him to the office, and he could get a look at her gams, but she turned back to her paperwork without another word. He marshaled his disappointment.

He plodded up the stairs. The first door on the left was of dark-stained, carved wood, and bore a brass plaque that read "Directors." He knocked, and then opened the door. Inside was a spacious office, with bookshelves lining three walls, the fourth wall an enormous picture window looking out over the rolling hills of upstate New York. In the distance were the purple peaks of the Shwangunk Mountains.

At the center of the room two desks faced each other. The two men in the room looked up at Fogarty's entrance. At one desk sat a tall man with sloping shoulders and a mop of black hair. Beside him stood a smaller, slighter man, older, his face gaunt, with deep-set eyes, receding gray hair, and a pencil mustache. Both wore dark, stylish suits, the crisp white shirts with Arrow collars that could split a hair, and the perfectly knotted silk ties. At least, Fogarty thought, the ties were silk. His hand involuntarily rose to his own tie, as he realized he didn't know what it was made of—though he was pretty sure it wasn't silk.

"Agent Fogarty," said the older man. "Welcome. I'm Dax Harnett. This is Roy Chancellor." They shook hands all around. "Please have a seat." He gestured toward a leather-covered armchair. The big man, Chancellor, took out a pipe and began to fill it. A knock came on the door, and it opened to admit the receptionist, who carried a silver tray with a coffeepot and cups. Turned out her legs looked as good as the rest of her, and Fogarty took the opportunity to appreciate them.

When they were settled with coffee, Chancellor's pipe going and Fogarty and Harnett firing up cigarettes, they got down to business.

"I've been the Bureau's SAC for Columbus for the past two years," Fogarty said.

"We know who you are," said Chancellor. "One of Hoover's cowboys."

Fogarty frowned at the term. J. Edgar Hoover's FBI had originally consisted mostly of earnest young men with law degrees, but by the early thirties, the bureau chief had realized he needed some agents with experience in the rougher areas of law enforcement, and he began hiring certain lawmen with experience at things like tracking and gunfights. Fogarty had been one of those hires, part of the crew the other agents, and nowadays the press, called "The Cowboys." Fogarty looked from one to the other of the men, unsure if Chancellor had meant to be insulting.

"No offense," said Harnett. "We also know you make collars and close cases, which is why Hoover gave you Columbus. What we don't know is why you need us."

"I'm on special assignment now," said Fogarty. "Mr. Hoover has put me in charge of the Torrance task force."

"Ah, yes, we've heard the stories," said Chancellor, nodding. "Multiple jobs at opposite ends of the state, mysterious disappearances, supposedly killed by the Cleveland police, and then turning up alive in Akron. Sounds like yellow journalism and superstitious rumors to me. Surely you don't buy these stories and attribute some supernatural agency to the Torrance gang?"

"I didn't, until they vanished when I was chasing them." Both men cocked skeptical eyebrows at this, and Fogarty hurried on, "I mean literally vanished. We were closing on them, barely a few yards from their car when it happened. There was a sound like an explosion, and a flash of light, and they were gone. Just disappeared. Not a trace left." The two men looked at each other. Fogarty had the feeling there was a silent conversation going on.

"That's interesting," said the older man. "It wasn't just an explosion? There was no shrapnel, no detritus?"

"None. Just a scorch mark on the road." Fogarty shook his head. "I gotta tell you guys, I'm not real comfortable with all this. I mean, you get down to cases, I guess I'm as superstitious as the next Irishman. I go to church... Well, I used to, anyway. But somehow I always sorta figured magic and miracles were all in the past, never figured to meet them on the job. Now it seems like the only possible explanation for the Torrance gang's escape was something supernatural. But Mr. Hoover would never accept such a suggestion, which is why I'm here on my own lookout."

"I'll be honest with you in return, Agent Fogarty," said Harnett. "Ninety percent of the cases we investigate turn out to have a rational explanation, though one no one had previously thought of. But there are that other ten percent, where we've encountered something science doesn't understand. There's no telling which yours is until we look at all the evidence."

"What else can you tell us?" asked Chancellor.

"Not much to tell. They disappeared, and that was that. We tore that whole area of the road apart, thinking they might have rigged someplace to hide, but there was nothing. We wondered if another gang had put a bomb in their car, but, as you say, there would have been some kind of remains, some shrapnel. There was nothing."

"You haven't seen them since?"

"No, this was last week, the Tiverton Bank job."

"Well," said Dax Harnett, "perhaps this does bear looking into. Our regular consultant rates would apply..."

"Um...," said Fogarty, "as I say, this isn't an official consultation. I don't think Mr. Hoover would exactly approve."

"On your own time and your own dime?" said Chancellor.

Fogarty nodded.

"Which means we must be discreet." said Dax Harnett. "And I think we can give you a certain courtesy discount."

Roy Chancellor frowned, and then grudgingly nodded. "Alright," he said. "I guess we can do that."

***

Eight miles outside of Columbus, on a small side road, one of the Bureau's dark gray Packards and a large black Duesenberg were parked. Wide fields extended to the horizon on either side of the roadway, plowed in furrows, but with no crops evident. Dax Harnett stood peering at the screen of a device the size of a small suitcase, which rested on the hood of the Duesenberg. "Definite disturbances in the magnetic field," he said.

"No kidding?" asked Fogarty. "What does that mean?"

"Beyond that something big happened here? Damned if I know."

Grinning, Chancellor said, "Then what good are you?"

"I attract the dames, of course." Dax Harnett said, and shut down the device. "Let's assume for the moment our gangster did disappear somehow. What disappears must reappear, or it does him no good. If there are magnetic anomalies at the point of departure, there must be similar effects at the point of arrival."

"Great," said Chancellor. "We'll just search the entire globe for another magnetic anomaly, and we'll have them." He shook his head. Then he looked up suddenly. "No, wait... You know, we might actually be able to do that. That machine the Russians put into space..."

"The satellite?" asked Harnett.

"Yeah... Doesn't it record magnetic data?"

"You think Moscow would cooperate?"

"Maybe—if we do an end run around the politicians, and go straight to the scientists. Be worth a wire to find out."

***

"Akron again," said Chancellor.

"What do you mean, 'again?'" asked Fogarty.

The big man from the Seward Agency was holding a dark sheet of plastic up against the window. The three of them were crammed into Fogarty's office. At least it had a window, even if the view wasn't much, just the alley and the building across. Just now Chancellor blocked that view with what looked like a big photographic negative he held up against the glass. It was the image transmitted electronically from Moscow. At first glance, it didn't look like anything, just a bunch of hazy abstract shapes. Faintly, behind the hazy lines, if you looked hard, you could make out the shape of Lake Erie.

"Akron was one of the places reported a mysterious sighting of Torrance when he'd supposedly been over the line in Fort Wayne at the same time. If your disappearance story is true, some of the other stories are probably true, too…"

"And some are baloney," said Fogarty. "How do we tell which is which?"

Harnett stepped to the window and peered at the negative. "We look for correspondences between your story and theirs," he said. "They both happened at night, or on a rainy day, or on the fifth of the month, or…" He pointed at the magnetic image. "Both places show magnetic anomalies during the same time period."

All three peered in silence at the black and white image for a time.

"Akron," muttered Harnett. "Wait a minute…" He shuffled through some of the files piled on Fogarty's desk, and produced an old report. "I thought so. Back in 1932, Torrance was a known associate of a Gypsy fortune teller named Magda Ouspenskya, who lived outside Akron. The Akron cops thought they were setting up some sort of con, but nothing ever came of it, at least not that got reported."

"Maybe I should make a visit to Akron," said Chancellor, "see what I can find out from the locals."

"Might want to visit the local Salvation Army first,"

said Harnett.

"You think they'd know anything?" Fogarty frowned.

"Nah," said Roy Chancellor, "but I'll need a different wardrobe."

"Meanwhile, you and I," Harnett said to Fogarty, "will look up this Madame Ouspenskya."

✱✱

Fogarty pulled the Packard to a stop before the old trailer that hunkered in an abandoned lot on the outskirts of Akron. He turned off the engine. The trailer looked as though it hadn't traveled the roads in many years, its sides faded to dull gray, its tires long flattened, weeds grown up around them.

"Do you know this Magda Ouspenskya?" Harnett asked.

"Had occasion to question her once, a few years ago," Fogarty allowed.

"No offense, but perhaps you'd better let me do the talking," said Harnett. "I've dealt with the Rom a bit, speak a little of their lingo."

"The Rom?"

"Short for Romany. It's what the Gypsies call themselves."

Fogarty glanced at him skeptically. "Yeah, well, anyway," he said, "Magda's no more a real Gypsy—um, excuse me, a real Rom—than I am a brain surgeon. She just likes to pose as one. Makes her seem more mysterious."

They got out and crossed to the trailer. At Fogarty's knock, the trailer door opened a crack, and a woman's face peered out. Thin and gaunt, she looked to be in her sixties, though Fogarty's file had said she was only forty-six. She eyed them up and down, and Fogarty knew she was making them for cops. He couldn't tell whether she recognized him, or just knew the look.

"What you want?" she said. "I pay this month already, get lost."

"We ain't Akron PD," said Fogarty, reaching for his

badge. Harnett put a hand on his arm.

"We're private," Harnett said. "Just want a consultation. Droboy tume Romale. Mandar tsera tai kater o Del mai but te aven tumenge."

"What?" The woman looked genuinely confused.

Harnett tried again. "Jeśli nie mówisz po Romani, nie jesteś naprawdę Rz. To nie znaczy, że nie masz wiedzy. We'll pay your usual fee."

"Większość Amerykanów nie wie Polski z Rosyjskiego z Suahili. You speak Polish, so for you, cheap rate, fifty dollar."

"Twenty-five."

"Forty."

"Thirty for the consultation. If you can do what we need done, much more."

"How much?"

"Don't you want to know what the work entails first?"

She peered at him for a moment, then nodded. She put out her hand. "Thirty first."

Fogarty glared at Harnett, but the detective calmly produced three ten spots, and handed them to the woman. She made the money vanish, stepped back, and opened the door wide.

They climbed up into the trailer. The space was small and cramped, but cleaner than Fogarty would have expected. There was a stove and a fold-down table covered with brightly patterned cloth, a crystal ball and a pack of cards upon it. On a shelf behind, a plaster cast of a skull— at least, Fogarty thought it was a plaster cast—was topped with a half-burned candle. A beaded curtain separated the sleeping area from the kitchen. The place smelled of incense and fried onions. Magda took the bench seat behind the table, and gestured Harnett to a battered wooden folding chair before it. Fogarty stood, his back to the door.

"I have a friend," said Harnett. "Not him," he added, when Magda's eyes darted to Fogarty. "Another man. He needs to travel, very quickly. More quickly than Mr. Edison's bullet train. Now he's here—*poof*—now he's there. Like travel on the astral, but in body."

"Instant transportation by magic?" She shook her head. "You waste your time, private detective man. It cannot be done."

"Oh, yes it can. I know it can. I've seen it. The only question is, can you do it? And, of course, how much would it cost?"

"Why do you not go to this person who did it before?"

"He's dead. Can you do it?"

The old woman sat back and looked at him silently for a long time. Finally, she began to laugh.

"So he found a way," she said.

"I beg your pardon?"

"You lie to Magda," she said. "But that's okay, Mr. Private Dick. Magda likes you. You and your G-man friend here, you after Jim Torrance, no?" She leaned forward, and suddenly her accent was gone. "Torrance, he came and asked for the same thing. I told him it couldn't be done. Believe me, with what he was willing to pay, if I could have done it, I wouldn't be living in this shithole. Jim wouldn't believe me. Said he'd find someone, somewhere, who could do it. But you flatfeet coming here, asking about this, you think I helped him do it? If I could have, I would have, but I don't have that kind of juice. I couldn't even tell him where to start looking. But I guess his search worked out for him, or you two wouldn't be here."

"So I don't suppose you could tell *us* where to start looking?"

"No. But if you take Magda's advice," she said, her accent back in place, "you won't go looking at all. Anyone powerful enough to do this thing, you don't want to mess with. That kind of power, they could squash you and your G-man friend like bugs."

***

Back in the car, Fogarty asked, "You really seen it done once?"

"Nah," said Harnett. "She was right. I was bull-shitting."

Fogarty nodded. "Thought so. But you think it's possible."

"Tell you the truth, I dunno for sure."

***

The boys in the poolrooms and bars around Akron thought "Ray Chance" was an okay guy, for a drifter. Ray showed up for a few days that weekend, played a few games of poker, shot a little pool, bought a few drinks. He was okay at poker, though he never won much—or lost very much, for that matter—but he was a graceful loser. At pool he did a little better, and always bought his opponent a round, win or lose. Most of the time they were playing for pennies or matchsticks, anyway. They all needed what little money they had for the drinks.

Tonight the big man was standing at the bar with Ty Westfield and Croaker Brandt, watching a young Polish guy slaughter Joey Beets at pool.

"You ever see a lightning flash on the ground?" asked Ray.

Ty and Croaker looked at each other, then back at Ray. "You makin' poetic about Jan here?" asked Ty.

"No, seriously. Like a big flash and explosion, say, on the street."

"You mean as opposed to in the sky?"

"Yeah."

"Can't say I have. There was a freak lightning strike last week. But we didn't see it, just heard it from indoors."

"Joey seen something like that once. Ain't you, Joey?" said Croaker.

Joey was not listening, as he'd finally caught a break when the Pole scratched, and was lining up a shot.

Croaker leaned closer to Ray and lowered his voice. "Joey seen it over the west end. He don't tell this part of it no more, 'cause the guys made fun at him for it, but when he first told it, after the flash and thunder, he seen a Ford there that wasn't there before. Then this car just drives off, as if it had been tooling down the road all along." Croaker nodded, winked, and sat back. Then he suddenly leaned back toward Ray again. "Don't tell him I told you," he whispered.

"I won't," said Ray.

***

"Duquesne Street?"

"That's what the fellow said." Chancellor had bathed and shaved and changed from the shabby, out-of-date suit he'd worn as Ray Chance into his regular, more stylish attire.

Harnett was peering at the image from Moscow's satellite. "Hard to tell without a map to the same scale," he said, "but far as I can tell, at least part of Duquesne Street should be inside the area we're interested in."

"What did the Gypsy have to say?" Chancellor asked.

"Torrance approached her to do it, she claims she sent him packing, said it couldn't be done," said Harnett.

"You believe her?"

"I think so. Not certain, but I think so."

"So," said Fogarty, "we got a lightning flash and mysterious automobile appearance a few months ago around that area, and then last week, the disappearance in Columbus, both times coinciding with geomagnetic weirdness and lightning and thunder in both places."

"Not a huge leap," said Harnett, "to intuit that, had there been someone to see it, there might have been an automobile appear out of a lightning flash in Duquesne Street shortly after one vanished from Columbus."

"Not guaranteed," said Chancellor, "but I wouldn't bet against it. I say we go have a look around Duquesne Street."

***

Duquesne was a quiet rural street. Nice, large houses, set back from the road, shaded by elm and maple, though many showed the effects of neglect, and several seemed abandoned. They parked the Packard and the Duesenberg on the side of the road near where Harnett thought the magnetic anomaly crossed it. All three got out and began walking down the road, eyes scanning the roadway and surroundings.

"What's your bet?" Chancellor asked Harnett as they started off. "Advanced science, or something super-natural?"

"Not enough evidence to even guess," said Harnett.

"I'm going with supernatural. Be more fun that way."

"Roy, your sense of fun is extremely perverse."

"Was I claiming otherwise? I was not."

Less than a half mile along, they found some odd debris. A shard of glass from a headlight. A peel of rubber. A window crank from an auto. Some small lumps of rotten meat, no bigger than Fogarty's thumb, several now smeared across the pavement. The needle and dial of a gas gauge. Fogarty picked up a small object that turned out to be a collar button. It could have been some random trash dropped in the road, but none of the three thought so.

"Not enough for an accident or an explosion," said Harnett, "and too much for anything else."

Chancellor held up a metal tube, the rear end of which seemed to have melted off.

"What the hell is that?" asked Fogarty.

"I'm sure you've seen one before," Harnett said, taking the black metal tube from Chancellor and holding it before Fogarty's eyes. "It's the business end of a Tommy gun."

"What the bleeding hell happened here?" Fogarty shook his head.

***

"W. Valenta," read the mailbox. The three investigators had continued down Duquesne Street, and stopped at the next driveway.

"Could that be *Wladsiu* Valenta?" said Chancellor.

"The inventor?" said Harnett.

"Yeah," said Chancellor.

"Yeah, pretty sure that's him," said Fogarty. "The office has a file on him, but I haven't read it."

"He's not as famous as Edison or Tesla, but he makes it into the magazines now and then," said Chancellor.

"Yeah?" asked Fogarty. "Like *Popular Science*, *Popular Mechanics*, that sort of thing?"

"And *Life Magazine*. They did a photo spread on his laboratory last year. You know he actually improved on some of Tesla's designs? He got 30% more efficiency out of the Niagara power station."

"Last I heard," said Harnett, "he'd invented a way to transmit moving pictures as well as sound through the airwaves."

They looked at the place before them. A long, winding drive led to an old but well-kept-up farmhouse. The barn had been expanded upon, and extended with an addition that nearly doubled its size, and above the top of the attached silo extended a shaft with a copper sphere at its tip.

"Yeah," said Chancellor. "It's gotta be."

There was no answer at the door of the farmhouse, so they walked to the barn that housed Valenta's laboratory. As they approached, there was a loud report, and Fogarty's hand involuntarily went for his gun. The sound was followed by a crackling and a hum.

"Not a gunshot," said Harnett dryly. "Some sort of machine."

Fogarty drew his gun anyway.

Chancellor's knock on the door went unanswered, to no one's surprise; whoever was inside could hardly have heard it over the pops, crashes, and buzzing of the electrical equipment. Chancellor tried the door and found it unlocked.

The inside of the lab was as it had been shown in the *Life* photo spread, though some of the machinery was different. At the center of the vast space loomed a tall column wrapped with copper wire, topped by a silver metal sphere, surrounded by a circle of twelve miniature versions of the big column. Bolts of lightning leaped between the sphere at the top of the central column and its smaller brothers in the circle.

To their left, at a bank of controls, stood a stout, gray-haired man in a leather apron, goggles, and work gloves. When he noticed them, he nodded, and held up a finger. Turning to the bank of controls, he began flipping switches and turning dials, and the sound and light display faded, leaving only a scent of ozone in the air. The man stripped off his goggles and gloves, and walked toward them.

"You are police?" he said. His English was heavily accented.

"Federal Bureau of Investigation," said Fogarty, flashing his badge.

"I am Valenta," said the scientist, nodding. "I knew someone would come." He held out his hands, side by side. "Arrest me, then, for I am guilty."

"Guilty of what, Sir?" asked Harnett

"Guilty of murder. And of—how do you say?—aiding and abetting those evil persons. It was my translocator, you see. James Torrance had heard rumors, and he thought of how it could help him get away with his crimes, instantly disappearing here, and appearing there."

"Wait a minute," said Fogarty. "You're saying you made a machine that could make Torrance appear and disappear?"

"My translocator, yes?" He gestured toward a machine at the other end of the lab. It was in a shambles, and looked like a coven of mad dwarves had attacked it with sledgehammers. "Send to Tiverton, Fort Wayne, other places, bring back."

"Why did you help him?" asked Harnett.

"He had Mary, my assistant's daughter. She was his hostage. I could not let her be harmed. So, I murder."

"Murder?"

"This time," the inventor explained, "I send to Columbus. They will be twenty minutes robbing bank, then I must bring them back. During twenty minutes, I go to house, where small, ugly young man, very attached to Torrance, much trusted, he holds Mary. I say, 'Terrible accident! Torrance hurt!' The young man, he rushes out all heedless, and, bang! I hit with iron rod." Valenta shook his head sadly. "He is dead, I fear. Body is now back in icehouse. Then I am going back to laboratory. I am beginning translocation process to return gang, but halfway through, I smash molecular transducer. Is key to whole process, that transducer. Now, they are gone."

"Gone?" said Fogarty.

"Neither here nor there, or perhaps part here, part there, part... Somewhere else, *between*. Most of them is no longer in this world. I have murder these men also, by my action. So. Arrest me."

"Mr. Valenta," said Fogarty, "I don't think we need to arrest you. As far as the moke in the house, it was clearly self defense, and the defense of an innocent kidnap victim. As to the gang... Well, there are no bodies, and, anyway, I don't believe there are any laws bearing on suspending someone *between*."

To Fogarty's surprise, Valenta looked outraged, as if he thought there really ought to be laws about transporting people and things through the between, and the illegality of leaving people in limbo, as it were. Still, he did not protest aloud.

***

Fogarty had gathered the sparse remains from Duquesne Street, and tried to convince the Bureau that the Torrance gang had been vaporized by a freak lightning strike. It was a hard sell without any bodies. Probably the only reason he was not laughed out of the Bureau was that he had the famous scientist Wladsiu Valenta backing him. That worthy attested that yes, this was possible, and in fact just the sort of freak lightning that might do so had appeared in Akron the other night.

The fingers had helped, too. FBI searchers eventually turned up two fingers, severed neatly at their bases, the raw ends apparently cauterized, in the gutter of Duquesne Street. The fingerprints were a match for Albert "Aces" Toohey, one of the charter members of Torrance's gang. Mr. Hoover and others at the Bureau had still remained skeptical, and the case file was kept open. However, after a year and some with no sign of any of the members of the Torrance gang, the file was quietly shelved.

Harnett and Chancellor had vanished after that first encounter with Valenta, and when the Seward Agency's bill arrived (marked Personal & Private for Mr. Daniel Fogarty), it was reasonable—Fogarty was able to pay it off with only a few monthly installments.

Fogarty remained ever after ambivalent about the case. The scientist Valenta had almost refused to testify, as it required him to lie. Fogarty was glad the Torrance gang was gone, but he couldn't help a little feeling of regret. He had hoped to bring them to justice, or kill them himself. And the truth was, he agreed with Chancellor. Magic would have been much more fun than science.

***

The fate of the gangsters haunted him for years. Locked up in prison—or gunned down by police bullets— would have been one thing. Suspended in some limbo between here and there was another thing entirely. It gave him the creeps, thinking about it. He had asked the professor about that once, and Valenta assured him that the gang could not possibly be still alive and conscious.

"With the Translocator," Valenta said, "molecules are disassembled here, reassembled there. In between, there are no persons, no mind to perceive anything, yes? Just a stream of molecules and atoms. There would be no consciousness until they are reassembled at the other end."

Though he wanted to believe the old Slav, Fogarty wasn't quite convinced. His faith taught him that men were more than their bodies, more than molecules and atoms. There was something else, an essence the priests called a soul. Where did the soul go, while the atoms and molecules were being translocated? Valenta, an atheist himself, had no answer. The soul was not his purview.

Fogarty, however, did believe in a soul. So where were the souls of the Torrance Gang? Not in Heaven, surely, after all their crimes and killings. In Hell? The church assured him that sinners went to Hell after death, and the gang were certainly sinners. But they had not died, not in any conventional sense, so where did that leave their souls? It was a question Fogarty was not qualified to even begin to try to answer. He had determined at one point to ask Father Connolly about this, but when the time came, he found himself unwilling and unable to fully explain the whole thing, and they ended up discussing the Cleveland Indians' chances this season instead. For Fogarty, there would never be a convincing answer to the question of what had become of the Torrance gang's souls.

Dan Fogarty died in a nursing home in 1958. The nurse who discovered he had passed found clasped in his hand an old-fashioned collar button.

AUTHOR'S NOTE

Duncan Eagleson is a writer, illustrator, and sculptor, maskmaker, and creator of the *Railwalker* series (railwalkercomics.com). He has written and illustrated the graphic novel version of Anne Rice's *The Witching Hour,* and his work has appeared in Neil Gaiman's *Sandman* and the DC/Piranha Press *Big Books* series, as well as on many book covers and film posters. He has published several short stories and is currently writing his fourth novel. His first novel, *Darkwalker,* is now available from Pink Narcissus Press.

MR. TESLA'S RADIO RAINMAKER
JEFF HECHT

"Got any ideas?" Leroy asked, looking at the newspaper he had pulled from his lunch pail.

"About what?" answered Elijah. It was such a slow day for the mechanics at Gil's Garage that they had time to talk after washing their greasy hands and eating lunch.

"About old Mr. Hoover's latest plan to put the country back to work with private enterprise." Leroy pointed to a story on the front page. "Mr. Rockefeller promised to pay a million dollars to the first man to make enough rain to wash away the Dust Bowl."

"Ain't our problem," said Elijah. "Long as people need to drive their cars, we're okay. Ain't many got the money to buy new ones these days. Fixin' cars sure beats pickin' cotton. That's what my dad said when he sent me to mechanic school. People like us can't talk our way into good jobs; we need a proper education in the right skills."

"Mr. Rockefeller is offering a whole lot of money. A good mechanic could fix something up. That Mr. Tesla, he wrote in a magazine that radio waves could make water rain out of the air. That's what they need there in the Dust Bowl, Eli. A radio rainmaker."

Elijah bit into his apple and chewed it slowly, thinking. Gravel crunched along the road, and the two looked up and saw Gil walking towards the garage. He had gone downtown in the morning with a shoebox of papers. He still had the shoebox, but now his shoulders were hunched, and his face grim. Gil walked silently past them, set the box in the office, and went into the back room.

They knew what he was doing. They had seen the metal flask he hid in an old tool cabinet. It was his refuge on a bad day, and this year had brought too many of those. They weren't even selling much gasoline. They went inside quietly and adjusted the pistons on the engine they were rebuilding. They were working on the gasket when Gil walked in.

"I'm closing the place, boys," Gil said, his blue eyes looking deep into their dark ones. "I'm sorry. I don't have enough to pay the bank, so they're foreclosing. I didn't tell the bank Dr. Harris owes me for rebuilding the engine, so finish it up and I'll give you what he pays me. I don't want the bastards at the bank to get it. You boys have been the smartest mechanics I've ever had. I'll tell anybody who asks me that you two are the best mechanics on Long Island."

***

Over dinner at the boarding house, Leroy asked the landlady, Mrs. Williams, if she could type a letter for him. She said it would cost him 25 cents, and he would have to buy the stamps and envelopes. He came back an hour later with a pencilled letter to Nicola Tesla, Hotel New Yorker, Manhattan.

"Dear Mr. Tesla,

My name is Leroy Johnson, and I am a trained mechanic on Long Island. I saw Herbert Hoover's plan to offer a million dollars for making rain fall in the Oklahoma dust bowl, and I thought immediately of what you wrote about sending electricity into the air to make rain. Mr. Tesla, I greatly admire you, and I want to work with you on this project. If you need another person to help, my cousin Elijah is also a trained mechanic and would like to work for you. We both are hard-working young men with degrees from the Tuskegee Institute in Alabama."

When Mrs. Williams finished, he asked her to add Gil's name as a reference. She added the address of the boarding house and her phone number, and he thanked her for that as he paid her.

"It's the least I can do for you and Mr. Elijah," she

said. "I heard about Mr. Gil's garage. You boys are good tenants, and I want you to have good jobs in these hard times."

***

"A telegram came for you this afternoon," Mrs. Williams said when Leroy and Elijah returned to the boarding house on Friday evening with a box of tools Gil had insisted they take from the garage. She got it from the hall table and handed it to Leroy.

He worked his finger into the envelope and opened it with a mechanic's care. He read it silently, his eyes widening and a smile forming. Then he looked up and announced, "Mr. Tesla wants us to come meet him at his hotel at 10 a.m. on Monday morning."

"Me, too?" Eli asked.

"Yes, indeed. He says he has important plans to discuss with us."

"Well, I'm still going to be careful, Leroy. I'm not going to go out for that steak dinner until I get my first pay envelope. You remember that garage in Queens?"

"You won't have to worry about Mr. Tesla, Eli. He's a very important inventor."

***

Leroy and Eli donned their Sunday suits and took the early train into Penn Station on Monday morning. They found a Sunday newspaper left in the seat and for a few minutes talked about barnstorming flyers and baseball players, but Leroy wanted to think about what to say.

"Mr. Tesla wrote about how antennas can radiate electrical energy into the air and make it rain. He tried that in Colorado once, but I don't know what happened to his equipment. When Mr. Hansell had his car in, he said that RCA has a big antenna and the most powerful radio transmitters that Mr. Tesla ever built stored in a warehouse. If we could get that equipment out to Oklahoma, we could make it rain on the Dust Bowl and get Mr. Hoover's reward."

"Don't RCA's radio telephones use those big

transmitters?"

"Mr. Hansell told me Radio Central uses new vacuum-tube amplifiers that emit hundreds of kilowatts at shorter frequencies. So they stored the old ones. Mr. Tesla says all he wants are to have his ideas used, and he designed the old RCA transmitters, so he would be happy to use them. He doesn't have any company any more, Eli. What he needs are a couple of smart and hard-working mechanics."

"I hope so," said Eli. "Long way back to Alabama, and I don't want to ride the rails again."

***

The hotel clerk sounded suspicious when they asked for Tesla. "What do you want to see him for?"

"We are mechanics who he invited to discuss a business venture," Leroy said, pulling the neatly folded telegram from his suit pocket and showing it to him.

The clerk donned his reading glasses and examined the telegram. Satisfied, he handed it back and picked up the house phone. After a brief exchange, he said, "Mr. Tesla will be down in a few minutes," and showed them where to sit.

Tall and very gaunt, Nicola Tesla looked older than his photographs. Dressed in an old-style suit, he carried a leather case and looked around. Leroy stood up, waved and walked over to introduce himself. The three then settled in chairs around a coffee table.

"Your last employer recommended you very highly," Tesla said, opening his case and pulling a folder of papers. "These are the plans for my transmitter at Wardenclyffe which was demolished in a horrible misunderstanding. I have revised them to use the latest developments in electricity, but I will need your help to build them." He showed Eli and Leroy articles from *Electrical Experimenter* that described his ideas, and spread a drawing of an electrical tower on the table.

Leroy and Eli studied the articles and drawings, then Leroy looked up. "Mr. Tesla, I spoke to Mr. Hansell at RCA in Rocky Point. He said they have some of your equipment from Wardenclyffe in their warehouse."

"They do?" Tesla said, his eyes lighting up. "I thought the government had destroyed it all. I did some projects for the Radio Corporation, so I will contact them. First let me tell you what we need."

Tesla turned back to the magazine pages to point out what he needed. "We will generate a powerful radio signal and use it to send energy wirelessly through the sky. We need a source of electricity to provide power, transformers to generate a high voltage, an oscillator and amplifier to generate the radio-frequency power, and an antenna to radiate the energy into the sky. There it will condense the water from the air and the water will fall from the sky as rain."

Leroy carefully wrote the details in a bound notebook with a number 2HB pencil, going right up to the edge of the page to save paper, and trying not to smudge the vital list of equipment they would need. Eli listened intently to Tesla, nodding as he read the diagrams.

When Tesla finally paused, Leroy put down his pencil and looked at him. "We would like to be your agents and collect the equipment. The newspaper said the tests will be in August, so we need to get the equipment to the test ground in Oklahoma in time to assemble it. We may need a line of credit to arrange shipment." It was an anxious moment; he didn't know how he could obtain credit. Surely Tesla must have contacts.

"That should be possible," Tesla said. "I will talk with Mr. Hansell about that when I call him about the equipment."

***

When they got back to the boarding house, Mrs. Williams handed Leroy a telegram. Mr. Hansell would see them at 9 a.m. sharp in his office. "Time to fire up the Model T," he told Eli. The two changed into old clothes and went out in the back yard to tune up their old car.

The car purred early in the morning when they

drove off to the RCA Lab, stopping to buy five gallons of gas and getting a nickel back from their dollar. They looked in awe at the radio towers that sent telephone calls across the ocean. "Only J. P. Morgan himself could afford using that phone," said Eli.

"Or Mr. Rockefeller," added Leroy, thinking of the prize money.

C. W. Hansell greeted them inside, a short solid man who unrolled blueprints on his desk and pointed knowingly at the drawings. "Here's the mechanical layout of the antenna," he said. "We have more blueprints for the radio-frequency transmitter. It's an old-fashioned long-wave system, but it has lots of power. We use short-wave now because it's more efficient for intercontinental transmission.

Leroy's finger traced the tower structure and the cables carrying the power. His eyes opened wide when he saw the dimensions. "This is *really* big."

Hansell nodded and smiled. "That's why we took down the old tower. You can't afford to waste things in these times, so we stored everything. But now we are thinking of new projects, so we could use the space. We have men here who can crate everything and load it into box cars. They also will paint RCA all over it, so the poor people out in the dust bowl will know that RCA engineering can beat General Electric."

He spread another blueprint on top of the first. "This shows the electrical connections. We have some others with more details. You're going to need them when you put it together in Oklahoma. And I really think you have something there. I've been watching how negative ions make some people feel better. All that radio power should start the rain falling, too."

"That's exactly what we think," said Leroy, with Eli nodding in agreement.

They rolled up the blueprints and promised to send shipping instructions as soon as they could. On their way home, they stopped and sent a telegram to Mr. Tesla.

***

"It's going to work," Leroy said the next morning, holding the telegram that had just come from Tesla. "The money we were saving to buy a garage is enough to travel to Oklahoma and stay there. RCA is going to ship all the transmitting equipment. Mr. Tesla must be rich, staying in that fancy hotel."

"Well," said Elijah, twiddling his thumbs and speaking very slow and thoughtfully. "I guess it wouldn't do any good to buy our own garage, anyway. Look what happened to Mr. Gil." He stood and stretched. "Let's do it."

They spent a day trying to work out the plans, and after dinner they drove to Gil's house and asked if he would like to work for them.

Gil first thought they were joking, but as they explained their plans he realized they were serious. He turned to his wife. "Honey, I'm not any use here, there aren't any jobs here, and I need something to do before I get tempted to shoot that damn banker. I want to do it." Then he turned to Leroy. "And I can help you with the business, so the damn bankers don't rob you blind."

***

Gil took the train to Oklahoma a week early, to get things organized. He arrived at the little train station driving a used panel truck that he had bought from a busted farmer heading west. "I paid what I would have paid back in New York, and he looked at me like I was crazy, and said that would get his family all the way to California," he told Leroy and Eli as they drove off. "I found some locals who are happy to work for us for a dollar a day. It's probably best to let them think they're working for me rather than they're working for you. Most of them look older than you are, and they won't believe you're the bosses and the brains of the operation."

"Mr. Tesla's the brains," Leroy protested.

But Eli caught the drift of Gil's words. "Mr. Tesla won't be with us all the time putting things together, Leroy. Mr. Gil is twenty years older and a lot whiter than we are. They'll pay him more mind. Oklahoma isn't the North, Leroy."

"And I have them working hard; the first 10 feet of the tower is already up, so you and Tesla can concentrate on the transmitter."

***

A week before the contest trials, the Tesla-RCA tower, as everyone now called it, rose its full 65 feet above the dusty plain. Reporters had arrived for the spectacle, and Nicola Tesla held court outside the Tesla Radio Rainmaking headquarters, hastily assembled by local workers a hundred feet from the base of the tower. It was another hot, dry day on the Oklahoma panhandle, but Tesla still wore his Manhattan suit and tie. Standing under a tarp, he had shed the hat he wore outside.

"The rainmaking radio is a wireless power transmitter," Tesla explained as reporters scribbled their notes. "Radio waves push and pull water molecules high in the air together so they condense into tiny floating droplets. The longer the radio waves oscillate, the more droplets condense at the peaks of the waves, forming liquid water that rains from the sky."

Leroy and Eli sat on folding chairs in back of the reporters, drinking iced tea as they took a break from working on the transmitter. The tower had come with full blueprints, so Gil could show the crew how to bolt the thing together. But the transmitter blueprints were incomplete, so they needed Tesla to tell them what went where. They were amazed how well he remembered details of something he had designed years ago.

"Is this like the long-wave transmitter you designed for the radio-telephone?" hollered one of the reporters, a burly gray-haired man who had shed his jacket and rolled up his sleeves in the heat. "Can you make rain that far away?"

"This uses the same frequency," Tesla said, "but we are beaming the power up into the clouds, over our heads, instead of parallel to the ground so radio signal can reach people's homes. I have designed the antenna wires in this tower in a different way, to focus the radio waves up into the clouds, where they will collect moisture that will fall as rain."

"Have you looked at the General Electric antenna?" Eli whispered to Leroy. "It looks like Dr. Langmuir stole the idea from Mr. Tesla. Even with a Nobel Prize, he can't invent his own antenna."

"Our antenna is better. Mr. Tesla explained the differences to me. Did you see their transmitter?"

Eli shook his head. "Is it any good?"

"Very good," Leroy whispered. "General Electric has more modern power equipment, and much better vacuum tubes. But they can't get the power up into the clouds."

"I worry more about the aviators," Eli said very softly, sipping his tea. "They say they can make it rain by throwing ashes from their plane down into a cloud. I heard one of them boasting how he was going to beat both of us that way."

"No way," whispered Leroy. "We're going to beat them cold."

"Will Tesla Radio Rainmaking win the prize?" a woman's voice shouted from up front. Neither Leroy nor Eli had seen a woman in the crowd of male reporters, so they stood, but saw only a single hand reaching above the heads of the men.

Tesla beamed a smile at her. "My dear woman," he said, "we are prepared to soak the soils of Oklahoma and I have no doubt we will win the prize."

***

"Mr. Tesla is very busy," Leroy told the man from the electric company.

"I got to talk with him," said the electrician, a heavy-set man in well-worn overalls. "He's the man that knows about this thing. I've read all his articles in *Electrical Experimenter*, and I have to know how many amps and volts he needs to run this transmitter so I can run a power line to it. If you don't have a big enough wire, it won't do nothin'. And I have to check if your wiring is safe, too."

"Mr. Tesla gave me very complete instructions," Leroy said. He opened his little black notebook to the page where he had written down the specifications and showed it to the electrician.

The electrician read the numbers and nodded. "That's a lot of power. I need to see your switches before I wire it up. And you have to have big fuses."

Leroy walked him through the building, showing him the switches, the fuses and the big transmitter itself.

The electrician pulled a big flashlight from his pocket to look inside the transmitter. Leroy and Eli had removed the dust and cobwebs, but they couldn't hide its age. Ten years was a long time in electricity. The electrician raised his furry eyebrows as he stared inside.

"I thought Mr. Tesla just built this," he said at last.

"He overhauled a transmitter he built earlier," Leroy said. Actually, Leroy and Eli had cleaned it, with guidance from Mr. Tesla, who insisted it was as good as new.

"Well, I know who Nicola Tesla is, and I can't argue with anything he does, but this time I have to wonder a little bit." The electrician switched off his flashlight and put it back into his overalls. "I'll get my gear and hook this up."

It took most of the afternoon to hook up the power. The electrician chatted as he worked, and Leroy listened real carefully after he heard the man say that he had spent the morning wiring up General Electric's transmitter.

"Dr. Langmuir designed two new tubes for the oscillator, and they have one for the amplifier that's a triode almost as big as my truck. Everything is bright and shiny new," the electrician said from the top of his wooden stepladder, then asked Leroy to hand him the end of a wire. "When's the big test?"

"We're waiting for the weather, sort of." Mr. Tesla had said his discharges needed just the right conditions to cause rain, and Leroy didn't want to give away any secrets.

"So are they," the electrician said. "But don't you

have to finish this in August to win the prize?"

Leroy admitted they did.

"Well, let's test this wiring now," said the electrician, clamping the wire into place.

Leroy looked at everything himself before he pulled the big switch. The meter showed he had enough voltage, and he turned up the rheostat enough to get some power flowing. It was good enough for now, and he didn't want to show the electrician too much or he would tell it all to GE.

***

Everything seemed to power up flawlessly in the morning. The oscillator and amplifier hummed at the 60-cycle line rate. The meter showed a stable voltage. Gil, standing a few hundred feet away beside a receiver on the back of the truck, waved a handkerchief to show he was picking up a strong signal.

"I don't like the smell of the oscillator," Tesla said.

Eli asked what he meant.

"It smells like something electrical getting too hot." When that drew a blank stare, Tesla added, "like when you crank a car starter and it doesn't want to move, but you keep cranking and it does, but rubs too hard and heats up so much that the insulator turns black."

Eli looked puzzled. "Nothing is moving inside."

"Electrons are moving," Tesla said. "They go in and out of the condenser when the circuit oscillates."

They opened the switch and let the circuit discharge. One side of the oscillator box felt hot. When Tesla decided it had discharged enough, they opened the metal box. The smell was stronger, and when they looked in, they could see the big condenser was black in places. Eli put a gloved hand on the case, then pulled it away quickly. "Hot!"

Tesla sniffed the warm air rising from the case. "It's the condenser."

They let it cool for half an hour, then tried again. The meter showed a stable voltage, but this time Gil didn't stand up and wave his handkerchief. The big antenna wasn't radiating a thing.

When they opened the case again, they saw the condenser was partly melted. They were digging through the crates of spare parts shipped from Long Island, hoping to find a spare, when they heard a loud "bang."

Tesla kept searching, but Leroy and Eli went outside. The odor of the burnt condenser mixed with dust, but neither could smell anything chemical. They walked by the hangars that had been built for the six aviators who had signed up. People were standing around, looking at the three planes that had already arrived. A reporter was asking if the daredevil pilot Howard Hughes might show up, but no one knew.

Leroy and Eli walked past the planes towards the General Electric workshop, and saw Gil coming toward them. "I didn't get any signal from you, so I wondered if something had gone wrong. But when I heard the bang it came from GE. Somebody inside the workshop was cussing like you wouldn't believe."

The three walked together back to their workshop, where they found Tesla digging through the crates shipped from New York. He was sure he had left several more condensers at RCA. They helped Tesla for a while, then sent Gil out for sandwiches.

Eventually, Tesla found a plain cardboard box labeled "condensers" under packing material at the bottom of a "spare electrical parts" crate. Inside were two large condensers and several small ones, all dusty. "I think the big ones were spares," he said. "They look almost the same. I think RCA supplied them when we installed the original transmitter."

Leroy examined them. "A little bit smaller, I think. We could do better buying some here."

Gil shook his head. "I already called the electrical shop where we bought the wiring. The clerk said they have to order condensers that size from Chicago. It will take a week."

Leroy suggested testing the two large spares. But

when Tesla connected them to a meter, both showed dead shorts.

***

The next morning Leroy woke early in the back room where he and Eli slept on cots, and put on his only remaining clean set of clothes. He had planned to wear it for the demonstration.

Eli looked at him. "Where you going? To a funeral?"

"I'm going to talk to Dr. Langmuir. General Electric must have a condenser somewhere."

Eli's jaw dropped.

"What else can we do, Eli? Together we may have enough to make one radio rainmaker."

"Maybe," Eli said, "maybe that does make sense." He paused, thinking further. "Maybe all four of us should go with you." He explained the plan to Gil and Tesla when they arrived about 20 minutes later. "Nothing else is going to work," Eli added. "Let him give it a try. Let us give it a try."

The four of them walked quietly past the airplanes. A fourth had arrived in the morning. The new aviator sat beside it on a stool drinking coffee, and watched them curiously.

Lights were on in the GE workshop, but the door was closed when they arrived. Leroy knocked, and when an unshaven man in work clothes opened the door, Leroy asked, "May we please see Dr. Langmuir?"

Looking tired and angry, the man glowered at Leroy. "We don't need no stinkin' niggers."

A second man appeared at the door, frowning at the words. It was a bleary-eyed and very rumpled Langmuir, who recognized Tesla and his companions and flushed. "These two colored gentlemen are engineers who work for Mr. Tesla," he said in an icy rage. "You, Schultz, are a red-necked fool. These men may be able to help us. That's the last straw. You're fired!" He beckoned the four in as Schultz stomped out.

Langmuir reached out and shook Leroy's hand, then

Tesla's, Eli's and Gil's. "I was looking forward to seeing which of us had the better rainmaker," he said. "Unfortunately, the big vacuum tubes in our amplifier blew. I designed them just for this test, and they worked back in Schenectady. But something went wrong with the wiring here and they all blew. We don't have any spares, and it would take at least a week for Schenectady to make new ones, so we can't make the deadline."

"You were our only competition on the ground," Leroy said, "but our oscillator burned out a condenser. So we don't have an oscillator, but we do have an amplifier. If we put our equipment together, we can win."

For a long minute, Langmuir looked surprised, then his tired face lighted up. "That is a wonderful idea. I can see the headlines. 'GE-Tesla team brings rain to the dust bowl.'"

"Tesla-GE," interrupted Tesla.

Langmuir turned to him and smiled. "And you license us for the patent."

Tesla nodded as Eli whispered to Gil.

"But we get the prize money," added Gil.

"I need twenty-five percent to keep GE management happy. And for that you get my oscillator with the latest vacuum tubes."

Eli whispered to Gil, who looked quickly at Tesla and Leroy. "Done!" Gil said, and all four of them shook hands with Langmuir.

***

The aviators started in the morning, after a meteorologist with the Weather Service measured the humidity and certified that the air contained enough water to precipitate. The first took off at 9 a.m., in an old biplane carrying twin barrels of powdered urea, which he swore was the best stuff to make rain. Not a drop fell. Two men flew in the second plane at 10 a.m., one using the controls, the other turning a contraption which ground rock salt into fine crystals and sprayed it into the air. It flew over the airfield and bits of the rock salt fell on the people beneath. Bits of the rock salt felt moist, but no rain followed. At 11 a.m. a plane sponsored by the National Coal Council took off, and a chain-smoking press agent passed out printed flyers telling how coal ash was the best material for rainmaking, and would fertilize the Earth as well as make rain. Their machine began spreading ash before it reached two hundred feet, and ran out before it reached 5000 feet. Not a drop of rain fell, and the press agent insisted they be given another test run the next day. Noon was the turn of a professor of meteorology from the University of Oklahoma, burning a special fuel that he claimed would condense moisture from the air and trigger downpours. He laid down an impressive cloud of smoke, but no rain followed.

After the last plane landed, the meteorologist measured the humidity again, and decided conditions were good enough for the ground test. Tesla and Langmuir led the judges to the workshop, identified by a freshly painted sign as "Tesla-GE Radio Rainmaking." The head judge inspected the towering antenna and indoor machinery, then pulled out his stop watch.

Standing beside Langmuir and Tesla, Leroy pulled the power switch when the judge clicked the stopwatch. The transmitter began to hum. Eli stood outside, with a pair of opera glasses, watching Gil standing by a monitor receiver on the truck. Leroy waited anxiously for word from Gil that the signal was going. The two minutes he waited from the time he pulled the switch until Eli stepped inside and waved his handkerchief in the air seemed endless. He looked around and saw Tesla watching the big machine hum. High voltage tinged the air with the smell of ozone. He wished he had had more time to test the new oscillator.

Then Eli was at his side, saying "Looking good out there, Leroy."

"It can't be raining." The clock showed that only 15 minutes had passed.

"No, but I can smell moisture building."

Leroy wondered about Eli, then he realized Eli wondered about him as well.

After another 15 minutes, the two stepped outside. Eli pointed up at a thick cloud high overhead. "I told you moisture was building." Leroy studied the cloud in quiet awe. After a few minutes they went back inside and spoke quietly to Tesla and Langmuir, who went out to see for themselves. They came back smiling and looking confident.

Leroy turned back to the machine, making sure nothing went wrong. He was watching the dials on the amplifier intently when he heard a familiar voice ask, "Where is Mr. Tesla?"

It was the electrician, and he looked pale. "May I help," Leroy asked.

"There's a storm brewing out there, and I've been looking at your antenna. It don't have proper lightning protection. You're going to have to shut your transmitter down to prevent a lightning strike."

"We can't do that. We're in a contest."

"That tower could get hit with a million volts. It's too close."

"We can't turn it off now." Success was too close for Leroy to give up.

"Then get everybody out so nobody is hurt. ATTENTION" the electrician shouted. "A THUNDERSTORM IS COMING. LIGHTNING MAY HIT THE ANTENNA AND THIS BUILDING. YOU MUST EVACUATE."

"I can't leave," Leroy said.

He felt a hand on his shoulder; it was Mr. Tesla, looking solemn. "Use the Faraday cage, Leroy. It will protect you." He pointed toward a rusty cylindrical structure with metal rods running up from the floor and curving together at the top. It had been in one of the crates, and Tesla had assembled it himself. "Keep your hands and arms inside."

Gil, Eli and Leroy quickly moved the cage to sit

beside the transmitter, and the two others helped Leroy nudge it close enough for him to watch the controls.

"YOU MUST EVACUATE" the electrician shouted. "This is a dangerous storm."

The others left quickly, leaving Leroy in the metal cage. It was five minutes before three, but out the window it looked almost as dark as night. He heard voices, people running, and someone shouting "STORM SHELTER." Then an eerie silence.

He felt the electricity first, saw the flash of light a split second later, then came the most intense clap of thunder he had ever felt. A moment later a brighter flash burst came inside the workshop as the transmitter blew. Silence followed, and a slowly fading afterglow echoed in his eyes.

Leroy stayed frozen in the cage, unable to see, worried that the energy of the lightning bolt might not have drained away, and fearful that it had destroyed Mr. Tesla's Radio Rainmaker before he could show it worked.

In the stillness, he thought he heard a raindrop on the roof. Then another, and another. They came faster and faster until they were beating a torrent. Then he heard people's voices outside, cheering.

Leroy joined in. "We won! We made the rain," he shouted. The door creaked open, a flashlight followed, and the cheers of success followed the light into the workshop.

AUTHOR'S NOTE

When Tom and Judith proposed this book, I asked myself what great technological feat I could invent for the Deco era. I thought of a time when radio was a wonder, and the dust bowl threatened to dry up middle America, and thus my idea evolved. I drafted some real scientists for the tale—the legendary Nicola Tesla, Irving Langmuir (a

1932 Nobel Laureate in Chemistry), and radio engineer C. W. Hansell, whose 300 lifetime patents were once second only to Thomas Edison's. But the real heroes are Leroy, Elijah, and Gil, ordinary people who rose up to the challenge to make it all happen. If only the real world worked like that.

LOSING AMELIA

REV DICERTO

15 August, 1936
To: Mrs. Amelia Earhart
From: W. von Braun
AASF Flight Base
Tucumcari, New Mexico

Dear Amelia,

I would first like to offer you congratulations on your recent test flight of the *Hermes A* rocket plane. I must confess it is always rewarding to witness you pushing one of Dr. Goddard's and my prototypes farther than any of the male pilots. I have yet to see any of the men demonstrate your flair and spirit. What is that word you Americans like so much? Moxie, I believe. Are we close enough friends that I may accuse you of possessing moxie?

I hope that your time in New York City is passing satisfactorily. With the current hectic pace of labors here, a visit east would do me a world of good right now. Dr. Goddard and I have been working around the clock, overseeing the construction of the newest version of the *Hermes*. Not, of course, that I am not glad to do the work! But still, I would very much like to see Broadway, the Rockettes. I hope to some day climb to the top of the Empire State building. I can only imagine what a spectacle it must be, looking down on Manhattan Island from a stationary perch 173 floors above the ground. I look forward to some day seeing the gleaming bridges, the roadways, even the air traffic, from such a vantage.

The reason for my letter is this: The final version of

the *Hermes* space plane is on target to be completed by early this coming winter. Dr. Goddard and I have decided that, once the craft has been built and successfully tested, we would like you, and none other, to be the person to put it through its paces. The *Hermes* is the most powerful rocket plane we have built to date, and Dr. Goddard and I think this will be an opportunity for you to achieve yet another first, Amelia. How would you like to be not only the first woman, but the first human being ever to fly a rocket plane around the Moon?

All that remains, apart from the final phases of construction on the space plane, is for Dr. Goddard and I to find a way to procure some truly powerful radio and radar equipment. If only the Second Republic of Poland did not have such strict laws regarding the export of their electronic technology; we might then be able to purchase one of Dr. Tesla's new devices. I shall have to look into other alternatives. Sadly, that will require a lowering of our standards, but we shall make out as best we may.

Respectfully,
Wernher von Braun

***

21 August, 1936

Dear Wernher,

You certainly know the key to a girl's heart, you crazy German! I can't tell you how happy your letter made me. What a chance!

What can I say, sir? I'm in!

Giddily yours,
Amelia Earhart

***

Translated from Polish

1 September, 1936

To: Mr. Teodor Lis
President, Warsaw Electrical and Radio Corporation
Warsaw, Poland
From: Amelia Earhart
New York, NY

Dear Mr. Lis,

I hope this missive finds you well. Please allow me to introduce myself.

I have been an aviator since the year 1923, and in that time have accomplished a number of feats that have gained me some small degree of fame. In 1925, a year after the first ever transatlantic flight by Charles Lindbergh, I had the honor to be the first woman to fly an aircraft across the Atlantic Ocean. Two years later I flew my Lockheed Vega 5b from Mexico City to Newark, New Jersey.

I have worked as a test pilot, a writer, teacher, and lecturer. In recent years, I have become increasingly involved with the U.S. Agency for Aeronautics and Space Flight. In that capacity I have served as the lead test pilot for the new rocket-powered space planes designed by Drs. Goddard and von Braun.

The two scientists have recently offered me the opportunity to attempt yet another first. Their *Hermes* space plane is nearly ready for its maiden voyage, having already completed a number of upper-atmosphere flights, and they have asked me would I care to be the first person to fly a rocket plane around the Moon and back. Just imagine it, Mr. Lis!

Naturally I leaped at the opportunity. However, a flight of such a distance is a risky proposition, and will require the use of sophisticated communication technology—technology which is simply beyond the means of American scientists to produce.

I have read extensively about the magnificent progress made in the transmission of radio waves in recent years by Dr. Tesla in your country. While your nation and mine are fiercely competitive with one another, I see here an opportunity for a collaboration. I would like to open a dialog with you over the borrowing, leasing, or purchase of one of your firm's most advanced radio units for the purpose of my flight. Such technology would enable a home base to remain in contact with the space plane throughout the flight. As I see it, Mr. Lis, both nations would gain immensely—the United States through the achievement of flight to, and around, our nearest celestial neighbor; and the Second Polish Republic through providing the near miraculous electronic technology necessary to safely make the attempt.

Please, sir, do consider this opportunity, and let me know the disposition of yourself and your firm on the matter at your earliest possible convenience.

Warmest Regards,
Amelia Earhart

***

14 September, 1936
From: Teodor Lis
Warsaw, Poland

Dear Mrs. Earhart,

Greetings from the Second Polish Republic, and many congratulations on your exciting opportunity.

Your accomplishments, Mrs. Earhart, are very well known here in Poland. With your words, "Sirs, please don't believe that I need one of *those* to fly this bird across that lake!" when sponsors urged a male navigator and pilot upon you before your groundbreaking transatlantic flight, you liberated an entire generation of Polish women—and our technology sector has profited immensely! And for those of us keen to enjoy the humor of our western neighbors, the slight gesture toward your pelvic region was neither lost nor unappreciated.

I hope you understand that the role of Warsaw Electrical and Radio Corporation has become very much entwined with that of our Republican government, as our functions, overseen by Dr. Tesla, have become deeply enmeshed within the defense of our great nation. Therefore it was necessary to take your request to the highest levels of our industrial-governmental complex. I have discussed your request with both President Dziedzic and Dr. Tesla.

It gives me great pleasure, Mrs. Earhart, to inform you that I have received permission to provide you with a Warsaw Electrical Marconi 17 radio unit for the duration of your mission. This, our newest model of long-range radio devices, consists of an "away" unit, to be housed in your rocket plane, and a "home" unit, much larger and more powerful, to be installed at your home base. The Marconi 17 is as yet not available in Poland for purchase, and is still considered to be in a prototype phase.

Moreover, as the Second Republic desires greatly to be associated with your historic journey, I have also been granted permission to furnish you with a Warsaw Electrical Niemczyk Class long-distance radar unit. This device, also still in its prototypical phase, will enable your home base to track your location throughout the entirety of your journey with an accuracy, at your furthest point from the Earth, of within one hundred kilometers.

My dear Mrs. Earhart, you gratify both Warsaw Electrical and the Second Republic with your willingness to include our technology in this most historic of endeavors. I wish you all success upon your journey, and I hope that, as you prepare for your day of departure, you will remember those who have contributed to your great achievement, and will maintain correspondence with your Polish supporters.

Wishing you God's protection and Godspeed,
Teodor Nikola Lis
***

Translated from Polish

14 December, 1936
From: Amelia Earhart
New York, NY

Dear Mr. Lis,

Of course I was grateful to learn of your, and your government's, great generosity toward me and my mission in furnishing it with both an advanced radio unit and the radar capabilities to track my spaceflight. But Mr. Lis, I have to say you have not been entirely honest with me! I traveled to New York City's Pier Nine myself last Thursday, just to witness the offloading of your equipment from the ship, which I had been informed had arrived the night before.

Well, I'm sure you can imagine my surprise! You wily rascal, you never told me that in addition to the equipment (and who could have expected the crates would have been so *big*? Each one could have contained an automobile, and there were seven of them!), you would also be sending a team of experts to install and operate the devices. Your Miss Kozlow and Miss Wiater are fine, well-mannered, forward-thinking young women, and greeted me with a respect that was as unexpected as it was flattering.

As an American, I have grown accustomed to outstanding, nearly futuristic feats of technology and construction; and of course I am better acquainted than most with my nation's achievements in flight, aeronautics, and aerospace design. But that same heritage leaves me lacking in familiarity with electrical engineering and electronics, the specialties of the people of the Second Republic. Therefore I am probably not the best suited of all recipients to judge the potential of the devices you have sent. However, if pure bulk, and the technical expertise displayed by the technicians, are to be used as a guide, I cannot doubt that you have done me and my nation a great service, and I look forward to piloting both of our greatest technical feats to date to a place beyond where humankind has yet trodden.

I am indebted to you, Mr. Lis. I look forward to our next communiqué.

In gratitude and admiration,
Amelia Earhart

***

Western Union telegraph, translated from Polish

16 December, 1936
From: Teodor Lis
To: Maja Kozlow
New York, NY

Maja Kozlow STOP   Remember agenda STOP Earhart flight is for testing purposes STOP Record all data regarding radar signal STOP Lis STOP

***

7 January, 1937
From: Teodor Lis
Warsaw, Poland

Dear Mrs. Earhart,

I am glad that you are getting along so well with Miss Kozlow and Miss Wiater. Treat them well! They were chosen not merely for their technical expertise, but also because each admires you as a personal hero. I had thought, in sending them, not only to honor you and your many accomplishments, but also to stoke the fire that burns within each of these young women, through enabling them to take part in your historic mission.

Please understand that the technical staff, as well as the equipment, are yours only on loan, until the termination of your mission. But while they are yours to use, may they serve you well.

I'm truly excited that your nation has offered mine
the opportunity to contribute equipment for your
mission, Mrs. Earhart. It is high time the world beyond the
borders of the Second Republic had an opportunity to see
what our scientists and engineers have accomplished—
and also high time for an exchange between some of our
technicians and yours. I feel an immense, personal pride
in this collaboration. Since 1910, when Dr. Tesla first
successfully tested his Wardenclyffe 1 Tower, and began
delivering free electricity wirelessly throughout the Second
Republic, our nation has received the most magnificent
influx of scientific minds. Much as all those European
scientists with an interest in engineering, flight, and
rocketry years ago migrated to the United States, those
with an interest in electricity and electronics flocked to
Poland. The migration from Germany was particularly
prodigious.

It seems to me now, looking back, as though for
many years the population of the German states had been
growing restive. I often wonder if Dr. Tesla's Peace Ray did
not head off a period of international conflict when he
used it in 1905 to destroy that division of German cavalry.
Two thousand burned horses, and half again as many
men, and twelve airships, may have been a trifle when
compared to the number who might otherwise have been
swept up. Why, my own assistant, a sulky Austrian, claims
that without the income he earns here directing
production at our Warsaw plant, he might never have
completed art school, and feels his own future might have
been a very dark one. Let us be glad dear Adolf is able to
go home of an evening and paint!

I propose an idea to you, Mrs. Earhart: Upon your
safe return to the Earth, and following the fanfare and the
tickertape parades, and all of the fancy banquets that you
shall be subjected to, will you grace me with a personal
interview? I shall furnish first-class tickets for you and Mr.
Putnam aboard the *Hindenburg*. Please come and be the
guest of myself, Dr. Tesla, and President Dziedzic. We

would be thrilled to hear the tale of your glorious exploit.

Yours in friendship,
Teodor Lis
***

Translated from Polish

1 February, 1937
From: Amelia Earhart
New York, NY

Dear Mr. Lis,
You, sir, have got yourself a date!
Amelia
***

1 March, 1937
From: Amelia Earhart
PanUSA Airship Terminal
Chicago, IL

My Dearest George,

It's a funny thing for me, dear, to be a passenger in the air. Of course, I have no experience whatsoever at piloting an airship like this, four hundred foot long, lighter than air, slow. I don't suppose it could be very difficult, though. I mean, the dashed things are ungodly slow. Still, there is a stately grace to them. This particular one, named by her owners the *Miranda*, is a lovely, modern- looking affair, all shining steel and chrome, with elegant, curved features, a sleek airbag, and four powerful screws in the area of her tail. Still, I'm not at all accustomed to being waited on during an air voyage.

I suppose a girl could get used to the champagne, though.

I have to say, it was positively thrilling to board an airship at the Empire State building. You have to take an elevator all the way up to the 145th floor. I'm used to being outdoors that high above the ground, from my days piloting biplanes. It's quite another thing to stand up there waiting for a lift, though, sipping coffee and looking out over the Manhattan skyline. Why, you can see clear to Connecticut!

But the building is gorgeous, George, and we should go and pay a visit when next we're in New York together. Promise me we'll do that, will you? All chrome and stainless steel archways, huge, rounded designs curving over you as you chat and await your ship.

And then this dot appears on the horizon, over the Hudson. It's silver, glimmering in the sunlight. And gradually it grows, and it grows, until it becomes plain that the thing coming toward you is simply colossal. And only when you realize how great an object it is do you then start to hear the sound of her massive diesel engines! And still she grows and she grows.

Finally she pulls up alongside the platform, and turns broadsides to you, and she actually stops in place, and bobs there like a ship at sea. Men in sharp uniforms run out and take the lines, and make her fast to a vast number of stanchions, just as though she were a ship on the water, fore and aft. And then a slender, gleaming, steel gangplank extends from her cabin and clangs into place by the gate.

Well, I could go on, but I'm probably boring you. Let me just say that Karolina, the radio operator, is the most delightful company. Maja, the radar technician, is somewhat more aloof, but she's pleasant enough in her own quiet way. I'd be hard pressed to imagine two sharper, brighter, more engaging young women. I would say they remind me of myself at their age, but I can't imagine I could have comprehended the technology that they understand so well. They simply rattle on about it, an hour at a time sometimes, leaving me positively in the dust. If my example really did influence so many young European women to take up the sciences and leave behind lives of subservience and low expectations, then whatever I have achieved in this life, I have done well. They are a comfort to me and a joy; and they speak of my upcoming mission with such great exuberance—particularly Karolina.

Well, dear husband, I won't tire you with any more trivial details. When next your wife stands upon *terra firma*, it will be at the AASF base at Tucumcari, New Mexico. There I shall finally see my new space plane, and begin my series of shakedown flights.

I eagerly look forward to your arrival there. The best to you on the road.

Your loving wife,
Amelia
***

Translated from Polish

3 April, 1937
From: Karolina Wiater
AASF Flight Base
Tucumcari, New Mexico

Dear Mr. Lis,

This assignment is a pleasure, and I am very grateful to you and to Dr. Tesla for permitting Maja and myself to take part in it. Mrs. Earhart is quite a dynamic personality!

The United States are every bit as grand as rumor has made them out to be. Vast highways crisscross the nation, six lanes wide, packed with automobiles of every description, glittering with chrome and putting out a powerful fume. And the buildings! Oh, Mr. Lis, you and Dr. Tesla must visit this magical place, when your busy schedules permit.

It is strange, though, living in a nation in which DC power is the chief source of electricity. Every few blocks, or every few miles in the country, one passes a large building housing another power generator. Why did these people not listen to Dr. Tesla in the 1890s? Their radios, such as they are, barely pick up a thing, aside from static! As for television, well, that is a thought that has not yet so much as occurred to any American scientist. The vacuum tubes here, Dr. Tesla could have assembled in his sleep in the 1880s.

As to the mission, it goes on admirably. We have assembled the radar installation and the home unit of the radio, and are well on our way to completing the installation of the away unit onboard the *Hermes* rocket plane. Mrs. Earhart has a habit of giving her aircraft personal names, I have learned; so in addition to its formal name, the *Hermes* craft is now familiarly referred to as *Judy*, I believe in honor of a childhood friend of Mrs. Earhart's.

Judy is a marvel to behold. Our biplanes in the Second Republic seem so primitive by comparison. This plane scarcely looks like an airplane at all to Maja and me.

She is a full two hundred-fifty meters long. I do not exaggerate, Mr. Lis. When first I beheld *Judy*, she was standing upright. No hangar in Poland could accommodate such a ship in the upright position; but these Americans, with their advanced engineering, have built a hangar capable of accommodating *Judy* either upright or prone.

Drs. Goddard and von Braun have assured me that *Judy* can carry sufficient fuel to bring her around the far side of the Moon and back to Earth, all the while under powered flight. Dr. von Braun intimated that it was largely because the bulk of this flight would occur outside of the Earth's atmosphere, where there is no air and therefore no resistance, that such a feat of engineering was even conceivable. The challenge of tracking *Judy* through her course around the Earth's satellite and back, a distance of roughly 540,000 miles, is a task Maja seems to look forward to with great anticipation. Communicating with Mrs. Earhart through the duration of the flight will bring me both pride and great pleasure.

But she is a lovely sight to behold, Mr. Lis. The rocket plane, I mean, not Mrs. Earhart. From a distance, she is pencil-thin, tapering from a point capped with a spear-like antenna to a tail section so narrow one could barely get one's hand inside. Every inch of her is gleaming, shining steel, as bright as polished silver. Her windscreen is the thickest glass I have ever seen, slightly tinted, running in an arc like a smiling mouth over her nose, never interrupting those perfect, sculpted lines. Her wings are nearly nonexistent. If *Judy* were a telephone pole, in terms of length and width, then either wing would be no broader than the width of my hand, though perhaps twice as long. Her tail raises perhaps twice as high, but the horizontal elements are only half as broad. In all, she is the most elegant vehicle I have ever laid eyes upon.

I am told that, upon the day of the historic lunar voyage, *Judy* will be half-laid upon a gantry set at an angle to the ground, like a cart at the base of a steep hill. A rocket-powered car will be set off, which will drag her at an ever-increasing speed on a sled up this mile-long ramp. At the apex of this slope the track will end. The car, having exhausted its supply of fuel, will simply fall away; however, *Judy*, having fired her rocket engines moments previously, will continue on, at such an angle as to be prepared to lift into the upper atmosphere with the slightest application of her power. In this way, *Judy* is spared the need to expend the massive amounts of dry fuel needed to accelerate her to the speed required for her to attain spaceflight.

What a clever people, these Americans!

Yours in faith and labor,
Karolina Wiater
                              ***
Translated from Polish

12 April, 1937
From: Maja Kozlow

AASF Flight Base
Tucumcari, New Mexico

Mr. Lis,

Sir, this missive is written to inform you that the *Hermes* space plane has been successfully test-flown. On 9 April, 1937, Mrs. Amelia Earhart ascended the scaffolding affixed to the side of the gantry supporting the craft. At 07:53 the rocket sled was fired.

The sled, sir, was in its initial phases frightfully slow, and at first I believed the craft would fail to attain flight. However, once its cargo was in motion, it rapidly gained speed. By the time it reached the end of its ramp, it was moving at a frightful pace, and the *Hermes* propelled herself from the gantry with a roar of her rocket engines and a sound like thunder, a thing which the technicians here refer to as a "sonic boom."

The plane flew admirably well, trailing a stream of flame and smoke. Mrs. Earhart made some sixteen turns around the AASF land here—located in a flat, broad, arid plain—before tearing off beyond the horizon. Each time the plane passed overhead, there was again that sound as of thunder, or a great explosion, that seemed to erupt of an instant, and then to fade as an ongoing roar of rocket engines.

Sir, the *Hermes* space plane is a formidable craft. Never have I seen such a streamlined, powerful machine, nor one better suited to its purpose.

The attitude among the American personnel is one of great elation, and Drs. Goddard and von Braun seem confident that their creation is equal to the task for which it was constructed. Mrs. Earhart is equally enthusiastic, filled with a confidence bordering upon arrogance—a distinctly American trait, I am coming to learn. Karolina, it would appear, has formed a bit of a crush on the pilot. I therefore advise you to adhere to the original plan, and keep any information regarding the less overt aspects of our mission from her. I will see that she knows what is required for her to fulfill her duties.

As for the equipment, it is functioning perfectly and just as expected. I never once lost sight of the rocket plane on the radar screen; the signal remained strong and solid. Karolina reports that the radio system also functioned perfectly, without so much as a tick of static.

I should point out that the Americans have placed monitors upon both Karolina's station and my own. They make no attempts to operate, interpret, or touch the equipment, but it seems plain that they will not trust data that they have not themselves witnessed. They continue to treat us with respect, however.

The next test flight has been planned tentatively for 20 April, 0:7:00, pending the analysis of flight data recorded by Karolina, the American observers, myself, and of course the headstrong Mrs. Earhart. Per your request, I will send a ping on band B once the flight is underway. I shall, of course, report at once should there be any new developments.

> In Patriotism,
> Maja Kozlow

***

21 April, 1937
From: Amelia Earhart
AASF Flight Base
Tucumcari, NM

My Darling George,

I'm so blue over your delays in Chicago! How I miss you, my dear. The past two weeks would have been so much more enjoyable with you present.

But blue or otherwise, I now have the confidence to say that the mission is most certainly going to go off! The first flight, the shakedown on the 9th, was a success, of course. But I wasn't even permitted to take my *Judy* out of the atmosphere. The good doctors wanted to test under safe conditions how the Polish electronics would function.

Well, they may have had their doubts, but I'd none of my own—neither of the technology of the Second Republic nor of the abilities of my dear Karolina and Maja. In any case, the equipment functioned swimmingly, and I was able to chat with Karolina throughout the entirety of the flight.

But the *Judy*, George! She's so lovely! I can hardly wait for you to see her. She's far and away the biggest craft I've yet to pilot, all gleaming steel, smoother and shinier than anything you've ever seen. I can't describe to you the sense of power I experience with the slightest movement of the throttle.

Yesterday I finally got to take her out of the atmosphere. I've been out there a dozen or so times, in other birds; but nothing has ever compared to this. The doctors finally let me really open her up. We need to see if she'll go as fast as we hope, you understand; I can only carry so much fuel, so we need to get a certain amount of speed out of a certain amount of gas.

According to Maja's radar, *Judy* nearly doubled the speed she needed for the trip! What a thrill, being up where it's all dark above, where you can see the horizon sloping away in every direction, where the airfield has vanished beyond a speck, lost somewhere in the mass that is the southwest of the United States. Then you bury the throttle, George, and you're pressed back into your seat… The Earth seems to turn below you. I haven't the words!

There was one small hiccup. About halfway through the flight, as I was describing the stars to Karolina—they look so different, darling, when you're up above the atmosphere—there came a hissing sound through my headphones, and gradually I lost Karolina's voice in a sea of static. Then the radio seemed to cut out entirely, even the static disappearing.

I was a bit unnerved. At that point, you're so far above the earth, maybe three hundred miles up, that seeing the place you took off from is an impossibility. And you're moving so fast. You need someone on the ground to guide you in; this is why we need the Polish radar. Our own imitations are alright for a trip as high as I was, and they functioned just fine; but any farther, and I'd be lost to them. And without the voice from home base, you're as good as lost.

Still, it was a sort of a peaceful feeling. There I was, hundreds of miles above the Earth, suddenly totally alone. I was afraid, George, but I was also calm in a way I can't describe. I suppose it was because I was at the stick of my lovely *Judy*. I mean, I was doing what God put me here to do, so I felt sure all would be right.

And that turned out to be the case. In two minutes, the static returned, and Karolina's voice faded back in as the static faded away; and then I was being guided back to the base by my new Polish friends. It was the most comforting sensation. I really can't wait for you to meet Karolina and Maja, George!

Well, I've got to go to a meeting with the doctors, now. Do try and wrap up quickly. I've got another two test flights before we start preparing *Judy* for the mission. We're thinking the actual flight will take place in July. And I want you here with me, George, as I get ready! This gal wants to kiss her man before she climbs those steps to fly to the stars and back.

Yours Longingly,
Amelia XO

***

Western Union telegram, translated from Polish

15 June, 1937
From: Maja Kozlow
Western Union Telegraph Office
Tucumcari, NM

Mr Lis STOP   All tests complete STOP   Radio

functional STOP   Radar functional STOP   Space plane functional STOP   During test flight 4 June radio contact lost radar contact lost STOP   Duration of signal loss four minutes STOP   Altitude at time of loss one thousand miles STOP   American observers aware of outages STOP   Seem to accept cover story about temporary solar interference STOP   Kozlow STOP

***

Translated from Polish

25 June, 1937
MEMO
To: Dr. N. Tesla, Facility Manager Adriana Dunajski
Wardenclyffe Tower #7
Bialystok, Second Polish Republic
From: Teodor Lis
Warsaw, Second Polish Republic

Dr. Tesla, Miss Dunajski,

All preliminary tests of the new #7 tower with regard to operation Deep Sky have been completed successfully. Operatives report radio and radar signals were interrupted as scheduled on all test missions. Reported timing and duration of outages matched test times precisely.

The final mission of operation Deep Sky has been scheduled for 1 July, commencing at 09:00. Wardenclyffe #7 should be prepared for final testing by that date. No further tests associated with Deep Sky have been scheduled prior to that date.

T. Lis

***

Transcripts from radio communications

Flight Base, Tucumcari, New Mexico

1 July 1937

09:25:00

Amelia Earhart: Well, boys and girls, this lady is off! I've lost my altimeter, so between that and the dark above me, I'd say I'm out of Earth's atmosphere.

Karolina Wiater: I have you on radar, Mrs. Earhart. Current altitude, three hundred-plus miles. You are on course.

AE: It's lovely up here. Not a ripple or a bump! I can't even see the base anymore.

Wernher von Braun [mission manager]: You will not experience any more turbulence, Amelia. Not outside of the atmosphere. You are in for a very smooth two days of flying.

AE: Right! Thank you, Wernher. Say, folks, is my husband there?

George Putnam: Right here, darling. How's it feel up there? You comfortable?

AE: My *Judy* fits me like a glove!

KW: Four hundred-plus miles, Mrs. Earhart.

AE: Come on, now, Kari! Call me Amelia, will you? I'm all alone up here. The least you can do is be friendly.

KW: Of course. I'm sorry, Amelia.

GP: You hang tight, now, dear. Keep your eyes on the road.

AE: (Laughs) Of course, dear. Not that there's a thing in the world to hit.

13:52:00

AE: (Static) ...said, can anybody read me down there?

KW: We lost you for a time, Amelia, but we have you back again.

AE: It's not as peaceful when I lose the radio, now.

KW: Why is that?

AE: Well, it's one thing losing contact when I'm a couple hundred miles above the ground. I mean, from that height, I could at least descend, find a place to set this bird down, you know? Now that I'm...

KW: Eighty-two-plus thousand miles.

AE: (Nervous chuckle) Yeah! Well, the loneliness isn't as nice at this point, if you understand. If something were to happen, I'd really be alone out here.

WvB: You understood this risk all along, Amelia.

AE: Sure, Wernher, but that doesn't make it any easier to bear. But say, how's the radar? Is that cutting out as well?

KW: Not at all. Maja says she has had you on screen since the moment you took off.

AE: Well, at least there's that! Thanks, honey.

17:21:00

WvB: How are you doing, Amelia?

AE: Just fine, Wernher. Though I must say, you boys might want to build in a bigger heater next time around.

WvB: You're cold?

AE: It's pretty chilly up here. I've got a bit of frost forming on the instruments, and on the inside of the windscreen.

WvB: I'm sorry. The heater is still working, though?

AE: Oh, yes. I can see it glowing. I can just imagine what it would be like up here without the thing! I'd be frozen solid.

WvB: What does the Earth look like?

AE: Well, it's still taking up most of the view to starboard, but it's definitely looking a bit puny. No question I'm away from it. Imagine how the Moon looks from the ground when it's full. I'd say about five times that size.

WvB: Be sure to take as many pictures as you can.

AE: I have been.

WvB: Thank you.

[Static crackles briefly]

AE: Kari, you haven't got any other objects on the screen, have you?

KW: No, Amelia. Just you, and of course the Moon. Why?

AE: I'm feeling kind of funny. My hair's standing up. Static electricity, I guess. But it's making my head spin and float a bit. Oh!

KW: What is it?

AE: Sparks, jumping from the instrument panel. Ouch! (Nervous chuckle) I just got a dratted shock! You *sure* I'm alone up here?

WvB: You might be experiencing some sort of an electromagnetic disturbance. Sunspots, maybe, or a solar flare.

[Static begins to interfere with sound]

AE: I don't like it. My mouth *[gap]* funny. Fingers *[gap]*... ...hear me at all?

KW: You're cutting out again, Amelia.

AE: [*Static*] ...even see the dratted Moon. Am *[gap]* on course?

KW: Yes, Amelia, you're still on course. Maja has been following you. You should be able to see the Moon just fine. Dr. von Braun, what is the problem?

WvB: I can't say. I don't like the electromagnetic interference. Perhaps you should tell her to abort and return to base until we can determine what it is she's running into.

KW: Amelia, Dr. von Braun wants you to turn around. He's concerned about the electromagnetic interference.

AE: [Static] ...around? *[gap]* ...see this thing through!

WvB: Amelia! I'm serious. You could be placing your life in jeopardy. I order you to turn that plane around!

[Static ends]

AE: I'm sorry, Wernher. I missed that. Didn't get a single word. My, but it's lovely up here! And look, there's the Moon again! (Sigh, as of relief) Glad that tingling feeling's gone.

2 July 1937
08:43

KW: Amelia, how are you doing?

AE: Just a bit chilled, hon. Has the radar cut out at all in the past hour?

KW: No, not in the past hour. Maja had you on the screen during the last radio blackout.

AE: Well, that's a relief. I can't get over these fuzzy patches. It's like the whole plane is electrified. It's gotten so that the past few times, I could barely even keep hold of the stick.

KW: Maybe you should have turned around when Dr. von Braun asked you to.

AE: I'm sorry, darling, you cut out again.

KW: (Sigh of resignation) Right. So... You're beyond the Moon now. What do you see?

AE: It's magnificent. The Moon is sort of a silhouette of itself, ringed with sunlight. Off to the upper right I see the Earth. It looks hardly any bigger than the full Moon looks from base. For a while it was completely hidden behind the Moon. It's lovely, Kari. All swirling clouds, with deep blue oceans. You can barely make out the land. Right now the Moon is mainly a dark mass.

KW: I can't wait to see the pictures.

AE: (Gasp) Oh, hang it!

KW: What is it?

AE: The buzzing is back. Ouch! The stick just shocked me again. My hair's on end.

KW: I wish you'd come back when the doctor told you to.

AE: Sorry, I missed that.

[Static appears in transmission]

KW: No you didn't.

AE: [Gap] ...Earth? I swear it was just over *[gap]...* Kari, are you reading...

KW: Amelia?

[Transmission dead for fifteen seconds]

AE: [blast of static] (Screams) ...burned my hands! I'm bleeding! My eyes! Kari, they hurt *[gap]...* can barely see a thing!

KW: Amelia! Come in! What is happening?

WvB: Is she still on radar?

Maja Kozlow: She's right there. Here's the moon, here's the plane.

WvB: Amelia! Can you read us?

[Blast of static]

AE: ...light all around me, like blue and green lightning streaking and flashing past my *[gap]* ...so sorry, team. I shouldn't be cracking like...

WvB: Amelia!

KW: Amelia! What is happening? Is the plane still functioning?

[Blast of static]

AE: ...flames. Blue flames, and smoke. *Judy* is shuddering. I think she may break...

KW: Amelia!

WvB: Mrs. Earhart!

[Blast of static followed by silence]

09:27

WvB: Miss Kozlow, please confirm that the space plane is still on radar.

MK: I still have her, sir.

WvB: Miss Wiater, no further radio signal in the past hour?

KW: Nothing, sir. (Sniffle)

09:38

MK: Dr. von Braun! It's split!

WvB: What's split?

MK: See? The blip representing the space plane. There are... three blips, now!

WvB: Traveling in roughly the same direction. Slightly divergent paths. Perhaps it's an echo. Can that happen?

MK: I do not know, sir.

KW: (Catching breath, as though crying) Perhaps it could, if there is something in space that can create an echo.

> 09:42
> *MK:* I've lost all the pieces.

> 12:38
> *WvB:* Any contact? Either of you?
> *MK:* Nothing since the three echoes vanished.
> *MK:* (Emotional breathing) Nothing in three hours.

***

Interoffice memo

2 July 1937, 12:53
AASF Flight Base, Tucumcari, New Mexico
To: Robert Goddard
From: W. von Braun

Hermes space plane believed lost, 2 July 1937, 08:43 hours. Monitoring of lunar environ with Warsaw radar and Earth atmosphere with US radar to continue.

I fear we have lost a hero this day.

Wernher

***

Letter seized in evidence, English

3 July, 1937
From: Karolina Wiater
AASF Flight Base
Tucumcari, New Mexico

Dear Mr. Putnam,

I hardly know where to begin, or how to write this letter to you. I have only known you for a few weeks; however, I was a great admirer of your wife and her many accomplishments. I like to think that in the few months I knew and worked with her, I was her friend.

First let me say that Amelia was one of the most beautiful and lively women it has ever been my pleasure to know. And you should know, Mr. Putnam, that for all her vivacity, your wife was never more pleased than when you arrived at the AASF base. She had seemed happy enough in the weeks spent testing her *Judy*, but once you arrived on base, she seemed to glow.

She looked so brave, Mr. Putnam, and so lovely, ascending the gantry to the cockpit of the rocket plane, dressed in her flight leathers, her scarf blowing in the wind. Her smile was like that of an angel as she waved at us all before climbing into her seat. It was an honor to stand beside you, sir, and witness such a great moment in the life of such an admirable woman.

I am not pleased at the part I played in Amelia's disappearance. I confess that I had suspected for a long time that some plot was in the works. It seems to me now, Mr. Putnam, looking over my own records and having stolen a few glimpses at those of my colleague Maja Kozlow, the radar operator, that the outages of radio communication and radar contact experienced during several of Amelia's test flights were timed events, of which Miss Kozlow was warned beforehand by our superiors in Poland.

In even setting so much to paper, I hope you understand that I risk my very life.

As I say, I suspected a plot; however, I never thought it would result in the disappearance or possible destruction of the *Judy*. I now believe that the planned outages were somehow connected with an experimental new facility back home, Wardenclyffe #7. Whether that facility houses some sort of signal jamming equipment, or a new, more powerful version of Dr. Tesla's Peace Ray, I do not know. Very little is known of what transpires at Wardenclyffe #7.

I only hope, Mr. Putnam, that you believe me when I say that I feel deep shame and regret over the loss of your wife, during what should have been the crowning achievement of her aviation career, and a great moment for all of humankind. While no one will ever know just what she experienced in the cockpit of the *Judy,* I cling to the belief that perhaps, despite her transmissions' failure to reach the Earth, my voice might have brought her some comfort before the space plane's disappearance.

It is with great sorrow that I join Miss Kozlow, whom I can scarcely bring myself to speak with, in dismantling our equipment. It is with regret that I leave your bereaved nation.

> Yours in Mourning,
> Karolina Wiater

***

11 July, 1937
From: Colonel Justin Gunn, Security Chief
AASF Flight Base
Tucumcari, New Mexico
To: General Adam Coleman, US Joint Chiefs of Staff
CC: Robert Goddard, Wernher von Braun, George Putnam

Gen. Coleman,

I am attaching a letter written to Mr. George Putnam, the husband of Flight Lieutenant Amelia Earhart, for your records.

Mr. Putnam, I apologize for the necessity of your receiving the letter in this fashion.

Based upon the information contained in Miss Wiater's letter, the Polish technicians involved in Operation Deep Sky have been detained, and their equipment confiscated. The radio and radar equipment are currently being examined by Drs. Goddard and von Braun, along with their staff, and it is hoped that American electronic technology will benefit greatly from what can be learned from these devices.

While it is as yet too soon to draw any definitive

conclusions, it seems plain, both from Miss Wiater's letter and from telegraph records seized since the disappearance of the *Hermes* rocket plane, that the technicians lent by the Second Republic of Poland were under orders to communicate secretly with superiors in Poland regarding details of Operation Deep Sky, and also not to interfere should any complications arise during the course of the mission. Upon questioning, it seems almost certain that the technician Maja Kozlow was fully complicit with orders from Poland that may have led to the loss of the space plane. Karolina Wiater may be found innocent of most charges, as it appears that she was not informed as to the nature of her team's true mission.

In the aftermath of the loss of America's most valued technological achievement, and the thwarting of her most ambitious mission of exploration—one intended to better the understanding of all of humankind of the nature of our universe—not to mention the loss of the beloved Flight Lieutenant Earhart, AASF superiors are requesting that all diplomatic options be exercised with the Second Republic. It is hoped that sanctions and international pressure will be levied upon Poland until information regarding the loss of the *Hermes* and the capabilities of the Wardenclyffe #7 installation are surrendered.

Gentlemen, we must not sit idly by and let our greatest technology, and our best and brightest pilot, be cast into the void.

Yours truly,
J. Gunn

***

16 July, 1937
From: General Adam Coleman, US Joint Chiefs of Staff
To: Colonel Justin Gunn

Justin,

Sorry I cannot copy your associates in Tucumcari on this message. Be aware that the diplomatic pressure to which you referred in your memo of the 11th has already been set into motion. To underscore our seriousness, President Roosevelt has ordered the deployment of 24,000 troops to eastern Germany. These will be augmented by a further 13,000 German troops, and a complement of 6,000 of Dr. von Braun's latest V9 rockets.

My friend, our President, all of America, and our allies in Europe and elsewhere will not rest until this matter is resolved.

Yours,
A.C.

AUTHOR'S NOTE

Rev DiCerto lives in a historic home in Connecticut with nine well-used guitars. He has been writing fantasy and science fiction since he could hold a pen, and started writing his first book at the age of ten (regrettably, it remains unfinished). Rev recently returned to writing after a number of years spent concentrating on composing, recording, and performing music with a number of bands.

ABOUT THE EDITORS

Tom Easton was the book columnist for the science fiction magazine *Analog* for 30 years. He holds a doctorate in theoretical biology from the University of Chicago and recently retired after thirty-one years as Professor of Science at Thomas College in Waterville, Maine. He now lives in the Boston area.

His latest nonfiction books are *Taking Sides: Clashing Views in Science, Technology, and Society* (McGraw-Hill, 12th ed., 2015), *Taking Sides: Clashing Views on Environmental Issues* (McGraw-Hill, 15th ed. Rev., 2014), and *Classic Editions Sources: Environmental Studies* (McGraw-Hill, 5th. Ed., 2014). His latest novels are *Firefight* (Betancourt, 2003) and *The Great Flying Saucer Conspiracy* (Wildside, 2002) (both available as e-books from Naked Reader Press).

Judith K. Dial was born in Hollywood, CA, a circumstance she's never quite overcome. Her parents read SF in an era when it wasn't quite respectable for adults to do so. Judith was a second-generation bookseller, and sold used fiction, specializing in science fiction, for many years —and accumulated far too many books. She is also a former technical writer, married, and lives in New England.

Tom Easton and Judith K. Dial are the editors of two previous anthologies: *Visions of Tomorrow* (Skyhorse, 2010) and *Impossible Futures* (Pink Narcissus, 2013).